# THE BREAKDOWN

# What Reviewers Say About Ronica Black's Work

### A Love that Leads to Home

"If you love a slow-burn romance where the characters are carefully dancing around each other while being incredibly adorable, this story is for you. It was an emotional read for me, and if you want a good heart-wrenching story, read it."—*Hsinju's Lit Log*

### Freedom to Love

"This is a great book. The police drama keeps you enthralled throughout but what I found captivating was the growing affection between the two main characters. Although they are both very different women, you find yourself holding your breath, hoping that they will find a way to be together."—*Lesbian Reading Room*

### The Practitioner

"*The Practitioner* by Ronica Black is the angsty sort of romance that I can easily get lost in. I wanted to fill a tub and bathe in all the feelings. Hell, if I had one of those fancy, waterproof Kindles, I just might have."—*Lesbian Review*

"The beginning of this novel captured my attention from the rather luscious description of a pint of Guinness. I cannot tell a lie, I almost immediately wanted to be drinking it. ...The first scene with the practitioner also pulled me in, making me sit up and pay attention to what was happening on the digital page. The relationship was like a low simmering fire, frequently doused by either Johnnie's personal angst, or Elaine's. This book was an overall enjoyable read and one which I would recommend to people wanting characters who practically breathe off the page."—*Library Thing*

**Snow Angel**

"A beautifully written, passionate and romantic novella." —*SunsetXCocktail*

"*Snow Angel* is a novella, and it flies by. It draws characters and scenes in large strokes, and it's good fun if you'd like a quick read that's particularly escapist."—*The Lesbrary*

**Under Her Wing**

"From the start Ronica Black had me. I loved everything about this story, from the emotional intensity to the amazingly hot sex scenes. The emotion between them is so real and tear jerking at times. And the love scenes are phenomenal. I feel I'm raving—but I enjoyed it that much. Highly recommended."—*Kitty Kat's Book Review Blog*

**"Emily" in Women of the Dark Streets**

"A darkly disturbing brush with questionable magic that leads to an astounding one-eighty-degree turnaround after an apparent attempt at suicide. Mindboggling!"—*Rainbow Book Reviews*

**The Seeker**

"Stalkers, child kidnappers and murderers all collide in this fast-paced, dual-plotted novel. This is not Black's first novel, and readers can only hope it will not be her last."—*Lambda Literary Review*

"Ronica Black's books just keep getting stronger and stronger. …This is such a tightly written plot-driven novel that readers will find themselves glued to the pages and ignoring phone calls. *The Seeker* is a great read, with an exciting plot, great characters, and great sex."—*Just About Write*

**Flesh and Bone**—*Lambda Literary Award Finalist*

"Ronica Black handles a traditional range of lesbian fantasies with gusto and sincerity. The reader wants to know these women as well as they come to know each other. When Black's characters ignore their realistic fears to follow their passion, this reader admires their chutzpah and cheers them on. …These stories make good bedtime reading, and could lead to sweet dreams. Read them and see."
—*Erotica Revealed*


**Chasing Love**

"Ronica Black's writing is fluid, and lots of dialogue makes this a fast read. If you like steamy erotica with intense sexual situations, you'll like *Chasing Love*."—*Queer Magazine Online*


**Hearts Aflame**

"Sleek storytelling and terrific characters are the backbone of Ronica Black's third and best novel, *Hearts Aflame*. Prepare to hop on for an emotional ride with this thrilling story of love in the outback. …Along with the romance of Krista and Rae, the secondary storylines such as Krista's fear of horses and an uncle suffering from Alzheimer's are told with depth and warmth. Black also draws in the reader by utilizing the weather as a metaphor for the sexual and emotional tension in all the storylines. Wonderful storytelling and rich characterization make this a high recommendation."—*Lambda Literary Review*

"*Hearts Aflame* takes the reader on the rough and tumble ride of the cattle drive. Heat, flood, and a sexual pervert are all part of the adventure. Heat also appears between Krista and Rae. The twists and turns of the plot engage the reader all the way to the satisfying conclusion."—*Just About Write*

"I like the author's writing style and she tells a good story. I was drawn in quickly and didn't lose interest at all. Black paints a great picture with her words and I was able to feel like I was sitting around the camp fire with the characters."—*C-Spot Reviews*

**Wild Abandon—*Lambda Literary Award Finalist***

"Black is a master at teasing the reader with her use of domination and desire. Black's first novel, *In Too Deep*, was a finalist for a 2005 Lammy. ...With *Wild Abandon*, the author continues her winning ways, writing like a seasoned pro. This is one romance I will not soon forget."—*Books to Watch Out For*

"This sequel to Ronica Black's debut novel, *In Too Deep*, is an electrifying thriller. The author's development as a fine storyteller shines with this tightly written story. ...[The mystery] keeps the story charged—never unraveling or leading us to a predictable conclusion. More than once I gasped in surprise at the dark and twisted paths this book took."—*Curve*

"Ronica Black, author of *In Too Deep*, has given her fans another fast paced novel of romance and danger. As previously, Black develops her characters fully, complete with their quirks and flaws. She is also skilled at allowing her characters to grow, and to find their way out of psychic holes. If you enjoy complex characters and passionate sex scenes, you'll love *Wild Abandon*."—*MegaScene*

"Black has managed to create two very sensual and compelling women. The backstory is intriguing, original, and quite well-developed. Yet, it doesn't detract from the primary premise of the novel—it is a sexually-charged romance about two very different and guarded women. Black carries the reader along at such a rapid pace that the rise and fall of each climactic moment successfully creates that suspension of disbelief which the reader seeks."
—*Midwest Book Review*

"Ronica Black has proven once again that she is an awesome storyteller with her new romance, *Wild Abandon*. With her second published novel, she has crafted an erotic, sensual and well-paced tale. ...Black is a master at teasing the reader with her use of domination and desire. Emotions pour endlessly from the pages, moving the plot forward at a pace that never slows or gets dull. But Black doesn't stop there. She is intent on giving the reader more. *Wild Abandon* hints at a plot twist early on, and while we know who it involves, we do not know what will happen, and how, until the last minute, effectively keeping us spellbound."
—*Just About Write*

### In Too Deep—*Lambda Literary Award Finalist*

"Ronica Black's debut novel *In Too Deep* has everything from nonstop action and intriguing well developed characters to steamy erotic love scenes. From the opening scenes where Black plunges the reader headfirst into the story to the explosive unexpected ending, *In Too Deep* has what it takes to rise to the top. Black has a winner with *In Too Deep*, one that will keep the reader turning the pages until the very last one."—*Independent Gay Writer*

"...an exciting, page turning read, full of mystery, sex, and suspense."—*MegaScene*

"...a challenging murder mystery—sections of this mixed-genre novel are hot, hot, hot. Black juggles the assorted elements of her first book with assured pacing and estimable panache."—*Q Syndicate*

"Black's characterization is skillful, and the sexual chemistry surrounding the three major characters is palpable and definitely hot-hot-hot...if you're looking for a solid read with ample amounts of eroticism and a red herring or two you're sure to find *In Too Deep* a satisfying read."—*L Word Literature*

"Ronica Black's debut novel, *In Too Deep*, is the outstanding first effort of a gifted writer who has a promising career ahead of her. Black shows extraordinary command in weaving a thoroughly engrossing tale around multi-faceted characters, intricate action and character-driven plots and subplots, sizzling sex that jumps off the page and stimulates libidos effortlessly, amidst brilliant storytelling. A clever mystery writer, Black has the reader guessing until the end."—*Midwest Book Review*

"Every time the reader has a handle on what's happening, Black throws in a curve, successfully devising a good mystery. The romance and sex add a special gift to the package rounding out the story for a totally satisfying read."—*Just About Write*

**Visit us at www.boldstrokesbooks.com**

# By the Author

# THE BREAKDOWN

*by*
## Ronica Black

2024

ISBN 13: 978-1-63679-675-8

This Trade Paperback Original Is Published By
Bold Strokes Books, Inc.
P.O. Box 249
Valley Falls, NY 12185

First Edition: September 2024

CREDITS
EDITOR: CINDY CRESAP
PRODUCTION DESIGN: SUSAN RAMUNDO
COVER DESIGN BY TAMMY SEIDICK

# Acknowledgments

To Bold Strokes Books, for all the support you continue to give me during my writing journey.

To my friends and family, for all the love and support. You mean the world to me.

## CHAPTER ONE

"Of course, I had to get the cart with the wonky wheel," Natalie Brewer said under her breath as she forcefully maneuvered around an end cap displaying cases of Pespi Zero Sugar. She hurried down the aisle, wheel squeaking, and grabbed a bag of Pepperidge Farm Milano Mint Chocolate cookies. They were her fave, and she'd hoped that finding something she liked would help to calm her anxiety a bit. But no such luck. Her heart was still beating damn near out of her chest.

"It's okay," she whispered, tossing the cookies in the cart and taking a wayward glance behind her. Sure enough, the man with the ball cap and shoulder-length blond hair came into view, entering the aisle. When he saw that he'd been spotted, he dropped his head, reached for a bag of sugar cookies, and pretended to read the label.

White-hot heat tingled up her neck to her face as she shoved the troublesome cart around another end cap, heading for the next aisle. Once there, she paused, forcing herself to act casual, to examine the different blocks of cheeses. The first few she didn't pay much attention to, too busy thinking about the mysterious man to give them much thought. But eventually, she calmed enough to focus on a nice block of Monterey Jack. She decided it was the one to go good with the fancy crackers she'd previously added to her cart. The pair would make a nice little snack, along with some white wine and some black grapes. Maybe she'd even cool off in the bath and soak in her favorite lavender bath salts as she indulged in the food. Yes, that sounded good. Maybe this day could be saved after all. That is, if the man with the hair would stop following her.

She flicked the rectangle of Monterey Jack into the cart and continued down the aisle, trying to keep her breathing steady, once again trying to convince herself that the man showing up on every aisle was just coincidence and that Allen, her ex-husband, was not having her followed. Again.

She paused to look at more cheese. She plucked a block of Kerrygold Dubliner Irish cheese. She'd never tried Irish cheese before. With a careless shrug, she tossed it into her cart and carried on. She was almost to the end of the aisle and so far, no man. Her heart fluttered with hope as she readied to turn the corner. But just as she was about to do so, she snuck a look back to double-check, unable to help herself. And there, just rounding the end cap, was the man. He quickly cast his gaze down and busied himself with the cream cheeses.

Furious, she gritted her teeth and shoved her cart quickly up to the checkout lane. Grocery shopping was over. She was sick of this shit. So damn sick of it. Allen was having her tailed again and they were making it more than obvious now, just to harass her, to frighten her, to anger her. Well, it was working, goddammit, because she couldn't help but feel all of those things. And with Allen upping his game to showing up and personally threatening her, along with damaging her property, like slashing her tires, she was more than fed up and frightened. She was terrified and hopeless.

But no one would help her and it wasn't like she hadn't tried. The cops said they couldn't prove anything in regard to Allen, but she had done as they'd suggested and taken out a restraining order. Little good that had done though. Allen had apparently just hired men to follow her. To do his dirty work for him. And now this asshole, this surfer-looking dude with hair better looking than her own, was tailing her like some annoying puppy. Jesus, when was it going to end?

She could, of course, give Allen what he wanted. She could cave and accept him back and remarry him. That would stop the current harassment, sure. But the physical and mental abuse would start up again, along with the jealousy and controlling behavior. Of this she had no doubt. She couldn't go through that again. She couldn't. She wouldn't survive.

She absently touched her neck, recalling the last time Allen had put his hands on her two weeks before when he'd forced his way into her apartment. He'd shoved her against the wall with a tight grip on her throat, telling her she could never leave, never escape him. She still had the yellow-and-purple bruising marking her skin from the encounter.

She swallowed hard, realizing that his threat was finally resonating.

Her cart protested loudly as she moved forward in line. A quick glance to her right showed that the man was now standing in the checkout lane parallel to her. He was holding a blue bottle of Powerade, his one and only purchase.

She rolled her eyes. Asshole.

She briefly considered leaving her cart and darting out the door. But she knew it was no use. She wasn't a fast runner and the man looked very fit, his surfer hair giving way to a surfer's athletic build. He'd dart out right after her, leaving his Powerade easily behind. Still, she was ready to flee. She'd packed a bag that morning with her laptop, a few days' worth of clothes and toiletries, and almost all of her savings, knowing if the chance came, she'd take off and speed away out of town. If only she could find a way to do it.

She inched forward to unload her cart. She was buying cookies, crackers, and cheese. Jesus. She hadn't even had the wherewithal to grab the wine or the grapes. Oh, well. She'd still try to have a nice relaxing bath.

But who was she kidding? She was too upset. There would be no relaxing. No nice cool bath to escape the scorching Phoenix heat. There would only be pacing up and down the hallway, while her roommate's nosy cat watched her with an all-too-sanctimonious glare. Then she'd go to her room and crash on the bed, staring up at the ceiling as the fan rotated around and around, doing very little to cool her. She'd think of her life and where it had all gone wrong, and there would be too many occurrences to count.

"Did you find everything you were looking for, Ms. Brewer?" the grocery clerk asked with a polite smile. Natalie stared at her for a moment, unsure as to how she knew her name. But then she remembered, she'd typed in her phone number for her discount membership so she could take advantage of all the sales.

"Yes, I did, thank you." She returned the smile and pulled her wallet out of her purse to leaf out some cash. She took her receipt, the few bags of groceries, and headed back out into the late August heat. She squinted against the brutal sun and tried like hell to pretend that it wasn't a hundred and seven degrees and that she wasn't out in it during the hottest part of the day.

*Please, God, allow this heat to let up. It's killing me and everyone else.*

With sweat beading her brow, she loaded up her pale yellow 2008 Chevy Aveo and climbed inside the sauna-like interior. She quickly cranked the car and blasted the AC, but it helped very little, blowing warm, rather than cold air. The car was in bad need of a freon charge. One more thing on her list that cost money she didn't have.

But she forged on.

She reversed out of the parking space and headed for the road. She was waiting there with her right turn signal on when she happened to catch a glimpse of the vehicle behind her in the rearview mirror.

"No," she said, though she wasn't surprised.

The surfer dude was behind her in a jacked up red truck.

She jutted her chin in defiance as her heart careened in her chest. Fucking Allen. Fucking fuck face Allen. She couldn't take it anymore. She just couldn't. She'd show him. Once and for all.

As soon as the road was clear to her left, she slammed on the gas and made a left turn instead of a right and peeled out across the roadway in front of oncoming traffic. Horns blared and tires screeched, but she didn't dare stop or look back, flooring her little Aveo, willing it to gain speed. She gripped the steering wheel tightly and prayed, and when her car had gained enough speed, she craned her neck to see the man in his truck still waiting in the grocery store turn lane. She smiled as she looked at herself in the mirror.

"Catch me now, asshole."

She pressed harder on the gas and made another quick turn. Then another. And soon she was on I-17 heading north out of the Phoenix city limits. But where was she going? She didn't know. She just needed to drive, to feel free for a little while, give herself time to think.

She drove for a long while and pulled off past the Rock Springs Cafe exit and drove along a dirt road for another twenty minutes. Storm clouds were building to the north, and they now looked ominous enough to strike. She'd been so focused on her thoughts that she'd failed to notice the clouds or the barren desert around her.

She stopped her vehicle and turned around in the middle of the road. She needed to head back. She honestly had nowhere to go. She couldn't afford to hide out in a hotel, though she wished like hell she could. No, her little defiant misadventure was over. But as she accelerated once again, her car hitched. A few seconds later, it hitched again and made an awful grinding noise. She looked at the gauges. The car was overheating and the check engine light was on. Her car should be used to the heat though, shouldn't it? Damned if she knew. She knew nothing about cars. Why hadn't anyone taught her about cars? Better yet, why hadn't she learned on her own?

She managed to steer the Chevy over to the side of the road just before it died.

"Great. Just great." She switched off the engine and tried to restart it. No dice. Only now there was white smoke rising from under the hood. She smacked the wheel again and cursed loudly.

Ahead of her, lightning split the deep blue sky and thunder rumbled viciously overhead. The interior of the car grew increasingly stifling, causing her to crank down her windows. But the outside air was just as stifling, and the acrid smell of the smoke made her cough.

She rested her head on the steering wheel, trying to think her way out of the predicament. She felt trapped, helpless, just like she had growing up in the foster care system. She'd had no control back then, no way out of those often times awful situations, and the feelings of déjà vu were almost overwhelming. She sat up and searched for her phone, but nothing came to mind as to how she could escape. She stared at the phone long and hard. Who would she call? What would she say?

Her roommate. She'd call Gayle and ask for her help.

She dialed her and placed the phone to her ear. But there was no connection. No service.

She threw the phone into the passenger floorboard and reached into one of the grocery bags. She dug out the Pepperidge Farm cookies and tore into the bag.

As she began to stuff her face with crunchy mint chocolate decadence, she closed her eyes and finally allowed herself to cry.

## CHAPTER TWO

"Vaughn, how you been?" Harry Townsend asked as he handed her her receipt.

"I've been getting by," she said as she took her bags full of saddle butter, coat conditioner, and horse treats. Normally she would've said she was fine. Most folks said they were just fine. But Vaughn was aware that Harry knew better, and she wasn't one to lie.

"Yeah?" he said, raising a bushy white eyebrow. "Anything you wanna share?"

Vaughn had known Harry Townsend all her life. He'd owned the feed and supply store in the Deer Valley area for over fifty years. He was a longtime family friend and she knew he was only asking out of concern.

She sighed as she adjusted her cowboy hat. "I suppose you heard about Ricky and Pedro." They were her two latest hires, and as of this morning, they were MIA.

Harry looked beyond her to where his grandson Riley had just entered the store. He nodded toward him. "Say, Ri. You hear anything about those new ranch hands over at Vaughn's?"

Riley sauntered over to the counter and pulled off his John Deere ball cap to scratch his head.

"They're over at the Cherry Blossom." He blushed, as if just saying the name of the run-down strip club was somehow sinning.

"The Cherry Blossom?" Harry let out.

Riley's blush deepened. "Yes, sir. They been there since lunch according to Bobby Dillinger."

Harry cleared his throat as if the name Bobby Dillinger had somehow choked him. "I wouldn't put too much on that now, Vaughn. Dillinger's no good."

"He's no good," Riley said. "But he wouldn't make something like that up. Besides, I seen Ricky's old pickup in the parking lot of the Cherry Blossom when I went to fill up across the street."

Vaughn sighed. "I should've known." She shouldn't have hired two men without decent references. But she'd been in a bind and needed the workers desperately. Now she was paying the price for taking such a risk while they were at the Cherry Blossom, eating cheap wings from the lunch buffet and drinking way too many cheap beers.

"It waddn't your fault, Vaughn," Harry said. "You were just trying to find some workers."

"I'm afraid it's a little more complicated than that, Harry. I been suspecting they were abusing drugs for some time now, the way they been acting on the job you see, so I told them I wanted a drug test. They refused and I threatened to fire them if they didn't comply."

"You did, did ya? Well, I don't blame you none for that, Vaughn. But it looks like they decided to save you the hassle of firing them."

"Seems so. They were mighty pissed when they left yesterday. So I can't say I'm too surprised that they didn't show today."

"I reckon not." He stroked his stubbled jaw. "You ain't the only one hurting for good workers neither."

"Yeah, I know." Truth was, every business around was looking for people who were still willing to put in a hard day's work. But they were few and far between since the COVID pandemic. At least that had been Vaughn's experience.

"I'll keep my ear to the ground for ya, Vaughn," Harry said. "See if I hear as to what their plans are, if anything."

"I appreciate that, Harry."

"I've got you all loaded up," Riley said, gesturing toward the door. He'd put the rest of her supplies in the bed of her truck, and she couldn't have been more grateful. It was hot as hell out and her back was already sore from all the chores she'd done earlier at the ranch.

She gave Riley a firm pat on the shoulder and pushed out the door. It jingled shut behind her as she glanced up at the darkening sky. Thunder rolled softly in the distance, due north. If she was right, and she usually was when it came to summer monsoons, her place would be getting hit soon. She piled her remaining supplies into the extended cab and crawled in behind the wheel. She mulled over what all she needed to do when she got home as she drove back toward the ranch. The chores seemed never-ending as of late and she was plain old exhausted. Add to that the fact that the ranch was in financial trouble, two of her best broodmares had run off that morning, which she had yet to locate, and she was damn near ready to collapse she was so overwhelmed. And she wondered, not for the first time, if Ricky and Pedro had anything to do with the missing mares. If they did, there would be hell to pay. Not showing up for work was one thing, but stealing from her was a whole other thing completely.

"What a day," she said with a sigh. And what was she going to do about Ricky and Pedro if they showed back up for work tomorrow? It had happened before. A guy named Zane she'd had working for her would no-show for a day or two and then miraculously reappear as if nothing had happened. She let it carry on for as long as she could tolerate before she finally let him go. She'd hurt for help after that for a good while until she'd found somebody new. Now she was in a similar quandary with what to do. Should she really fire their sorry asses if they returned and refused the drug test? Or give them a stern warning and allow them to continue to work? She was rubbing her tired eyes as she drove down the private road toward her ranch when she saw it.

She leaned forward in her seat, trying for better focus. But it was what she'd originally thought. Smoke. She slowed as she grew closer, panicked that it was the beginnings of a wild fire. But it wasn't a wildfire. It was a small yellow car parked off the side of the road, facing her. She crept alongside it, not expecting to see anyone, not out in this heat, and not with such heavy smoke billowing out of the vehicle. But there she was. A woman. A lone woman sitting behind the wheel crying.

Vaughn braked and reversed. She pulled off the road and killed her engine.

"What in the hell are you doing out here?" Vaughn whispered, hesitating to ask her that directly. After a short inner debate though, she eventually decided to climb out of her truck and cross the road to do just that. Her boots kicked up dust as she walked, and the woman hurriedly wiped at her face as she saw Vaughn approach.

"I'm fine," the woman let out, startling Vaughn. "I'm okay, really. No need to bother."

Vaughn stopped next to the car, grimacing at the irritating pungency of the smoke. "You aren't a bother," she said, searching her face for clues as to who she was and why she was on her private road. But none seemed to be forthcoming, leaving Vaughn with nothing to do but take in her short, raven-black hair and captivating green eyes. She was a beauty.

"Really," the woman said. "I'm okay."

Vaughn forced herself to focus, and as the woman turned to look at her again, Vaughn noticed what looked like bruising on her neck. Vaughn wondered what it was from, or rather, *who* it was from. "It doesn't look it," she said, shifting her gaze back to the smoking hood. The woman followed her line of sight.

"Oh, it'll be fine."

The woman was being ridiculous. "I don't think so."

"It will," the woman insisted. "I'm just going to wait it out."

Vaughn checked the surrounding desert, concerned that maybe whoever had left those marks was hiding somewhere nearby. But she saw no one. "Really?"

"Sure."

Thunder cracked loudly overhead. Vaughn looked up just as fat drops of rain began to fall and slap the dry earth. Vaughn held out her palms, enjoying the feel of the cold droplets but worrying about her mares. She needed to get home; she didn't have time to wait on this beautiful but battered stranger. Still, something told her to stay, that the woman needed help even though she wasn't directly asking for it.

"Yeah, well, just so you know, no one else is likely to come by here this evening." She leveled her gaze at her. "No one besides me."

The woman seemed to think that over and, for a second, Vaughn thought she'd caused her enough concern to concede that help was needed. But then she put on the plastic smile again. "That's okay."

Vaughn glanced back at the engine. Orange flames were now tickling the edges of the hood. She reached for the door handle.

"Enough small talk," Vaughn said. "It's time to get out of the car."

"What?" She appeared alarmed. "No."

"Ma'am, the car is on fire. It's dangerous to remain inside."

"On fire?" She looked through the windshield, trying to see. "I don't—"

"Come on, you've got to get out now." Vaughn opened the door and reached for her arm, but the woman pulled away from her.

"I can do it," she said.

Vaughn held up her hands. "Okay."

The woman reached into the passenger seat to grab her purse and some grocery bags. Vaughn eyed the burning engine, worried she wasn't moving fast enough.

"Come on, now," she said. "You've got to hurry."

The woman stood with the bags in tow. Vaughn tried to help her, but the woman pointed at the hatchback instead. "My bag," she said. "And my laptop. They're in the back."

Vaughn hurried to the back, popped the door, and retrieved the bags. And just as they began to walk away from the car, there was an enormous bang and the woman smashed into Vaughn in sheer fright, careening them both onto their backs on the dirt road. Heavy drops of rain pelted Vaughn as she blinked for focus. Once up on her elbows, Vaughn could see that the hood had blown and the entire front end of the car was now engulfed in flames. She secured her hat and crawled to her feet, already able to feel the pressing heat from the fire, and helped the woman stand.

"Come on, we need to get away from the car," Vaughn said as she led the woman toward her truck. They grabbed the bags and stood watching the car burn for a moment, the white smoke now churning black, rising into the dark blueberry sky.

"I don't understand," the woman said, tearing up again. "It was running fine yesterday. And today, just out of nowhere, it started to overheat."

"It's hard telling," Vaughn said. "Just be thankful you're okay."

"Yeah, that's a bit hard to do right now. That was my only mode of transportation." She wiped her tears with the back of her arm, lifting the grocery bags to do so. Vaughn gently took the bags from her, now carrying them all.

"I'm Vaughn, by the way. Vaughn Ruger."

"Natalie Brewer."

"Hi, Natalie."

Vaughn went to place the bags in the extended cab of her truck.

"What are you doing?" Natalie asked.

"I'm loading up your goods."

"Why?"

"Because I'm giving you a ride. Figured you'd just come with me to my place to wait for help. I'm just up the road a ways. 'Less you want to wait for the fire department. They'll probably arrive soon enough."

"I thought you said no one else would be out this way."

"That was before your car blew, ma'am. Now with the heavy smoke and flames, the fire department will surely be notified. The wildfire risk is too high for them not to respond. So, what do you think? You want to come with me, or wait for them?"

Vaughn stared up at the sky again as she waited for Natalie to decide. Thunder boomed and more lightning veined the sky. Vaughn held onto her hat as small pellets of hail began to fall. She tried to lead Natalie to her truck by the elbow, but Natalie remained still, looking down at the hail as if in complete disbelief.

"This can't be happening," she said.

"You coming?" Vaughn asked as she crawled inside the safety of her truck.

Natalie glanced back at her and, after giving her a defeated look, finally rounded the truck and joined her. She crawled in next to Vaughn and slammed the door and they both sat in silence for a moment, gathering their thoughts. Vaughn grabbed a towel from the cab behind her and handed it over. Natalie took it eagerly and wiped her face while Vaughn rubbed her own face with her damp hands.

"Some storm, eh?" Vaughn said, turning down the radio.

"Mm." Natalie appeared to be lost in thought, staring out through the hail-assaulted windshield. "I can't believe this is happening."

"Bad day?"

"The worst."

Vaughn started the truck. Natalie swung her head around. She looked back to her burning car. "Ah, shit, my phone!" She started to reach for the door handle, but Vaughn stopped her.

"Wait, you can't go."

"I need my phone!"

Vaughn tightened her grip on her arm. "It's too dangerous."

"Let me go!"

But another loud bang shook the truck and they both crouched in response. When they looked back over at the car, Vaughn saw that the entire thing was now burning, leaving no room for debate about going for the phone.

"No!" Natalie said. "No, no, no!"

Vaughn tried to comfort her, but Natalie wanted no part of it. She just kept saying no and crying, tears streaming down her face. Vaughn, clueless as to what to do with the beautiful woman sobbing in her vehicle, did the only thing she could do. She drove away, leaving the burning Chevy on the side of the road to be consumed by the fire.

Natalie watched out the back window for a long while before she faced front again. She wiped at her tear-stained cheeks and sniffled.

"I know it doesn't seem like it right now, but it's going to be okay," Vaughn said softly, more worried about the marks on her neck than the burning car.

"Please don't speak of things you can't possibly know."

Vaughn tried again. "The car, it's replaceable and—"

"I didn't have full coverage," she stated. "I couldn't afford it."

"Oh."

"See? It's not all going to be okay. None of it is."

Vaughn remained silent. Natalie looked at the surrounding desert as the storm carried on, strong winds now jostling the truck.

"Are you okay?" Vaughn asked. "Did someone…hurt you?"

Natalie touched her neck but didn't speak right away.

"Because you're safe now. And we can call the police when—"

"No!"

"Okay," Vaughn said, not wanting to frighten her.

"I can't let him know where I am," Natalie said, almost to herself. "I can't let anyone know."

Vaughn let the comment go, sensing that she was more like a scared, cornered animal than a rational human being. One wrong move and she'd scamper, never to be seen again.

"How far to your place?" Natalie asked.

Vaughn pointed. "Just right up here."

They pulled onto the ranch road, this one leading them to the broad wrought iron entryway with the words Midnight Mine Ranch spelled out overhead. Vaughn climbed out briefly to open the gate below and returned to the truck.

Natalie mouthed the words of the ranch aloud as they drove through.

"Neat name," she finally said.

"Thanks."

"It's yours?" she asked.

"Yes, ma'am. Been in my family for three generations."

"Wow." She looked at her. "What kind of ranch is it?"

Vaughn slowed the wiper speed as the hail stopped falling. She drove down the front drive, through the countless cottonless cottonwood trees and the large corrals that flanked them. And beyond those, stood the stables. "Horse ranch," she said. "We breed the finest quarter horses around."

Natalie's eyes grew wide and she stared back out the window, presumably to look for said horses.

"You like horses?" Vaughn asked, once again thinking about her missing broodmares. She'd put a good portion of her horses in the stables before she'd left, knowing a storm was due to blow in. But a few remained turned out, and according to what she could see, her missing broodmares still weren't among them.

"I love them."

"Really? You ride?"

She shook her head.

"Ever?"

"No. I uh...never got the chance."

Vaughn found that bit of news particularly sad. She wanted to offer her some lessons, but she thought better of it. Natalie was already upset at having to come to her home. She didn't want to push things.

Vaughn slowed as they came upon the main house, which was a Spanish-style hacienda, with white stuccoed walls and a red-tiled roof. The walls were in bad need of a paint job and the roof needed some repairs, but money had been tight as of late and she hadn't been able to afford to get those things done. She hoped, when the cooler weather came, that she'd be able to do most of the repairs herself.

"Who's that?" Natalie asked as Vaughn's grandmother, June, walked out through the courtyard to wait next to the driveway.

"That's June," Vaughn said. "My gram."

Natalie looked at Vaughn in disbelief. "Your grandmother? She's looks great."

Vaughn chuckled. "That she does." They watched as Gram sank her hands into the back pockets of her jeans as she waited for them to climb out of the truck. She was dressed similarly to Vaughn, in a T-shirt and jeans and cowboy boots. Her wild white hair was blowing in the wind, and she had that all-too-familiar look upon her face as she silently questioned who was riding shotgun next to Vaughn.

"I hope I look that good when I'm her age," Natalie said.

Vaughn killed the engine and opened her door. "We should all be that lucky."

Natalie climbed out the passenger side as Vaughn secured her cowboy hat on her head and gave a nod to Gram. "Those mares come back?"

"Mojo did," she said. "I stabled her up."

"Great," Vaughn said, inhaling the fresh scent of rain and recently watered earth. "One down, one to go."

Thunder rumbled overheard, though it sounded farther away now. Maybe the storm was letting up. Summer monsoons didn't usually last very long, so she was hoping she was right. The sooner she could get on the four-wheeler to go looking for Hazel, the remaining broodmare, the better.

"Who's this?" Gram asked as Natalie joined them.

"Hi, I'm Natalie." She extended her hand.

"June Ruger. Nice to meet you."

Natalie gave a shy smile. "You as well."

Vaughn watched as Gram sussed her out. Though Gram was eighty-five, she was every bit as fit as Vaughn was, and that included her mind, which was still sharp as a tack. So Vaughn wasn't surprised when she focused in on Natalie's bruises right away, but didn't speak of them.

"What brings you out this way, Natalie?"

"My car—uh—it kind of blew up."

Gram's eyebrows lifted. "Oh?"

"It actually did," Vaughn clarified. "We left it on fire up by the turnoff."

"Well, my goodness," Gram said. "Do I need to put in a call to the fire department?"

"Wouldn't hurt," Vaughn said.

Gram looked back at Natalie. "Are you okay, darlin'?"

"I—" She crumbled into tears as if she'd been holding in the real pain for far too long and could no longer contain it. Gram embraced her and looked curiously to Vaughn.

Vaughn knew then that it was going to be a long night and that Hazel might have to just wait.

## CHAPTER THREE

Natalie finished towel drying her hair and smoothed down the soft, old T-shirt and a pair of jeans she'd changed into. She looked at herself in the mirror and wiped away the remnants of mascara from around her eyes. She'd seen way better days, but there was nothing she could do about it now.

She ran a comb through her damp hair, trying to clear her mind. A knock came from the bathroom door.

"You doing okay, darlin'?" It was June, checking on her.

Natalie gave herself one last look and extinguished the lights. She opened the door and emerged. June stood waiting for her with a caring smile.

"Fine, thanks," Natalie said. June grazed her arm.

"Good, I'm glad." She led her down the hall of the cool, cozy home and into the kitchen. Vaughn stood at the worn pale yellow counter, sipping from a mug of coffee. Though it was hot outside, the coffee smelled delicious.

Natalie climbed onto a barstool and noted that Vaughn had changed clothes as well. Now she was in a black tee with faded jeans rather than a dirty white tee and dark jeans. She seemed to look fetching regardless of what she was wearing. In a rugged cowgirl sort of way.

She slid Natalie a mug of hot coffee.

"Thank you," Natalie said, wrapping her hands around the hot cup of joe. "You've both been...so kind."

June waved her off. "Shoot, that's nothing, sugar. We're just being hospitable."

Natalie sipped her coffee. It was divine. "Still, you've been kind. Thank you."

"You're welcome," Vaughn said, sipping from her own mug. Her cowboy hat hung by the door, and she appeared to have brushed her hair, combing it away from her face and tucking the sun-streaked brown strands behind her ears, which seemed to accent her angled jaw. But her eyes were what were the most striking. They were a light, piercing blue, and they felt as though they were pinning Natalie to her seat.

Natalie offered a self-conscious smile and broke Vaughn's gaze by staring into her steaming coffee.

"Oh," Vaughn said, reaching across the counter for the cordless phone. "I suppose you need to use this." She slid the phone to her, much like she'd done the mug of coffee.

Natalie stared at the phone, unsure as to what to do. She didn't exactly have family she could call. And close friends? Well, she'd lost those when she'd married Allen. He'd been sure to run them off and she'd yet to reconnect, trying hard instead to rebuild her financial security. So, who was she going to call? An Uber? Sure, she could. But she'd just end up back at home, where she was sure the man would be waiting in his truck, starting the whole cycle over again. Only now, she had no vehicle, no way to escape, even if she wanted to try.

*Fuck.*

She lifted the phone and dialed the only person she knew who would halfway give a shit. Gayle, her roommate of less than a year, answered on the third ring.

"I told you, I don't like dick pics," she said by way of greeting.

Natalie stammered, confused. "Uh, what?"

"Who is this?"

"Gayle, it's Nat."

"Nat?"

"Natalie. Your roommate."

"Oh, right. Thought you were someone else."

*Apparently.*

Gayle bit into something that sounded crunchy and chewed in Natalie's ear.

"Listen, Gayle, I've had a bit of a mishap with my car. I'm okay, but I'm—"

"Mishap? What, did it blow up or something?" More crunching. Natalie winced and realized that calling her was probably a mistake. Gayle didn't pay much mind to her or take things seriously on a good day, so what made her think she would now?

"Yes, actually, it did."

"What? No way!" She laughed. "Jesus, Nat."

"It's really not funny." This was a mistake. The last thing she needed was to be laughed at for her misfortune. Fucking Gayle. She could almost picture her, sitting on the couch, munching on a bag of chips after having smoked a fat joint, binge-watching some reality show with the volume up incredibly loud, doing her best to ignore the rest of the planet.

"That's crazy," she said. "I mean—it seriously blew up?"

"Crazy or not, it happened," Natalie said. "And I don't appreciate the laughter." Silence. More crunching. Natalie decided to put an end to the torture. "Anyway, just wanted to let you know that I'm okay and that…. I might not be back for a while." Natalie could've elaborated further, Gayle knowing about her recent troubles with Allen, but Natalie didn't think it wise to share everything with her at the moment, just in case he decided to come around. If Gayle was one thing, it was a blabbermouth. Intentional or not. And Natalie didn't want her involved in this. It was for Gayle's own protection as it was hers.

The statement seemed to have got Gayle's attention.

"What?"

"So, you can have that friend of yours stay temporarily if you want." Gayle had an on-again, off-again boyfriend she'd really been wanting to come and stay, but Natalie had always refused because the apartment was too small and she didn't want another human to pick up after. One child was enough.

"You serious?"

"He can cover my rent for a while." She wasn't totally sure about this, but she was sure about one thing. She did not want to go home. And with Gayle's boyfriend paying half the rent, Natalie could now spend her money on somewhere else to stay.

"Great, Nat, thanks. Er, when will you be back?"

"I don't know. But I'll give you as much of a heads-up as I can."

"Okay."

"Good-bye, Gayle."

"Bye."

Natalie handed the phone back to Vaughn, who seemed surprised that the call had ended so soon.

"Roommate," Natalie said.

Vaughn eyed the phone. "Did you want to call someone else for a ride?"

Natalie shook her head, as the realization that she had no one and nowhere to go struck again. Tears brimmed as she searched her mind for a plan. And they threatened to fall as she thought of Allen and his threats.

"Would you like for me to give you a ride?" Vaughn asked.

"No, you don't have to do that—" Vaughn was being so kind.

These people—they were so nice. Why couldn't she have good people like these in her life? After all, she was a good person, wasn't she?

June touched her arm again and Natalie turned to face her, her chest now burning with the pent-up pain. The older woman with the wild white hair was looking at her with the kindest, sweetest face she'd ever seen.

"You okay, darlin'?"

Natalie tried to speak, but instead she fell into her gaze and fell into sobs. June drew her to her and held her tight, quietly soothing her as she patted her back. Natalie clung to her, feeling secure in her wiry frame, wishing she'd had someone to embrace her like this all those many years ago when she'd lost her father. And then again as she'd gone from foster home to foster home.

"Shh, there, there," June whispered. Natalie withdrew and wiped her eyes. June tried to help, using her rough-feeling fingers to smooth away the tears. "Why don't you tell us what's going on with you?"

Natalie gulped a breath of air, caught on the tail end of a sob, and settled once again onto the barstool. Her heart raced like a tiny bird's in her rib cage, but something told her she could trust these people. Perhaps it was their kindness, or maybe their vibrant, caring eyes. She wasn't sure. She just knew that she felt…safe.

"I don't know where to start," she said.

"At the beginning," June said with an encouraging smile.

"If I did that, we'd be here all day."

"That's okay," June said.

Natalie calmed her breathing. "I'll share with you what's going on now. I'm recently divorced," she said. "It's been less than a year and my husband, er, my ex-husband, doesn't want to let me go."

"Uh-oh," June said, giving a knowing look to Vaughn.

Natalie waited to see if they were going to share what they were thinking, but when they didn't, she continued. "He's been harassing me, stalking me even. Calling me at all hours of the day and night. And he…" She stroked her neck. "Did this. I reported him, but a friend of his lied and provided an alibi for him, so the best I could do was get a restraining order against him. Now he's having *other* people follow me and harass me and I just can't take it anymore. I'm going nuts. So, earlier today when I saw that I was once again being followed, I lost my tail and drove out here, just to get away for a little while. Only, my car decided to implode on me and well, here I am. Thankfully, I'd already packed an emergency bag full of necessities."

June looked to Vaughn again. They exchanged a long glance. June spoke to Natalie once again. "Sounds like you've been through a lot, sugar. I'm so sorry."

"Me, too," Vaughn said. "No one deserves that."

Natalie stifled a cry. "Thanks, but I feel bad. I shouldn't be burdening you all with this. It's just that, I feel like I'm losing it.

Ever since I started crying in the car, I can't seem to stop. I'm just totally breaking down."

"That's understandable," Vaughn said. "When you've been traumatized like you have."

"What are you going to do now?" June asked. "Do you have a plan?"

Natalie snorted. "Disappear?"

June squeezed her arm. "I wish you could, sugar. I wish you could."

There was a brief silence. Then Vaughn pulled June aside and they whispered together off in the corner. Natalie stared at the counter, feeling exposed and vulnerable. She'd just shared some of her deepest troubles with these people and now they were discussing her. She couldn't help it, but she felt ashamed. She shouldn't be in this position. But this was how her life had seemed to always go. She'd just always had to deal with the worst of circumstances, including her time with Allen. God, why had she ever bought into his bullshit?

*Because he promised me a life beyond all the bullshit I'd been through.*

Vaughn and June returned with June placing a hand on her shoulder, as if to reassure her, but it did little to calm her nerves.

"You do believe me, don't you?" The last thing she wanted was for these two nice people to worry about her lying. "I can show you the copy of the restraining order. I have it."

Vaughn spoke. "You can show it to us if you'd like. But it's not necessary. We believe you. We've had some experience in this area, unfortunately, with a close family member. We remember what it's like. The pain, the anguish, the constant looking over your shoulder. And we don't want you to have to do that. So, we've talked it over and we think you should stay with us, in our guesthouse. We're not using it and it would give you a safe place to hide for a while…"

Natalie spoke up, her need to reassure *them* now instant and overwhelming. "I could pay rent. I mean, not much, but I'd give you what I could, and I'd be glad to help out around the ranch. I know I don't know much, but I'm a fast learner."

Vaughn smiled.

June chuckled. "Well, Vaughn's a heck of a teacher and we could use an extra hand. And you deserve to feel safe in the place where you lay your head. Everyone does."

Natalie held back more tears, ones of gratitude. She felt hopeful for the first time in ages. "I really appreciate this," she said. "You have no idea."

"Do you need to get anything else from your place?" Vaughn asked.

"No. And even if I did, I wouldn't go back. I wouldn't risk it. Besides, I don't need much."

"She can get whatever else she may need here," June said. "Or we can pick it up for her."

"That work for you?" Vaughn asked.

Vaughn and June were going out on a limb for her. They didn't even know her, yet they were willing to help. Her luck was finally changing. "If it works for you."

June patted her shoulder. "It's a deal." She headed for the front door. "I'll let you and Vaughn work out the rest while I go hunt down Hazel."

"I can do that, Gram," Vaughn said, making a move for the door.

"No, no. You stay and work things out with Natalie. I'll be just fine." She shrugged into a light raincoat and tamed her unruly hair beneath a black cowboy hat. Then, with one last smile and a wink toward Vaughn, she was out the door and back into the stormy night.

"She's very nice," Natalie said. "You both are."

"Like she said," Vaughn said. "We're just being hospitable."

Natalie laughed. "You mean you're always this nice to strange women you pick up off the side of the road?"

"Mm, you seem to be the exception."

"Guess I'm just lucky."

"Guess so." A grin lifted the corner of her mouth just before she sipped more coffee.

They began to discuss rent and the particulars of Natalie's stay. Though embarrassing, Natalie told her of limited finances, explaining that she'd been laid off from her job at the credit card company, but that she was still able to support herself with her side hustle. She wrote blogs for a few companies, promoting their products, and now that she was able to do that mostly full time, she was pulling in a livable salary. She still had to live by a strict budget, which she explained to Vaughn, so that meant only a certain amount could be spent on rent. Vaughn, thankfully, understood and offered her an affordable amount.

Vaughn led her out to the guesthouse, which was nestled behind the main house. It was a small Spanish-style cottage with a matching color scheme to the bigger house. She could see that the front was once rich with vegetation and some wildflowers, but had since given way to mostly dead plants and weeds, no doubt due to the relentless summer heat. Nevertheless, it looked like a nice place and the inside looked cozy and comfortable, though stifling hot. Vaughn showed her around, turning on the AC, flipping on lights and fans, and removing furniture covers. The floor was covered in dark tile and the furniture was older and worn. An arched wood burning fireplace adorned the wall of the small living room, flanked by a heavy-looking armchair and a small sofa. Natalie immediately pictured herself there, curled up with a hot cup of coffee and a good book, fire or not.

The bedroom was equally as cozy with a full-sized bed, a chair, and a night table. A beautiful painting of a dark-haired woman in a red Mexican-style dress hung on the wall.

"And here's the bathroom," Vaughn said. "Extra toothbrushes, toothpaste, shampoo, and soap, are all in the cabinet here, along with the towels."

Natalie peered inside just before Vaughn switched off the light.

"And that should do it. We'll get you stocked up with groceries tomorrow. And your cheeses? They weren't kept cool enough I'm afraid. I wouldn't eat them if I were you."

Natalie laughed. "Those were kind of a silly buy anyway." She'd only hung on to them for fear they'd be her only means of food for a while. She just couldn't afford to throw away money.

Vaughn sank her hands into her pockets. "You sure? Because we have some Monterey Jack in our fridge if you'd like some?"

"Really?" She realized just how hungry she was, and she still had her crackers. "I think I'll take you up on that."

"Come on," Vaughn said with a wave as they once again headed for the door. "We'll get you all taken care of."

Natalie smiled as she followed her out into the stormy night.

*You don't have to ask me twice, Vaughn Ruger.*

## CHAPTER FOUR

S he sure seems like a nice young gal," Gram said, referring to their new guest, Natalie, as Vaughn drained a third horse bucket and poured in some apple cider vinegar to scrub it with.

"Yes, she does. A bit browbeat, but nice nonetheless."

Gram helped scrub away the lingering algae in another bucket. It was nearing ten at night and Vaughn was finally on the last of the daily chores after having found Natalie on the private road. The chores were the ones Ricky and Pedro were responsible for and here she was trying like hell to finish them up. She'd already mucked out the stalls in both stables and given the horses their supplements. She'd double-checked all the fans, made sure there was no storm damage, and now it was time to clean out all the water buckets in the stables.

"I figured you were thinking the same as I was as far as Natalie's concerned," Gram said.

Vaughn didn't really want to get into it, but she knew Gram wouldn't let up until it was discussed. And she was right. They'd been thinking along the same lines. "I suppose."

"Have you spoken to her lately?"

She was referring to Sissy, Vaughn's aunt. She'd moved away a few years before due to a horrible divorce and her story had sounded a lot like Natalie's.

"I haven't. You?"

Gram sighed. "Not in a while."

"I'm sure she's fine." She was sure of no such thing. But Sissy kept to herself. There wasn't much they could do.

"Maybe," Gram said. "She's just so different since..."

"I know," Vaughn said.

"She's never going to be the same."

"'Fraid not."

Gram straightened. "I hope Natalie doesn't suffer the same effects." Gone was the free-spirited extroverted Sissy they'd all known and loved. What remained was a quiet, reserved woman who had very little time or trust for anyone. It was heartbreaking.

"It's hard telling, Gram," Vaughn said as she continued to scrub. "But he's already put his hands on her and we know how that can escalate."

"Mm-hm."

"But if he can't find her, then it shouldn't be a problem."

"And if he does find her?"

"We call the cops. He won't be stepping foot on this ranch if I can help it."

Gram pressed her lips together.

"What?" Vaughn asked, sensing she was holding something back, which she rarely did.

"I'm just worried about the initial visit from him. The visit to let us know he's found her."

Vaughn straightened. "We call the cops. As soon as we set eyes on him."

"And while we wait for the police?"

Vaughn shook her head. "It probably won't come to that, Gram."

"Just to be sure, I'm going to keep the guns loaded."

Vaughn looked at her incredulously.

"You don't know this man," Gram said. "Nor do we really know this woman."

"You're catastrophizing."

"And you're downplaying a possibly very serious situation."

"Hey, I didn't hear you protesting."

"Because I think you're right. We should help her. But we should also be cautious. That's all I'm saying, child."

Vaughn closed her eyes. "Okay. We'll be careful. Keep our eyes open."

"And the guns loaded."

They worked some more and moved on to the next few buckets before Gram spoke again. "She's pretty, too."

Vaughn met her gaze. "Who?"

"Natalie."

"So?"

"So, you noticed."

"Doesn't mean anything."

June grinned. "Been a long time since you've admitted a woman was good-looking."

"Yeah, well, like I said. Doesn't mean anything."

"You're probably right. Best to leave it alone. She's got some trouble to contend with before she's available."

Vaughn laughed. "Jesus, Gram."

"What? I'm conceding. She's off the market."

"Even if she was on the market, as you say, I wouldn't be interested."

"Why not?"

"Because—well, we don't even know her for starters."

"But we invited her to stay in our guesthouse, did we not?"

"We—"

"Uh-huh."

Vaughn rolled her eyes.

"I know you well, Vaughn Marie Ruger. So don't even try to get anything past me."

"I just thought she could use the help." Vaughn said. "And that maybe the extra money would help us too."

"Kill two birds with one stone."

"Yes."

They worked some more in silence.

"You said you found Hazel?" Vaughn asked, the muscles in her back burning from overexertion. Her back pain was getting worse with every day, but she tried to hide that from Gram. She wondered though, how much worse it was going to get and whether or not she could keep hiding it.

"I did and I've been meaning to talk to you about that. She was out beyond the east fence line with a wire tangled around her ankle. It cut into her a bit."

"Shit." Vaughn stopped scrubbing. Just what they needed, an injured horse.

"I cut it loose, and tended to her, but you'll need to double-check her wound."

"It bad?"

"Just a small cut. Nothing serious."

They backed away as Vaughn rinsed out the buckets.

"I thought for a while there that maybe Ricky and Pedro had taken Hazel and Mojo both," Vaughn said, wiping her brow with the back of her arm. The storm had left a heavy, humid feel to the air. Something Phoenicians did not appreciate, and the big floor fans in the stables weren't doing much to help.

"I was thinking the same thing," Gram said.

"You don't think they let them out of the corral and into the field do you?"

Gram held her brush out for Vaughn to rinse. "I don't rightly know, Vaughn. Those boys…it's hard telling."

Vaughn was just about to agree with her when she heard someone enter the stables.

"Is that vinegar I smell?" Natalie asked as she joined them.

"It is," Vaughn answered as she handed the hose over to Gram to finish filling the buckets. She saw the questions on Natalie's face. She was wondering about the vinegar. "It helps clean and prevent algae growth and we also add it to help with the horses' digestion."

"Huh. I never would've guessed," Natalie said, crossing her arms over her chest.

"Thought for sure you'd be asleep," Vaughn said. They'd talked for a while more after she'd shown Natalie the guesthouse. They'd had some cheese and crackers and mainly spoke of the running of the ranch. Natalie had thanked Vaughn again and wished her a good night before returning to the guest cottage.

Vaughn wicked away more sweat from her forehead, removing her cowboy hat to do so.

"Couldn't sleep," Natalie said. "And I heard you two out moving around so I thought I'd see if I could help."

"There's nothing left to do tonight," Gram said. "'Less you wanna help Vaughn tend to some cuts on Hazel."

Natalie looked at Vaughn with hope in her eyes. "Can I?"

Vaughn shrugged, not used to people getting excited over treating some minor cuts. "Sure." She led Natalie to one of the supply shelves where they housed the first aid materials. She walked down to Hazel's stall, gave her some gentle pats, and opened the door to enter. Vaughn carefully cleaned her hands with antiseptic gel before she got started removing the taped-on gauze. Luckily, from what she could see, the wound on Hazel's leg wasn't very deep.

"Here you go," Vaughn said, handing the hand sanitizer to Natalie.

Natalie cleaned her hands and hesitantly stepped inside the stall. "Is this okay?" she asked, as if each step might rattle the horse.

"You're fine," Vaughn said, smiling to herself. "Hazel doesn't spook easy."

"Oh. Good to know."

Vaughn knelt closer and reached back toward Natalie. "You want to hand me that wound cleaner there? The white bottle. And some gauze?"

Natalie did as instructed and Vaughn began cleaning the wound. She knew that Gram had already done so, but it never hurt to do it twice. Hazel took a few miniscule steps but otherwise remained in place.

"Good girl," Vaughn cooed. "That's a good girl."

"How did she hurt herself?" Natalie asked.

"She got tangled up in some wire."

"That sounds painful."

"It does, doesn't it?" Vaughn sprayed on more cleaner and dabbed the last cut with the gauze. "She's lucky this is mostly superficial."

"How did she, you know, come across the wire?"

"She most likely got too close to the outside fence line when that storm rolled in. She wasn't supposed to be out that way, but there she was. That's where Gram found her."

"Does that happen often? Horses going where they aren't supposed to?"

Vaughn reached back again and met her curious gaze. "No. Not often. Will you hand me that Silvet Silver Spray now? The gray bottle."

Natalie handed it over. Vaughn applied it generously to the wound and straightened, trash in hand. "That should do it."

Natalie smiled as if feeling truly accomplished. "She's all better?"

"Should be, in about a week or so. We'll keep her duties light until then."

Vaughn exited the stall, allowed Natalie to follow, and closed it up and threw away the used gauze. She cleaned her hands again and led them out of the stables. She'd hoped for a gentle breeze outside to help stir the heavy feel to the air, but she was met with disappointment. Maybe a ride on the Quadrunner would help.

"I need to ride out to where Hazel was found to check that fence line before I turn in," she said.

"Mind if I come along?" Natalie asked. "I'd love to see more of the ranch."

Vaughn appreciated her eagerness to help, but she was tired, bordering on exhausted, and the thought of Natalie clinging to her on the back of the four-wheeler sent her head spinning to places it shouldn't go.

"You wouldn't be able to see much tonight," Vaughn said. "And I really need to make it a quick check."

The letdown wasn't well disguised on Natalie's face. But she lightheartedly smiled, nonetheless. "Raincheck?"

"Sure."

"Okay." She began to walk slowly away. "I guess I'll see you tomorrow."

"We'll be up bright and early," Vaughn said.

"I will too, then."

"Hey, Natalie," Vaughn called.

"Yeah?" She appeared hopeful, like maybe Vaughn had changed her mind about her coming with.

"Did the house get cooled off enough to sleep?" She couldn't believe she hadn't thought of the temperature in the cottage sooner. It had been closed up for weeks with the AC off to save money. And now she expected a guest to sleep in it after only a few hours of the air cooling.

"It's doable," Natalie said.

"Because we have an extra bedroom. In the main house, if you'd like to sleep there for the night."

Natalie seemed grateful but resigned. "I'll be okay, thanks."

"You sure?"

"I'm sure."

Vaughn waved and Natalie returned it before she walked away for good. Vaughn watched her go, thinking about the crazy day and how it had all turned out. She never would've imagined coming across a beautiful woman on the side of the road, car on fire, needing a place to stay. As Gram would say, you couldn't make this shit up.

She tugged on her cowboy hat and climbed on the four-wheeler. And as she rode out to the far edge of the ranch, Natalie crossed her mind once again. She thought about the way her dark bangs hung over her eyes and the way she brushed them back as if it were a nervous habit. She thought about her laugh. Though hesitant at times, it resonated and left Vaughn feeling lighthearted and full of laughter herself. She thought of her bruises and her story about a violent ex-husband. It hurt her heart to think about someone doing that to her, or any woman for that matter.

She slowed as she came to the edge of the east property, shining her Maglite along the fence line. She spotted the loose wire almost immediately; a tangle of it had settled at the base of the fence. She crawled off the four-wheeler, slipped on her leather gloves, and cut the wire free. Hazel was lucky she didn't get tangled and caught up in the fencing in the heat of the day. That would have been very bad indeed. And still she wondered, how the hell the horses got out to the pasture to begin with.

With the wayward wire in hand, she walked over to the Quadrunner and secured the wire to the back. She headed back to the house, ready to call it a night, with Natalie Brewer already on her mind once again.

# CHAPTER FIVE

*N*atalie shifted on the sofa and brought the soft fleece throw to her chest to snuggle up in. The night was warm, but the apartment was chilled since Gayle kept the AC set to "morgue." Natalie had opened the front door a little to even out the temperature since Gayle wasn't home. Boomer, Gayle's fat cat, was home however, and he jumped down from the back of the couch to stand at the screen door. He meowed as if he wanted to go out.

"No, Boomer, you can't go." He was forever asking to go outside, but she and Gayle were concerned about the nearby coyotes, so they were diligent about keeping him safe indoors.

He meowed again, longer and louder, angling his furry orange head back at her.

"You can't go. So, give it a rest, okay?" At this rate, she'd have to shut the door. She didn't want to listen to him crying all night.

She snuggled deeper into the sofa with the throw and thumbed up the volume on an episode of Alone on Netflix. She wasn't quite sure why, but watching individuals battle the elements of nature while completely alone resonated with her. She could do without the hunting scenes, but she rather enjoyed the show and enjoyed seeing how the contestants overcame various obstacles. She'd had to overcome quite a few herself in life, and she was having to do so again, so she enjoyed watching people battle the odds.

Boomer cried again and she smacked her forehead in frustration. "Boomer. For the love of God." But the light to the front porch clicked on, surprising her. It was motion-sensor, but she didn't see anyone nearby.

"Probably just a bird," she said as she returned her attention to the program. The porch light, which she could see out of the corner of her eye, switched off and she relaxed. Boomer began pawing at the screen door, rattling it and scaring her to death.

"Boom!" she shouted, as she tore off the throw and marched to the door. The porch light remained off, but she heard a scattering noise, like dry leaves scraping across concrete. "There's nothing out there," she said, although she wasn't so sure. "And you can't go out."

He cried again and she shooed him away from the door. He returned at once, pawing again at the metal screen. She knelt and scooped him up. She carried him to the couch and set him down. But Boomer darted for the door again and the light once again clicked on.

"Alright," she said. "I've had enough." She turned off the porch light and went to lock the screen door, intent on shutting the main door as well, but to her shock, the screen door was yanked open, and she was shoved quickly back inside, tripping over her feet. The fall to the floor was forceful and painful and she scrambled for bearing. But before she could even sit up, her ex-husband, Allen, was on top of her, pinning her to the ground.

She tried to call for help, but he stifled her mouth with a leather-clad hand.

"Shut up," he seethed. "Shut the fuck up. You scream, I'll kill you. Understand?"

She blinked at him, fighting for breath. He released her and stood, tugging her up alongside him, spinning her so she was against the wall, held in place with his hand to her throat.

She stared into his eyes. They looked wide and demented, the pupils fully dilated. Spittle dotted the corner of his tight mouth.

"You think you can get away from me? Do you? Well, you're wrong. You can't ever escape me, Nat, you hear me?" He smiled wickedly and she was certain he was going to kill her. The shiny blade he brandished next to her face all but convinced her. And *when he caressed her cheek with the back of the blade, her heart nearly tripped over itself.*

*"Please," she managed, his grip growing tighter. She could hardly swallow, and black spots were now dancing in her vision. "Don't hurt me."*

*"Don't hurt me," he mimicked her. "God, you're pathetic. Always playing the victim. Poor little Natalie. Boo-hoo. My daddy died when I was little. I had to go into foster care and live with strangers and they were so mean to me. Boo-hoo-hoo." He brought her forward and thrust her back again. She hit her head against the wall. She clawed at his hand, desperate for release, desperate for a full breath of air. But he didn't let up.*

*"You're mine, got it? You'll always be mine. You'll never get away. Ever. And if you try, I'll kill you, and I'll make it painful." Once again, he brandished the knife, tracing it down her cheek, cutting her ever so slightly so that warm blood trickled down from a stinging wound.*

*He released her and backed away. He pointed at her with the knife. "Don't you forget it."*

*Allen walked out, letting the screen slam shut behind him. Knowing her life depended on it, she ran to the door and bolted it shut.*

*She turned and slid down to the floor and cried. Boomer peeked out from the bedroom where he'd run to hide. He meowed at her, but it sounded faint, and different. Not at all like a cat.*

*He did it again, and again.*

*She couldn't place it but....*

The noise grew louder, and Natalie turned over in bed, confused. She opened her eyes and tried to focus. Again, the noise. This time she recognized it. It was a rooster. She rubbed her eyes and sat up, searching her surroundings. Her heart rate slowed as she remembered where she was.

"I'm at the ranch," she breathed, palm to forehead. She hugged herself as she made her way to the bathroom, the AC now a little too cold for her. She'd run it all night, desperate for the house to cool and now it seemed it was. Too much so.

After she relieved herself and brushed her teeth, she walked to the thermostat and thumbed it up a bit. She slid into her jean shorts and an old worn tee. Next, she stepped into her sneakers and headed for the door. The light of dawn greeted her with rays of golden sunshine as she stepped outside. The rooster crowed again and she smiled, never having heard one so close before. She breathed in the warm morning air as she walked farther out, following an overgrown stone footpath. She caught sight of the rooster along the fence to what she assumed was the chicken coop. He called out again.

"Morning," a voice said from the other direction.

Natalie turned and saw Vaughn approaching in a rugged-looking four-wheeler with two bench seats. It said Gator along the side. She was pulling bales of hay by way of a small trailer. "Wanna ride?"

"You bet." Natalie climbed on board thinking that this was better than a ride on the Quadrunner Vaughn had used last night, and they zoomed around the chicken coop to the main corral. Two men were there filling the troughs with fresh water. When Vaughn pulled inside, the men slid on gloves and began snatching small amounts of hay and placing them in large tubs that hung along the metal bars of the pen.

"This here's Benny, and that's Greer," Vaughn said, introducing the men. "Fellas, this is Natalie. She's going to be staying with us for a while."

The guys nodded, tipping their cowboy hats at her. One offered his hand but Natalie chose to wave instead. She was wary of men now, even ones that had done nothing to her. She had Allen to thank for that. She briefly closed her eyes as she recalled her dream and the way he'd choked her and threatened her with the knife. She'd left the knife out of her explanation to Vaughn and Gram, too ashamed to mention it. She knew it was awful, that he'd gone way too far. But she still hadn't wanted to see their reactions in hearing about it. Mainly because there was a part of her that still somehow felt responsible for his behavior. Like maybe she'd brought it on herself. That's what Allen had always told her anyway and she realized now that she'd started to wonder if it was true.

"We're getting ready to turn the horses out," Vaughn said, giving her a glance. "You okay?"

"Hm? Yeah, fine."

"You sure?

Natalie met her gaze and forced herself back to the present. "I'm good. What do you mean by turn the horses out?"

"Let them outside."

"Oh."

Vaughn stared at her for a moment longer, as if to confirm she was really okay, and then climbed out of the Gator to unhook the trailer, leaving it with Benny and Greer. She crawled back in the four-wheeler and drove them to the entrance of the stables and got out. Natalie hurried to follow her inside. Vaughn moved quickly and Natalie knew she'd have to be more mindful of that. Vaughn had things to do, important things, and it seemed she didn't want to dillydally around. Natalie had just caught up with her when they came to a stall with a woman inside with a tawny-colored horse.

"Morning," Vaughn said to the woman.

"Morning."

"Suzanne, this is Natalie. Natalie, Suzanne."

"Hello," Natalie said, feeling comfortable enough to extend her hand. Suzanne took it and shook heartily.

"Hi."

"Natalie is going to be staying in the guesthouse for a while," Vaughn said.

"Great." She smiled and continued petting the horse. "Welcome."

"Thanks." Natalie reached up and stroked the beautiful horse. "Who's this?"

"This is Oliver," Suzanne said. "He's our resident heartbreaker."

"Oh?" Natalie said. "I can believe it. He's magnificent."

Vaughn leaned on the stall and crossed her arms over her chest. "How is he this morning?" She looked to Natalie to explain. "He's had some colic here recently."

"Oh, no."

"Oh, it's okay," Suzanne said. "The vet said it's just gas. He seems better this morning. He took a little hay and we'll try again in a couple of hours."

Vaughn gave Oliver a pat and walked away. Natalie quickly said good-bye to Suzanne and followed Vaughn who, thankfully, stopped to open the next stall. She entered and slid a halter on another beautiful amber horse. "This is O'Malley," she said, stroking him. "He's our old man."

"Aw," Natalie said, stroking his graying muzzle. "He's sweet."

"He's actually quite grumpy."

"No, I'm sure he's just misunderstood."

"Ha. He'll like you."

Vaughn gently led O'Malley out of the stall, and they walked him to the corral where Benny, the leaner fellow, came and took his lead. Natalie stood with Vaughn for a moment and watched. The rising sun glinted off O'Malley's tawny hide, making it look like warm, rich honey.

"These horses," Natalie said. "They're so majestic." She knew she sounded wistful, almost silly, but she couldn't help it. She was truly moved by these creatures.

She felt Vaughn's eyes on her. "You really like them?"

Natalie nodded. "I do."

"You're going to fit in just fine around here." She placed a soft hand on her shoulder, causing Natalie to angle her head. "Come on, you can help lead the rest of the horses out."

Natalie, Vaughn, and Greer headed back inside the stable and brought out horse after horse, with Vaughn showing Natalie how to ease on the harnesses and slowly lead them out into the corral. Natalie smiled as she walked, feeling proud and honored to be leading each horse. She felt dignified and purposeful and her smile, she felt, couldn't be any more genuine.

"Come on," she cooed, directing the last horse out. She ticked at him, as she'd heard Vaughn do and the horse, whose name was Beauregard, followed her slowly. He, too, was up in years and slow moving. But his eyes were deep and rich, and she could tell he was taking her in and trusting her. They reached the corral and she gave him a few soft strokes on his velvety muzzle. "The pleasure was all mine," she whispered to him. He bobbed his head. She laughed. "I'll come back for you later, okay?" She left him and joined Vaughn at the gate.

"And the rest of the horses?" Natalie asked, motioning back toward the stables.

"We feed them inside and then they go out a little later, when the others are out to pasture. They just need a little extra one on one attention."

Vaughn started heading for the house.

"What now?" Natalie asked, catching up to her.

"Now we eat," she said. "Breakfast time."

## CHAPTER SIX

Natalie stood awkwardly at the kitchen counter as everyone moved around her like ants on a mission. Benny brushed by her with a heavy-looking pewter plate in hand and sat his scrawny body down at the table, removing his hat to hang on the back of the chair. He joined Greer in heaping a hefty spoonful of eggs onto his plate.

"Help yourself," Vaughn said, as she too breezed by her, plate in hand. She also sat at the round table and removed her hat to hang on the back of her chair.

"Yes, child, here," June said, handing Natalie a plate. "You better get in there or there'll be nothing left."

"Hey, Dumb and Dumber aren't here, so can I have their share?" Benny asked. Natalie assumed he was referring to the missing ranch hands that Vaughn had spoken of earlier. Seems she had two workers who weren't keen on showing up to work.

"You think I made enough for those two?" June said, making herself comfortable at the table. She patted the seat next to her, encouraging Natalie to join them. "Not likely," she said. "You don't work, you don't eat."

Greer laughed as he bit into a crispy strip of bacon. "I'll work extra hard then."

"You better," June said. "With your appetite." Greer's heavy cheeks bloomed with red. He was as husky as Benny was scrawny. Natalie found them both to be young and endearing. She was a little less intimidated by them now. They were just kids, maybe nineteen or twenty, with the whole world ahead of them. And they acted as such. She stifled a laugh as they continued to ramble as they ate, their sweat-soaked hair sticking up in places due to their hats. Boys. They were just boys really. They seemed okay enough.

"Child," June said, scooping out a heap of scrambled eggs for Natalie. "Eat." She dropped them on her plate and passed her the bacon and some country salted ham. "You're gonna need energy to work on this ranch."

Natalie took two strips of bacon, but June grimaced at her and added a slice of ham. She did the same with a biscuit. It wasn't that the food didn't look and smell delicious. It's just that Natalie wasn't used to eating such a big breakfast so early.

"Thank you," she said, a little overwhelmed at June piling her plate with food.

"You're welcome," June said. She smacked Benny on the arm, causing him to howl. "You hear that? She said thank you. Wouldn't hurt you two to do the same every once in a while."

"Thank you, Miss June," Benny muttered, rubbing his arm.

"Yeah, thanks," Greer added with a full mouth.

"That's more like it," June said. She took a bite of her own eggs, chewed and swallowed. "Ungrateful lot. You'd think you was raised in a barn."

Vaughn chuckled.

"And you," June said, pointing her fork at her. "You ought to do better, too."

"Me?"

"It wouldn't kill you to bring the eggs in for me in the morning. That damn rooster you brought home has it out for me."

Vaughn laughed, hand to her chest. "He does, doesn't he?"

"Blasted thing. I ought to get the broom after him. Show him who's boss."

"I'd pay to see that," Greer said.

"Me, too," Benny said.

"Just never you mind," June said. "It's bad enough I have to deal with that rooster. I don't want to have to contend with you two as well."

"Yes, ma'am," Benny said.

That seemed to be the end of the matter because they ate in silence for a while after that, with the boys chewing like it was their last meal and slurping on their orange juice and milk like they were dying of thirst. Natalie had never seen people eat so ravenously before. One would think they were going to a fire.

The boys finished, taking one last biscuit from the bowl as they rose from the table and secured their hats on their heads. They thanked June for breakfast again and hurried out the kitchen door, letting it slam shut behind them. The curtains swayed on the little rectangle of a window as Natalie stared after them, mouth agape.

"They got work to do," Vaughn said, grabbing her attention. "Work doesn't wait."

Natalie looked to her plate and forked more egg. She wasn't sure if she should keep eating or join the boys to help with the waiting work. June seemed to sense her conundrum.

"Eat, child," she said. She chewed her ham. "It can wait for you."

Vaughn sipped her juice. "We're understaffed. That's why they're in such a hurry to return to work. They've got a lot to do."

Natalie took a bite. She toyed with her remaining eggs. Vaughn was watching her.

"You not hungry?"

"I'm not used to eating so much so early."

"Just you wait," Vaughn said.

"You'll be starved by lunch," June said. "And even hungrier come supper."

"Maybe," Natalie said. "But I just can't eat any more right now. It was very good though. Thank you." She'd eaten some eggs, her bacon, and her biscuit. But she couldn't finish the ham or the rest of her eggs.

"You're mighty welcome," June said. She chewed on in silence. Then, to Vaughn, "What are you going to do about replacing those hands?"

Vaughn cut into her ham, scraping her plate. "Not much I can do today. Got too much to cover."

"We need workers."

"We do. But what do you suggest I do? Go down to that strip club and haul their asses out by their ears?"

"Wouldn't hurt."

"Wouldn't do no good, either. We need people who want to work. Not just work for a week and then blow all their money partying."

June swallowed. "You talk to people about it?"

"I did. They said they'd put the word out and keep their eyes and ears open."

"What about putting an ad in the paper?"

Vaughn looked at her. "Gram, they don't really do that anymore."

"Why not?"

"Because not many people read the paper. It's all online now."

"Well, I can't help you there. And you're not very good at that technological mumbo jumbo either."

Natalie spoke up. "I can do it for you."

They stopped eating and stared at her.

Natalie explained. "I know how to do it and I can get your request out and onto several sites."

"Think we'll get any hits?" Vaughn asked. "Because I haven't had much interest from anyone in the past year or so. And those that I do get don't stick around for long."

"It's worth a shot." Natalie thought for a moment. "Do you have a website?"

"You mean for the ranch?"

She nodded.

"I do."

"And you manage it and keep it up to date?"

Vaughn reddened. "Haven't had much time lately and like Gram said, I'm not very knowledgeable when it comes to that stuff. So I'm afraid what's up right now is not very impressive."

"How do you get your clients then?"

"Mostly word of mouth," June said. "Our reputation usually speaks for itself."

"That's good," Natalie said. "But you could probably do a whole lot better if you sell yourself online. Make people want to buy their horses here. Make people want to come work for you."

Vaughn studied her. "I'm not sure I know what you mean by 'sell.'"

"I can show you."

"You know this kind of stuff?" June asked.

"It's actually how I support myself right now. I write blogs and reviews for numerous companies promoting them and their products. I could do the same for you. Really amp up your website and garner you some more business as well as potential employees."

"That would be a nice change," June said, looking to Vaughn. "Wouldn't it, Vaughn?"

"I don't know," Vaughn said. "I don't have the time and—"

"Which is why I'm offering." But Natalie understood her hesitancy. Vaughn didn't know her and didn't yet trust her. She wasn't willing to let just anyone revamp her website. It was her life. Her livelihood. "I can show you some of my current work and create a sample website for you to take a look at."

"I don't see how that would hurt anything," June said.

Vaughn set her elbows on the table and folded her hands. "I reckon not."

"Great," Natalie said. "I can get started now if you like and then join you later for chores?"

"The sooner we get some more help around here the better," June said.

Vaughn steepled her fingers. "Sure."

Natalie smiled, thrilled to be given the chance to help. She rose to take her plate and silverware to the sink. She turned back to them as she ran the water. "Would you like me to help you clean up from breakfast first?" June had, after all, cooked for her and fed her. It was the right thing to do.

June stood and began gathering the remaining dishes. "That won't be necessary. You go on now and get busy on that computer of yours. We need workers more than I need help with the dishes."

Natalie rinsed her plate and dried her hands. "Okay."

"You come around noon for lunch," June said, crossing to the sink with her arms full. Natalie tried to help her but she side-stepped her. "You just worry about getting to work and then showing up for lunch."

"Yes, ma'am."

June smiled. "You're learning fast."

Natalie looked to Vaughn who gave her a nod, quietly dismissing her, and Natalie headed for the kitchen door. For the first time in years, she felt excited at the idea of helping someone with something she actually knew how to do. And helping Vaughn and June, at the moment, felt like everything to her.

## CHAPTER SEVEN

Vaughn took another batch of hay and deposited it in the last of the feed buckets along the side of the corral. She took a break and leaned along the railing, removing her hat to wipe her brow with the back of her arm. It wasn't even ten a.m. and the heat was already oppressive. It hung heavy in the air with the remnants of last night's humidity ruining her usually hot and bone-dry mornings. But that was August in the Valley of the Sun. Hot *and* humid, caused by the occasional monsoon. She supposed she ought to be used to it by now, being a valley native, but the humidity was never welcome. And August, well, August was always just a bitch of a month to plow through.

One of the horses neighed as if in agreement. It was Charlie and she was slowly walking up to her. "Hey, girl." Vaughn peeled off her gloves and stroked Charlie's neck. She was a stunner of a horse, with a shiny black coat and rich, glossy eyes. "You come to stand in the shade with me? It's hot, huh? Too hot." A few of the other horses had come to stand on her side of the corral as well, seeking the shade of the ramadas, the morning heat already too much for them. "How 'bout a cool down?" Vaughn walked over to the hose and uncoiled it. She hollered at Benny to turn on the faucet at the stable. She felt the water, noted the warm temperature, and waited a few minutes for it to run cooler, then she sprayed Charlie down. "There you go," she said. "Feel good?"

She adjusted the nozzle to create a mist and continued to wet Charlie down. Soon a few of the other horses sauntered up to her for their own cool down. A hot breeze began to blow through and Vaughn smiled, knowing it would help in cooling the horses with their wet skin. "There you go, you guys should be good for a while." She yelled again for Benny to turn off the water and rewound the hose. She was wiping her hands off on her jeans when Benny whistled at her and pointed beyond the corrals. She followed his line of sight and saw a vehicle pulling up on the drive. She squinted, trying to make out who it was in the white SUV. She left the corral and was halfway to the car before she could make out the writing on the side. The vehicle was with the fire department. Vaughn silently cursed and looked back toward the guesthouse. Natalie was nowhere to be seen.

A man climbed from the SUV carrying a hard-cased folder. He adjusted his sunglasses and stuck out his hand.

"Wesley Locke," he said. "Fire investigations. You Vaughn Ruger?"

Vaughn shook his hand and sank hers in her back pocket, nervous.

"Sure am. What brings you out this way?"

"Someone here called in a car fire yesterday evening and I was just following up."

"Right." She'd almost forgotten that Gram had called in to report the fire. So much had happened it had slipped her mind, which was unusual for her. She was usually very keen and on top of things. Natalie's presence had disrupted not just her home life, but her thoughts as well. She briefly wondered what else she would disrupt.

"The caller was…" He opened the folder and flipped to the correct page. "June Ruger."

"She's my grandmother. But she isn't the one who saw the fire. That was me. I came upon it as I was returning from town."

He made a note. "Did you happen to see the driver of the vehicle?"

Vaughn wavered. She didn't like to lie, but Natalie's location might be blown if she didn't. Thoughts of Aunt Sissy and all the trouble she'd gone through with her divorce came once again. She thought of how damaged she seemed to be from it all. The bruises on Natalie's neck also came to mind. No, she couldn't tell. She couldn't do that to Natalie.

She shook her head. She might not have done enough to support her aunt during her rough divorce, but at least now she could try to make up for that by helping Natalie.

Wesley glanced up at her over the rim of his sunglasses as he paused his pen mid stroke. "No?"

She shook her head again, unable to voice the lie.

"You just saw the vehicle then?"

"Yes, sir. I saw the vehicle."

He scribbled some more and closed his folder. "Did you see anything else unusual? Another vehicle maybe?"

"No, sir. It was storming so I didn't stick around. I just continued on home." She felt her face flush with guilt and she prayed he wouldn't notice.

"Guess the driver found another way home." He secured the folder against his hip and slid his pen into his shirt pocket. He dug into his back pocket and retrieved a business card. "Call me if you think of anything else. Anything at all."

"I will."

"Thank you for your time." He shook her hand again.

"No problem." He walked away, turning to look at Vaughn one last time as he was climbing in his SUV. She waved, watched him drive away, and headed back toward the corral. She had her head down, staring at the ground when she heard her name. She looked to her right and saw Natalie jogging up to her from the vicinity of the guesthouse. She seemed breathless when she reached her, but Vaughn could tell it wasn't from the brief exertion of the run.

"Who was that?" she asked, looking back at the retreating vehicle. Its tires were kicking up dust as it drove back down the long drive and out of sight.

"A fire investigator."

"Shit. Really?" Her eyes grew wide as she searched Vaughn's face. "What did you tell him?"

"I told him I didn't see anyone. That I just saw the fire and continued on home."

"Oh my God, thank you. Thank you so much."

Vaughn stared off into the blowing trees, feeling uncomfortable about the whole encounter. "You're welcome." She started walking again. Natalie followed.

"Are you okay?"

"Sure."

"You don't sound it."

"No? How do I sound?"

"You sound kind of pissed."

"Nope."

"You sure?"

"Yep."

Natalie lightly gripped her arm, causing her to pause. Vaughn held her gaze for only a moment before she looked away. She didn't want to upset her or cause any trouble. It was best left alone. Besides, she wasn't one to hash things out. She preferred to let things be.

"Tell me," Natalie insisted. "Please."

Vaughn chewed her lip, debating. She felt Natalie's grip tighten on her arm as she pleaded again. She could tell Natalie wasn't going to let her off the hook, so she spoke freely.

"I don't like lying," she said. "Under any circumstances."

Natalie seemed at a loss. She stammered. "I—don't either. But this is different. I'm—trying to hide—he—" She stopped. "If it bothers you, I can go. I don't have to stay. I don't want to make you uncomfortable."

Vaughn looked into her eyes. They were so crystal clear and green, almost the color of her mother's birthstone ring. The one she always wore unless she was painting. She hadn't seen that ring or her mother in close to a year. She suddenly longed for her to visit and she wondered what she would think of Natalie.

"You don't have to leave," she said. She wanted her to stay, wanted her to remain safe. Yet, she wasn't quite sure why she felt so protective of her. Was it because of her aunt and her experience? Or was it something more?

"Vaughn, I really don't want you to do things that make you uncomfortable. And lying…I understand why you don't want to. I hate lies. Allen…he lied to me about nearly everything. I—" She shook her head. "I understand." She dropped her hand.

"Just forget about it," Vaughn said. "It's over. Over and done with. He shouldn't have a need to come back."

"Yes, but he's going to know it was my car, if he doesn't already. There's the license plate and the VIN number. I'm doomed."

"He didn't mention your name," Vaughn said. "Or even suggest that you were here."

"Still, Allen could find out that my car was found. He has ways. Private detectives and shady friends who do things for him. I don't know what I was thinking believing I could hide from him."

"Hey," Vaughn said, resting a hand on her shoulder. "Try not to worry about it, okay? Should he come here, we'll deal with it. And I've been thinking…" She looked back toward the driveway. "I'm going to put up some no trespassing signs and lock the gate. Maybe put a little camera up so we know when someone is approaching. I've been meaning to do it, to prevent theft and such. We've had some trouble in the past. And with those ranch hands still out there doing God knows what…it's best if I do something to deter them from coming back. They aren't welcome here anymore."

Natalie seemed grateful. Her eyes softened and sparkled in the sunlight. "I'll stay as long as you're okay with it. But the second you aren't, I want you to tell me and I'll go. I'll be gone so fast you won't even know I was here. Deal?"

She extended her hand. Vaughn eyed it for a second and then took it in her own. It was smooth and warm. Not at all like her own or anyone else's she knew.

"Great," Natalie said. "Thanks."

She hitched her thumb over her shoulder. "I'm going to go get back to it. You good?"

Vaughn adjusted her hat, trying to ignore the emptiness she felt in releasing her soft hand. "Yep, I'm good."

"I'll see you at lunch?" She started walking back toward the guesthouse.

"You will."

She smiled and turned to continue on her way.

Vaughn watched her go, amused at her liveliness and good spirits. For a woman who was dealing with so much trauma and trouble, she sure seemed to be handling things well.

As she started her own walk back to the horses, she thought about Natalie and her future. If only things could work out for her so she could truly be happy and not have to worry so much.

If only.

## CHAPTER EIGHT

I don't care if she said no!" Allen Beaufort screamed into the phone line. "Just get her to refinance with that higher rate, otherwise you not only lose this client, but you lose your job as well." He slammed down the receiver and ran his hand through his hair as he leaned back in his reclining office chair.

"Idiots," he seethed, looking out the window of his sixth-floor office. How could everybody be such idiots? Granted, this new one was just starting out, but my God, when he first started he had no problem talking clients into anything. High interest rates? No problem. Hidden fees? No big deal. Balloon payments? Piece of cake. All this new girl had to do was promise to fix a problem if the client refinanced with a higher rate. Jesus, it should be a cake walk. It would be for him. Maybe he should just do it himself.

No. The girl had to learn, and he couldn't run a profitable lending business if he had to run around wiping everyone's noses. Lately however, that seemed to be all he was doing. Especially when it came to his female employees. They seemed to have the most trouble in getting things done. They often complained of feeling dishonest or doing things that went against their morals. Jesus. Most of the time he fired those people. He really wished he could hire all men, because the women were too weak. Wasn't that the case when it came down to anything though?

Christ on a cracker.

But he had to keep employing women. It made him look good and the clients, especially the ones who were more hesitant, seemed to respond better to them.

His phone beeped and his secretary came on over the speaker. Speaking of women, boy was he glad he'd hired her. She was as sexy as she was efficient. "Mr. Beaufort, Tom is here to see you."

"Tom?"

He heard her muffle the phone as she spoke to the visitor. "He said he has the information you've been waiting for."

*Right. Tom.*

"Send him in."

A few seconds lapsed before the dark oak door to his office opened and the young kid with the long blond hair walked in. Allen wanted to yank him by that hair and force him into a barber's chair for a good haircut, but he'd been assured by his contact, Nico Fritz, that this was the go-to guy for surveillance so he left it alone.

"Sit," Allen barked as he leaned forward in his chair. He rested his elbows on the desk and waited. The kid didn't look good, wouldn't meet his eyes. So he knew the news was bad. "Spill it," he said.

Tom hesitated and readjusted himself in the seat. He had on a ball cap and a tank top with a bright pair of board shorts. He looked like he should be on a beach, not hunting down his ex-wife. But maybe that was the point.

"Well?"

Tom cleared his throat and finally crossed an ankle over his knee. He bobbed his Nike-covered foot. "She's gone."

Allen blinked, unsure if he heard correctly. "I'm sorry, I must've misheard. What did you say?"

"She's gone, sir."

"What do you mean, gone?"

He visibly swallowed and again shook his foot. "She's, uh—not at home or—anywhere."

"She has to be somewhere. Surely you know that. I mean, the woman doesn't go anywhere but to the goddamned store and that apartment of hers. So, you're mistaken, my friend. She is not *gone.*"

"I can't find her. I've looked everywhere. I—lost her on the way home from the grocery store yesterday. She—"

Allen held up his palm to stop him. "You *lost* her?"

"Yes, sir. She—pulled out in front of traffic and sped off. I couldn't follow. And by the time I did—she was gone."

Allen chuckled softly, fuming inside. Hot blood spread beneath his skin and he swore he could literally burst into flames at any second. He slammed his hand down on the table and the beach boy jerked. "She's gone and she's been gone since yesterday?"

"I—I waited it out at her apartment all night, thinking she would eventually return. I didn't want to bother you—"

"You didn't want to bother me? Have you lost your fucking mind, Tom?"

Tom didn't speak. He seemed it wise not to answer.

Allen stood, palms on his desk. He leaned forward. "You're supposed to be the best. I'm paying you as if you are the best. So what the hell is going on here, Tommy? Are you the best or are you just a fraud, sent here to take my money?"

"I'm the best—sir. I swear."

"Then I suggest you get the hell out of my office and you go find my ex-wife before I come across this desk and rip your goddamned throat out."

Tom stood and trembled. He backed away toward the door. "Yes, sir. Right on it, sir." He ran into the door, struggled to pull it open, and walked out. Allen collapsed into his chair and picked up a pencil. He snapped it in half with his thumb and threw it across the room. Then he picked up the phone and dialed.

Tom might be the best at surveillance, but he knew someone who was better at something far worse. He grinned as the line was answered.

## Chapter Nine

June shook some cumin, garlic powder, onion powder, oregano, and paprika into a pan of sizzling ground beef. She stirred the contents with her wooden spoon, inhaling the cumin as it mingled with the other spices. She hummed as she added the last of the spices. The crushed red pepper. She finished stirring the ground beef and checked on the Mexican rice. After giving that one last good stir, she opened the oven for the taco shells. They were just beginning to brown so she, with an oven glove on, slid them out and set them on a cooling rack on the counter. Next, she removed the glove and stirred her pot of refried beans on the back burner. They, like everything except for the taco shells, were homemade. Vaughn insisted on it. The child never had liked the processed version of anything, especially refried beans.

June left the stove and cut up the lettuce and tomatoes at the cutting board on the kitchen island. She got out the cheese and sour cream and set the table. She returned to the stove and turned off all the burners, wiped her hands on her apron, and walked outside to ring the bell for lunch. It only took a few rings for the boys to come jogging toward the house, hungry for a midday meal. Vaughn soon followed, looking a little worse for wear and June wondered if her back was hurting. Poor child needed to see a doctor, but she knew she'd fight her on it, so most of the time she didn't even try to press her about it. She was just as stubborn as her headstrong mother, and there was no convincing that woman of doing anything she didn't have a mind to do.

"What's for lunch, Miss June?" Benny asked, tugging off his hat. His skin was coated in sweat, and he had a metallic smell to him that let her know he'd been working hard.

"Tacos."

He smiled at her. "Whew-ee. I sure do love your tacos."

"You love everything I cook, Benny. Who you kidding?"

"That I do, ma'am." He headed inside as Greer joined her on the porch.

"Did I hear you say tacos, Miss June?"

"You did."

"Whoo-hoo!" He hurried inside, wiping the sweat from his face with his faded bandana.

"What's got the boys so excited?" Vaughn asked. She was squinting in the sunlight and her arms and cheeks were tinged red. She looked like she needed a good soak in the bath and a cool lemonade to sip on. But June could offer her neither at the moment. There was still too much to be done.

"You know them. Food in general gets them all excited."

"True. But just out of curiosity, what did you make today?"

"Tacos."

"Oh, boy. That does sound good. Thanks, Gram."

"Got you all excited too, huh?" She playfully whipped her with the apron she'd untied from her waist.

Vaughn looked out toward the guesthouse. "Natalie here?"

"Not yet." June checked her watch. It was noon. "She'll come. Don't worry."

"I wasn't worried."

But June knew better. She didn't voice it. She just followed her inside and got busy helping everyone to their plates and glasses of iced tea.

The boys made three tacos each and spooned out big heapings of beans and rice. They sat and started scarfing the meal down, chatting loudly about the day's work so far. Vaughn made her plate quietly and kept eyeing the kitchen door. June rested a hand on her arm.

"Maybe you should just go get her."

"What? No, she'll come."

"Well, you seem concerned and maybe she's lost track of time."

"You think?" She again looked toward the door. Natalie gave a little knock just then, and entered. She had on a pair of black-rimmed glasses, giving her a cute studious look. It made Vaughn glance at her twice and June smiled.

"Grab a plate and help yourself to some tacos," June said as she welcomed her inside. "And you don't have to knock. You can just come in anytime. Our casa es su casa."

Natalie returned the smile, though it looked a bit shy, and took her plate to the stove. She made herself two tacos and helped herself to a small portion of rice. She sat at the table and sipped her tea as June made her own plate and joined them.

"How's your day going?" June asked, directing her question to Natalie as the other three continued to eat.

"It's going great," she said, seeming to perk up. "I've been working on a mock website all morning. I'm hoping you'll like it."

"I'm sure we will," June said. She was pleased to see Natalie so happy. She seemed to be in her element with the website work, just as Vaughn was with the outdoors.

"It's ready if you want to take a look after lunch," Natalie said.

June looked to Vaughn and answered. "I'm sure Vaughn would like that very much." She stared at her until she got the hint to speak.

"Yeah, sure. I'll take a look."

Natalie smiled as if pleased and took a bite from her taco. She'd piled it high with lettuce and cheese but no tomato. June mentally made a note of her likes and dislikes since she was the resident cook. She wanted Natalie's stay to be a pleasant one. Poor child had enough to worry about as it was and she looked like she could use a few good, hearty meals in addition to a safe place to rest her head. She wondered briefly what her ex-husband was like and what had drawn Natalie to him. She seemed like such an intelligent young woman, one who could tell a rabbit from a rattlesnake, so why had she fallen for such a bad seed? She was curious about her story and hoped she would learn it in due time. But until then, she was going to do her damndest to keep her safe.

"So, you seem to enjoy the work with computers," June said. "That's fascinating. I can't even work a cell phone."

Natalie chuckled. "I could teach you some things. It's really not that hard."

"On the computer? Lord, I don't know."

"I'll keep it simple, I promise." She held up her fingers. "Scout's honor."

"What kind of things could you teach me?" She'd never had much use for computers or cell phones. She liked doing things the old-fashioned way, which meant speaking to someone face-to-face whenever she could. All this technology kept people at a distance, and it wasn't healthy. Relationships shouldn't be built on a keystroke. They should be built on a good, firm handshake.

"I could show you how to check the email from the website and how to respond to people who have interest. That way you could keep tabs on your visitors and interest every day."

"That does sound good," June said. "What do you think?" she asked Vaughn.

"Sounds okay to me. It would sure help me out. I don't have time for the website as it is. Nor do I know what I'm doing."

"So we've understood," June said. "Not that I'll be much better. But somebody's got to do it."

"I can help you for as long as I'm here," Natalie said.

"We'd appreciate that," June said.

"And by the time I'm gone, you'll be an old pro at it."

"That sounds great, but I don't like the word old," June said with a laugh.

Natalie lowered her fork as if she'd done something wrong. "I'm sorry. I didn't mean anything by it."

Vaughn looked as alarmed as June felt and she spoke. "She knows, Natalie. No need to worry."

"Yes, child, I was only teasing." June patted her forearm, concerned at how browbeaten the poor woman seemed to be. She looked like a scared little rabbit. Good God, what had her ex-husband done to her?

Natalie set her fork on her plate and sat quietly. If she was trying to recover, she was doing it inwardly. June refilled her tea and encouraged her to drink.

"A little extra tea never hurt anyone."

"Thank you."

"You need to stay hydrated as well as fed." She eyed her half-eaten taco. "Eat up, darlin'. It's getting cold."

Natalie seemed to slowly snap out of her cloudy mood. She lifted her taco to her mouth and finished eating it without speaking. Benny and Greer started up again, both of them yammering on about something or other as they went to the stove for more beans, tacos, and rice.

"You boys save one more taco for Natalie," June said.

"Oh, no, I'm fine," Natalie said. "Really."

"Then save one for me," Vaughn said.

"There's two," Benny called back.

"Good," Vaughn said as she bit into her second taco. She chewed carefully, her gaze fixed on Natalie. She looked worried, like she wasn't quite sure what to do to make Natalie feel more at ease. June tried to remedy it on her own.

"Vaughn will show you more of the ropes around here after lunch. After you show her the website."

"That sounds great," Natalie said. "And I was thinking about what you said this morning. About the eggs. I could gather them in the mornings for you. If you like."

June felt her eyebrows lift. "Why, that would be wonderful. Wouldn't it, Vaughn?"

"It would. I only hope Diablo likes her better than he likes you though." She grinned as she took a bite of rice. "He's pretty territorial."

"Oh," Natalie said. "I didn't consider that."

"I'm sure he'll like you just fine," Vaughn said after she swallowed. She winked at her and Natalie blushed. June noticed and hid her own smile. Natalie seemed to be greatly affected by Vaughn. She wondered if there was an attraction there. June didn't know much about women loving women. Only what she'd seen with

Vaughn in the past. But she did know that women loved fiercely and deeply. And she'd hoped for a long while now that Vaughn would find someone good and true to love her that way.

Was it Natalie? She didn't know. But she did seem to be kind. If not a bit shy and reserved. Vaughn was right however, she had too much going on with her ex-husband to be concerned about anything else. Much less another relationship.

It was too bad though. June was growing very fond of her. And it seemed, if she was reading things right, and she usually did, that Vaughn was growing fond of her as well.

She'd have to wait things out and see. As her own mother used to say, only time would tell.

## CHAPTER TEN

Natalie finished eating and offered again to help June clean up, but she refused, encouraging her and Vaughn to go back to the guesthouse to see what she'd come up with as far as a website. Natalie set her plate in the sink and waited patiently for Vaughn to do the same. When she did, Natalie opened the kitchen door and smiled politely at Vaughn as she walked through, perching her cowboy hat back atop her head.

"Why, thank you, ma'am," Vaughn said with a smile all her own. "Not used to doors being opened for me." They walked slowly back toward the guesthouse.

"No?"

"Huh-uh. I'm usually the one opening them."

"Well, maybe that should change," Natalie said, squinting into the noonday sun. "It's nice to have a door opened for you every once in a while."

"Is it now?" Vaughn laughed. "I guess maybe you're right."

The day was turning into a scorcher, and Natalie was glad when they reached the door to the bungalow. She let them inside and led the way to her laptop on the small kitchen table. She sat and motioned for Vaughn to sit next to her. Vaughn did so and removed her hat and set it on her knee.

"Let's see what you've got here," Vaughn said, leaning toward her.

Natalie felt her breath quicken at Vaughn's nearness. She smelled of sweat and hay and dirt, a strange elixir that seemed to meld with her pheromones. It sent Natalie's head spinning.

"Again, it's just a workup," Natalie said, trying to hide her nerves. "A mock site. It's not published, but if you like it, all it would take is a press of a key to make it live." She woke her screen and brought up the website. The first page was a welcome page with a stock photo of a sprawling ranch along with some eye-catching font spelling out Midnight Mine Ranch. She had to admit the page was beautiful. It would really garner some attention if it went live. However, she had another idea before she wanted that to happen.

"This is a stock photo," she said. "But I think the page would look great with a picture of your ranch."

"Mine?"

"It's beautiful here, Vaughn. You should show it off. Maybe a sweeping pic with some of your horses in the background. And on these subsequent pages, we could use pics of the stables and corrals as well as the horses. What do you think?"

Vaughn seemed to be deep in thought. Natalie persisted.

"We could get someone out here to take the pics. A photographer. Do it up real professional like. I have to admit I'm not much of a photographer myself, but it wouldn't be difficult to find someone."

"It costs though," Vaughn said softly.

"It would, yes. But pictures of your own ranch would really sell the place and grab the interest of customers." Natalie stammered, trying not to lose her. "We would have to pay for these stock images too, you know. So…I don't know any other way unless you do—"

"I have some photos," she said, staring blankly at the screen.

"You do? Of the ranch?"

Vaughn blinked. "Yes."

"That's great. Can I see them?"

"I'll have to rustle them up."

"They're put away?"

Vaughn finally looked at her and Natalie saw pain in her eyes. Deep pain. The kind of pain that one would try hard to keep down.

She knew that kind of pain and recognized it for what it was. She let the matter go.

"Okay, just bring them by when you're ready." She clicked on the mousepad, showing Vaughn the other pages. "As you can see here—"

"I'll have them for you tomorrow."

Natalie stammered. "O—kay. As I was saying—"

Vaughn stood. "Looks good."

"But you haven't even seen all of the pages."

"It looks good," she said again, securing her hat on her head. "You're hired." She turned to go.

"But, Vaughn."

"Do what you have to do to get the site ready for tomorrow. I'll get those photos to you first thing so you can add them quickly."

Natalie chased her to the door. "Don't you want to see some of my other work first?"

Vaughn turned to face her. "Your work looks good to me, Natalie. Real good. You seem to know what you're doing."

"I—thank you."

"Keep up the good work."

Natalie fought for words, unwilling to let her go. "What about the chores? I'm supposed to help you this afternoon."

"I'd rather you work on the site."

"But I need information. How to list the horses, photos of the horses, information about the horses, etc. I can't just do this will-nilly."

"Get what you can from June. The rest I'll give you tonight after chores." She pulled open the door, letting in the harsh glow of sunlight. She tipped her hat at her. "Thanks, Natalie. You're really doing us a big favor."

"You're doing me a big favor," Natalie whispered.

"Yeah, well, I guess we can call it even, eh?" She walked out the door and left Natalie standing alone.

Natalie watched her walk away, wondering what had prompted the sudden and abrupt departure. It had something to do with the photos, she was sure of it. But what, she didn't know. She'd have to remember to tread carefully when Vaughn brought them over. She didn't want to scare her off. If anything, she wanted her to stick around. She liked her easy company, and she found herself more than curious about her. She seemed so strait-laced and reserved, yet she was forward and assertive when she needed to be. She wasn't someone a person could walk all over, that was for sure, and Natalie admired her for that. Natalie had always been more of a doormat. She'd had trouble telling people no and standing up for herself. She thought maybe it was because she feared rejection or upsetting people, preferring to just keep the peace instead. Because upset people did upset things. She'd learned that lesson once or twice.

She eased the door closed and made her way back into the tiny kitchen where she filled a mug with water and set it in the microwave. She heated it for two minutes and plucked it out to bob a single serving bag of vanilla tea in it. When the tea had steeped enough, she opened a jar of desert mesquite honey that June had given her when she'd brought over some groceries and scooped out a spoonful. She stirred it into the tea and returned to her seat. She sipped on the hot tea, allowing it to coat her throat as she scanned through the mock site. She had a lot to do and not much time to do it in. She decided she'd do what she could alone and call June over for the remaining information. She hated to bother her, knowing she had her own chores to do around the ranch, but Vaughn was right, this site needed to be up as quickly as possible. They needed workers as well as buyers.

"Shit." She hadn't even been able to show Vaughn her samples of job listings or some of the potential employees she'd found on a site already. Why had Vaughn taken off so suddenly? It only made things more difficult.

Natalie sipped her tea and stared out the front window. She could see Vaughn back in the corral, brushing down a horse. Just what secrets did she hold? Were they as deep and dark as her own? Was that even possible?

Whatever they were, they'd surfaced some today. She'd seen them firsthand, swimming in Vaughn's eyes and they'd looked extremely painful.

"What are you hiding, Vaughn Ruger?"

She took another sip of her tea and jerked as a knock came from the door. She set down her mug and walked to pull open the door. June stood there holding a stack of leather-bound folders. "Knock, knock," she said as she breezed inside, her wild white hair whipping around her face.

"June," Natalie managed to breathe. "I wasn't expecting you so soon."

"Well, Vaughn said you needed me, so here I am."

"Yes, well." Natalie struggled to get her bearings and closed the door to return to her seat. She brought up the website again and went into the first page, ready to edit. "I need to know all about the horses," she said. "Anything and everything you can tell me."

June lifted Natalie's cup of tea and crossed back to the kitchen. "I'll make us both more tea then. Because we're both going to be here a while."

Natalie pressed first one cheek then the other cheek to her shoulders, stretching her neck. Evening was fast approaching; she could tell by the position of the sun out the window. She and June had been sitting at the table, working at the computer for hours now and her neck and shoulders were paying the price. She raised her arms in a big stretch. June stood and did the same.

"Lord, child, are we done? My eyes are about to cross from looking at that screen."

Natalie swiped the mouse pad a few more times and saved their progress. All that was left to do now was to add the photos. "We're done," she said, relieved herself. She was ready for a break.

"If I drink anymore of that tea, I'll turn into a vanilla bean," June said. She gathered all the folders full of information about the horses and the ranch finances and headed for the door. "Guess I better go get supper started," she said. "Or I'll have some pissed off cowboys clamoring at my door."

"They eat supper here too?"

"Benny and Greer get three squares a day. It's part of their pay and part of the deal we made with their folks. 'Sides, those two, they don't know the first thing about cooking. So if they don't eat here, they eat junk, and they show up to work looking like strung out skeletons and performing just as bad. Doesn't do us any good when they're like that."

"I guess not."

"You come on over now when you're ready."

"I can help you now," Natalie said. "If you like."

"Why, sure, child. I'd love the company." She opened the door. "Might as well bring that contraption with you so you can show Vaughn."

"Right." Natalie closed her laptop and carried it with her to the door. She and June headed out back to the main house.

"We're having pot roast and taters for supper. I needed something to just cook in the slow cooker while we worked."

"Sounds delicious," Natalie said. They entered the house via the back door and she inhaled. "Smells yummy too."

June laughed. "Yummy. You're too cute, child."

Natalie felt herself flush. They came to the kitchen. It was sparkling clean. June had done a good job of cleaning up after the mess of the tacos at lunch. "Uh, where should I put my computer?"

"In here." June led them into a dimly lit living room, clad with a dark leather sofa and matching chairs. A large wooden desk sat nestled in the corner. June left the folders on the desk and turned to her. "You can leave it here," she said motioning her over. Natalie placed the laptop on the desk and followed her back into the kitchen where they both washed their hands. June pointed to where the dishware and silverware were and Natalie set the table with cloth napkins and all. She retrieved glasses and filled them all with ice and cold brewed tea while June readied the pot roast and boiled the potatoes to mash. Soon it was time for dinner to be served and Natalie saw the boys approaching from out the kitchen window.

"I sure am excited to see what Vaughn thinks of that finished website," June said as she poked at the roast with a large fork.

Natalie glanced over at her. "Oh, it's not finished. I still have to add the photos."

"Photos?"

She'd forgotten to mention the photos. That they weren't going to use the stock ones. "Yes, of the ranch. Vaughn said she had some. She just had to find them."

June stopped poking the meat. "She did, did she?"

"Is something wrong?" What was it about those photos?

"No, nothing's wrong."

"Vaughn had a similar reaction," Natalie said. "She got up and left suddenly. So, I assumed there was something about the photos she didn't want to discuss."

June put the lid back on the slow cooker, but she didn't turn to look at Natalie. Instead, she unfolded and refolded a dish towel. "Vaughn's a photographer. Or used to be. She was a damn good one too. Won some awards and such a long time ago."

"That's incredible."

"It is. It was."

"What happened?"

She finally faced her and her wrinkled face was slack with sadness. "That's a story for another day, Natalie dear."

Natalie felt her pulse beat in her neck. There was definitely something about the photos. Something bad. She felt guilty for asking. "I'm sorry, I shouldn't have asked."

"It's alright, child. You didn't know. Just...don't ask Vaughn, okay? When she gives you those photos, don't ask about them. Just...it's a big deal her giving you those."

"I understand."

"No, child, I'm afraid you don't. But I don't expect you to."

Benny opened the door and bounded in, his face red and slick, his hat-hair mussed and sweaty. "What's for supper, Miss June?"

"Sit your scrawny ass down and you'll find out." She swatted him with the dish towel and he hollered and hurried to his seat. Greer quickly followed suit, only he stopped to give June a sweaty kiss on the cheek.

She protested playfully. "Why, a sweaty kiss from a stinky young man, thank you, Greer."

He grinned. "There's more where that came from, Miss June."

"Oh, I have no doubt that there is."

Vaughn came in the door walking slowly, hand on the back of her hip. She was limping. "Smells good," she said.

June rushed to her. "That blasted back of yours," she said. "You sit now, you hear?"

"I hear." Vaughn sat carefully and June took her plate and filled it full of food for her.

"Why'd you boys let her bale the hay, huh? You know she's got a bad back."

"She wouldn't listen," Greer said. "We tried to stop her."

"Well, try harder."

"It's not their fault, Gram," Vaughn said. "We're all doing the best we can."

Natalie sat at the table, watching the exchange. It seemed her world wasn't the only one full of trouble. Vaughn's seemed to be as well. With the money troubles she'd heard firsthand from June, to needing good workers, to her back, it seemed her life was chock full of trouble.

Natalie could only hope that she wasn't adding to that.

## CHAPTER ELEVEN

Dinner was a noisy, fun-loving affair, and Natalie enjoyed herself immensely. As expected, Benny and Greer were great entertainment, telling all sorts of stories about the ranch and even a few about Vaughn herself. Natalie's favorite was the tale about Vaughn out on the trail, running to catch up with her horse, when she rolled on a small rock and fell onto the arm of a cactus, getting needles stuck in her backside. She'd had to bend over and allow Greer to pluck them out so she could get back on her horse.

Needless to say, Vaughn didn't like the telling of that story very much, especially when Natalie was almost in tears with laughter. June had laughed too, at Vaughn's expense, but it was all in good fun and it was nice to hear that Vaughn, just like everyone else, had the occasional mishap as well. Natalie had had her on such a pedestal, having such great respect for her, that she'd begun to think that she walked on water. So hearing that she was indeed human, and just like her in some respects, helped her to relax a little.

So, when she'd followed her into the living room after supper, and at June's insistence, she wasn't as nervous as she'd previously been in being so close to her.

"Supper was sure nice," Natalie said with ease as they neared the desk.

"It was."

Vaughn motioned for Natalie to sit in the office chair, while she pulled up a little ottoman. "I should probably go and shower first, so you don't have to smell me," she said as she sat beside her at the laptop.

"It's okay," Natalie said. "I li—er, don't mind."

Vaughn glanced at her in confusion, but let the matter go it seemed, because she focused on the computer screen. "Show me what you got."

Natalie woke the screen. "Well, as you remember, we have all the stock photos up on the mock site, but you can see here that June and I added a bunch of information on the horses and the ranch itself. She went from page to page, showing Vaughn everything she and June had managed to do that afternoon.

"You did a great job. It's really very impressive."

"It will be even more so, after we add your photos." Natalie said, worried she'd said too much, forgetting to heed June's warning.

Vaughn stared at the computer for a long moment, causing Natalie's nerves to wreak havoc on her insides.

"Right. The photos." She stood and turned toward an oak filing cabinet nestled against the wall. "They should be in here." She opened a deep drawer and riffled through some files before pulling out a thick one. She set it on the desk and opened it. There, in the file, were dozens of beautiful 8x10 photographs of the ranch. Natalie couldn't help but comment.

"These are incredible, Vaughn." She leaned forward, trying for a better look as Vaughn thumbed through them, but Vaughn closed the file before she could see most of them.

"We need the digitals though, don't we?" Vaughn said.

Natalie was taken aback at being shut out from the photos. "Uh, yes. Digitals would be preferable. But, Vaughn, these are—" She tried to touch the file, to open it once again, but Vaughn snatched it away and slid it back into the drawer.

"—amazing," Natalie finished, letting her voice drop off.

"I'll get the digitals." Vaughn opened one of the desk drawers and rummaged through it. She came up with a handful of USB drives and studied the tags attached to them. When she found the one she was looking for, she handed it to Natalie. "This should do it."

Natalie took the drive. "Thanks."

Vaughn let out a big breath. "Right. I'm just going to go shower now."

"You mean…you aren't going to help with the photos?" They'd just sat down, and even decided that Vaughn didn't need to shower right away. What was happening?

"You choose," she said. "You're the one with the eye for these things."

"But you're the one who—" Natalie stopped speaking and the pain she'd seen earlier in Vaughn's eyes resurfaced. She spoke again softly, hoping to rid her of that pain. "Sure, I can do it on my own, if that's what you prefer."

"I do," Vaughn said. She rounded the desk and walked out of the room. Natalie sat for a moment dumbfounded.

She still had no answers and what's worse was the awful hurt she'd seen overcome Vaughn. Just what was it about these damn photos?

She was determined to find out. She closed the laptop and slid the thumb drive into her pocket. Then she walked into the kitchen and set her computer on the clean table and joined June at the kitchen sink where she was cleaning the dishes from supper.

"Scooch over, lady," Natalie said, nudging her with her hip.

"Well, look who's grown a pair of ovaries all of a sudden," June said.

Natalie laughed.

"I told you I didn't need no help," June said.

"I know. But it looks like you do, so you're getting it, like it or not."

"I'm beginning to like you," June said, handing her a soapy plate to rinse.

"I'm beginning to like you too," Natalie said in return.

"Things go alright with Vaughn?"

Natalie shrugged. "She gave me the photos on a flash drive and then went to shower. So, to answer your question…I have no idea."

"I was afraid of as much. She's a hard nut to crack, that one."

"Seems so."

"And when it comes to some things, well there's just no way to get in."

"Like the photos?" Natalie asked.

"Like the photos."

Natalie angled her head as she dried the clean plate and stacked it with some others. "What is it about the photos, June? Why do they upset her so much?"

"I'm not sure I should say, child. Vaughn being so private and what not."

"I understand. I just…I saw the pain in her eyes and I…I guess I just don't want to hurt her by saying or doing the wrong thing."

June refilled the sink with hot water, causing the soap bubbles to rise on her side of the sink. She started in on washing again.

"I reckon I can tell you a little."

Natalie waited, breath held.

"Vaughn had a woman, some years ago, who she was in love with. Deeply in love."

"That sounds nice," Natalie said as butterflies began to flutter in her stomach. Vaughn liked women. She'd suspected as much but hadn't been sure. Now she knew and it was causing those butterflies to do backflips.

"It was nice for a time. Vaughn was working the ranch and taking photos in her off time. They were real good too. Professional quality. She had people clamoring to her for photos, so much so that she started her own little side business and earned her some extra money. Times was good. She was happy. The happiest I'd ever seen her. But this woman…this no-good woman, Jeanie…she…" June shook her head. "She left. She up and left. Just took off and disappeared, leaving no word as to where she'd gone. Well, Vaughn was up in arms, convinced something had happened to her. She called the police, hired a detective, the whole nine yards. But come to find out, the woman, she'd gone off on her own. To Mexico. And not only that, but she'd taken Vaughn's money with her, along with her identity. And what hurt Vaughn the most, was the fact that she'd had another lover waiting in the wings."

"Oh, no."

"Yeah. And you know what? She'd been seeing this other woman for nearly the whole time she and Vaughn had been together. Plus, she'd been the one running Vaughn's website for the photography business. So stealing her identity as the photographer and taking all the money Vaughn had made from sales wasn't that hard for her. Not that hard at all."

"That's terrible." Natalie felt ill. As if she'd somehow done something wrong in making the mock website. No wonder Vaughn had looked so pained. She'd been the victim of someone very manipulative and dishonest.

*Just like me.*

"I'm so sorry, June. I had no idea."

"Of course you didn't, child."

"I should've never offered to do a website. I should've—"

"Don't be silly. We need a good website. And Vaughn, she's had no interest in doing it. I think she's rather traumatized from the whole thing to be honest, so she doesn't want to do it. Which is why, you showing me a thing or two about it is a good thing. For the time being anyway."

Natalie took the final dish from her and rinsed it. Then, in a daze, she dried it and set it with the others.

"I'm not sure what to do, June," she confessed. "With the website and the photos. Like I said, I don't want to hurt her. But I was hoping to have her input on which photos to choose. She's the one with the best eye, since she's the photographer. Besides, it's her ranch. She should be the one to decide."

June pulled the drain from the sink and watched in a daze as the water and soap receded. "I think you're going to have to decide those things for yourself, Natalie. Vaughn's just too pained. She told you as much, didn't she?"

"She said I should choose."

"Well, then." She ran the faucet and rinsed out the sink. She met Natalie's gaze. "I guess that's what you're gonna have to do."

"Okay," Natalie breathed. "I guess I will." She dried her hands on the dish towel and handed it to June who did the same.

June hung the towel on the oven handle. "You might as well get used to it," she said. "Vaughn's not one to open up."

Natalie crossed to the table and picked up her computer. She headed for the kitchen door. "I'm beginning to see that," she said. She opened the door and bid June a good night. She stepped out into the evening air, allowing the oven-like heat to encase her, and walked quietly to the guesthouse, all the while thinking of Vaughn and her pain.

## CHAPTER TWELVE

Vaughn awoke and soaked in the shower for a long while, hoping the hot water would loosen her tight back. She hadn't slept well, due to her back, but the water was soothing, and quickly waking her. She had a lot to do that day and rising before dawn was just par for the course. So was showering each morning, even though she'd showered the night before as well. She found it invigorating and it also helped with her back.

She finished and dried and dressed. Then grabbed a bottle of cold water from the fridge, swallowed two Advil, and slipped out the kitchen door after starting the coffee machine for Gram. Daylight was just beginning to break, the night turning from black to midnight blue, and soon, as perceived just over the horizon, a pale blue. She inhaled the fresh air, thanked God for the forecast of a cooler day, and headed for the stables. But as she walked, she snuck a look at the guesthouse and noticed a light on. Natalie must be up. She was impressed. She thought for sure the city slicker would need to be roused to gather the eggs. But it seemed she was wrong. The door to the guesthouse opened as she was watching and she glanced away, hoping not to be caught looking. But Natalie spotted her and called out.

"Good morning," she said, hurrying to catch up to her.

"Morning."

"It's beautiful out, isn't it?"

She had on jeans today and a pair of sneakers. Vaughn couldn't help but notice. Natalie followed her line of sight. She lifted a foot.

"June ordered me some rugged hiking boots from Amazon," she said. "For work on the ranch. Thought they'd be better than my sneakers."

"They will," Vaughn said.

"I thought about boots, like yours, but I heard they're hard to break in and I didn't want sore feet. I want to be able to help a lot, so I need to be in good shape all the way around."

"Ah."

Natalie looked over at her. "You don't say much, do you?"

Vaughn kept walking, looking ahead. "I do when it's called for."

"And it's not called for now?"

Vaughn finally glanced at her. "What would you like me to say?"

"I don't know. I'm just trying to make conversation. But I get it. You don't know me well at all, so why share?"

They came to the chicken coop and slowed as Diablo, Vaughn's small, red rooster jumped up onto the fence and began to crow. The little guy was loud and he was putting his whole body into it. It made Natalie laugh and Vaughn couldn't help but smile.

"That's Diablo," she said.

"Devil." Natalie chuckled. "Does he live up to his name?"

"He does."

"I sure hope he likes me."

"Walk in there with confidence and you'll be fine. The only reason he doesn't like Gram is because she once had to chase him out of the coop and keep him away from the chickens."

"Oh."

"Gram will sure appreciate you getting the eggs for her."

"I'm here to help." She smiled softly at her. "You know, I finished the web site last night."

"Oh?"

"I just need your permission to have it go live."

"You have it."

"You sure you don't want to look at it first?"

"I trust you."

Natalie seemed surprised at the statement. "Thanks. I hope it does you proud."

"I'm sure it will."

Natalie hesitated at the gate to the coop, as if she was going to say something more. Vaughn waited, but she must've changed her mind because she gave a little wave and walked inside, leaving Vaughn behind.

Vaughn watched her go, making sure Diablo didn't give her any trouble, and then headed off sipping her water. She entered the stables, turned on the lights, and walked down to the very last stall to begin her work.

After she mucked the first row of stalls and spoke briefly to the boys who'd arrived shortly after she'd started, she heard Gram ring the bell for breakfast. Vaughn leaned the hay fork up against the wall and headed for the house. When she came to the corral, she was surprised to see Natalie grooming one of the horses the boys had let out.

"Am I doing it right?" she asked, brushing down Charlie.

"Looks pretty good to me," Vaughn said. Her gaze traveled over Natalie's lithe body, shown off perfectly in the tight jeans and short-sleeved shirt she had on. She moved with grace and ease and Vaughn caught herself staring and forced her eyes to refocus on Charlie. But her mind kept replaying the vision of Natalie moving, the way her muscles in her sinewy arms shifted as she brushed, the delicate flare of her hips, and the way her shirt lifted slightly when she stretched, exposing her smooth, pale torso. Vaughn cleared her tightening throat.

"You can finish that after breakfast," she said, walking on. She needed to escape, to clear her head for a moment. Natalie was off limits, for more reasons than one, and she couldn't afford to get caught up in an attraction to her, even if she kept that attraction to herself. She had very important things to focus on, and rolling in the hay, or even dreaming about rolling in the hay with Natalie, was not among them.

"Hey, wait up." Natalie set down the brush and hurried out of the corral to join her. "You want to take a peek at the website after breakfast? I haven't been back in to publish it yet."

"Why not?" Vaughn had thought for sure she'd told her to go ahead.

"I got caught up in doing chores."

Vaughn didn't speak, just clenched her jaw. She really needed that website up and running. "Fine."

"Great. I'll also show you some of the job listings I want to publish."

"Okay."

Natalie seemed to sense her mood. "I'm sorry, Vaughn, I just don't want to do anything without you getting a look see first."

"And why is that?"

"Because…it's your ranch and—"

Vaughn stopped. "Gram told you, didn't she?"

Natalie shifted her gaze and Vaughn knew. "Christ."

"She didn't tell me a lot," Natalie hurried to say. "Just that… you were betrayed. And I don't want to cause any trouble. I don't want to risk doing something you don't like."

"Fine, I'll look things over." They walked up onto the porch where Gram stood waiting with her apron on, wringing it with her hands. She was smiling, but Vaughn could tell she'd heard some of their conversation.

"Gram," Vaughn said by way of greeting. She was furious at her for telling Natalie about Jeanie and more furious at not knowing just how much she had told her.

"Vaughn."

"You and me," Vaughn said. "We'll talk. Later."

"Alrighty."

The three of them headed inside and the boys bounded up behind them. Vaughn held the door open for everyone and just before she closed it, she closed her eyes and sighed. It was going to be a long day.

After breakfast Vaughn walked quietly back to the guesthouse with Natalie to look over her work. They hadn't spoken at breakfast, both of them choosing to sit and listen to Gram and the boys rather than talk. Gram had sensed Vaughn's mood too, especially after Vaughn had told her they needed to talk, and she'd watched her and Natalie both closely across the table. She'd wanted to speak to them, to illicit conversation, Vaughn could tell, but she'd wisely refrained, leaving things be. And now it seemed, that Natalie, too, was wary about speaking to her, because they walked in silence and things remained that way until they got inside and sat at the small kitchen table.

Natalie opened her laptop and woke the screen. She brought up the website and turned the laptop to face Vaughn. Vaughn looked at it quietly, checking out all the pages as Natalie coursed through them, explaining things.

The site was brilliant and beautiful and very professional looking. Vaughn was moved, almost to tears. It wasn't just her photos, the ones she'd avoided looking at for two years, that had moved her, it was Natalie's work, her attention to detail, her above and beyond effort. She'd really done her a huge favor and she was sitting there patiently waiting for Vaughn to speak, awaiting her approval with a look of terrible trepidation.

*Christ, am I that scary? Have I been a big ass about this?*

Vaughn looked at her. "It's…" She nearly choked, her throat tight with rising emotion. "Wonderful."

Natalie's face softened and her eyebrows lifted. "Really?"

"Yes."

She let out a small yelp and threw her arms around Vaughn, hugging her tight. "Oh my God, thank you," she said into her ear. "I'm so glad you like it." She drew away, smiling at her, but Vaughn was too shocked and too moved to return the smile. She was too busy trying to control her reaction at having Natalie in her arms. Of feeling her firm body pressed against hers and inhaling the scent of her soap and shampoo. It had stirred her, and her mind was spinning. She hadn't been prepared to feel these feelings. Hadn't been prepared at all. So, she did the only thing she could do. She stood and scooped her hat up off the table.

"Wait," Natalie said, looking incredulous. "Don't leave. Not again."

"I really should get back to it," Vaughn said, trying to avoid her heavy gaze. Why did she have to have eyes like she did? So crystal clear and green? Like a lush, green meadow leading up to a lake?

"No," Natalie said, clenching her wrist. "Sit." She tugged on her and insisted she return to her seat.

Vaughn sank back down into the chair, but she didn't remove her hat.

"Now, I'm going to push this button and publish the website. You ready?" She hovered the cursor over a yellow button that said PUBLISH.

Vaughn nodded.

Natalie published the site and smiled. "We're online!" She clapped. She stopped when she saw that Vaughn didn't join in. "Okay, now I'll show you the job listings I worked up."

She brought up the listings and let Vaughn read them over. She'd done a surprisingly good job considering she knew nothing about ranching. "They're great," Vaughn said. "Only add this to this one." And she rattled off more of a job description and Natalie typed it up. When she finished, she showed Vaughn the sites she was going to post them to. "I also thought that maybe we should print them up so you could take them and post them at places you frequent. Like the feed store and tractor supply, etc."

"Okay, sure. Good idea."

Natalie sent the pages to Gram's new email so Vaughn could download them and print them in the house.

They sat in silence after that with the air heavy between them, and Vaughn could feel the electricity of a mutual attraction. Natalie kept looking at her with her captivating eyes, while brushing her dark bangs away from her face. It was obvious that she wanted to speak, but she seemed at a loss for words. Vaughn, too, didn't know what to say. She stood once again.

"I better go."

Natalie joined her and they walked toward the door.

"Thanks for coming by to look."

Vaughn gripped the doorknob. "Thanks for all your hard work. What do I owe you?" She was eager to pay her, to even things out. Natalie had done her such a favor, and she'd done a damn good job at it to boot. Vaughn dug in her back pocket for her wallet. She opened it and began leafing through her cash. A website fee wasn't in the budget, but she'd have to sacrifice. They really needed the website and this new one would bring in some much-needed business, she was sure of it.

Natalie covered Vaughn's hand with her own and lowered it along with the wallet.

"No charge," she said softly.

"I need to pay you something. You did such a good job."

"No, really," Natalie said. "You don't owe me a thing."

"But you did me such a big favor."

"And like I said, you're doing one for me. We're even."

"You—sure?"

"Positive."

Vaughn closed her wallet and slipped it back into her pocket. She opened the door.

"I'll join you as soon as I post those job listings," Natalie said.

Vaughn nodded. Then she gave a small smile and walked out into the bright, morning sun.

## CHAPTER THIRTEEN

Titus "Tito" Alvarez waited quietly in the doorway of Allen Brewer's home. It was a large house by normal standards, fancy, the kind of house rich white men seemed to prefer, but Tito knew he nearly dwarfed the massive front door with his size. Something that gave him great comfort.

"Tito, good to see you," Allen said, trying to give him an embrace. Tito stood very still, and Allen drew away, forcing a smile. "Come in, come in." He waved him inside and walked to the wet bar in the living room. Evening had set in already, sunset coming earlier now that it was September, and Allen had yet to switch on the main lights, so the room was backlit only in blueberry accent light. He fumbled with two tumblers, as if he were nervous, and began pouring himself a little Petron Tequila Burdeos Anejo.

"Tequila?" he asked, as if Tito couldn't read the bottle. "It's the good stuff."

Tito walked slowly into the room and stood next to a chair. He didn't answer, just flexed his fists, making the tattoos on his forearms dance. He caught a glimpse of himself in the mirror behind the bar and took in his large head with a tight flat top haircut, pock-mocked cheeks, and a neck the size of most men's thighs. His eyes were what got to people though. They always had. They'd been described by some as dead eyes.

"Okay, one glass of the good stuff, coming right up." Allen poured him a generous helping, despite Tito's silence on the matter.

He rounded the bar to hand it to him and sat on the sofa and crossed his legs to sip from his own glass. "Please, sit."

Tito stared him down as he sank into the chair across from him.

"Bet you're wondering why I called."

Tito didn't respond. He knew what was up. Nico Fitz had filled him in on Allen's missing wife, despite Allen have gone around him to contact Tito. But one couldn't keep much from Nico. The man seemed to know all. And Allen would be wise to remember that.

"I have a job for you," Allen continued. "An important job. I need you to find my wife. She's, uh, taken it upon herself to skip town, you see. And that's unacceptable."

Tito sat very still, staring at him. Then he swallowed his tequila in one big shot. Allen blinked at him. "Would you like another?"

Tito shook his head. Allen seemed to relax. "I'll pay you generously, of course, just as I have before. But I need her found quickly. Because I don't like it when she's gone. The house feels…" He spread his arms. "Empty." He smiled. "I feel empty. You feel me?"

Tito sat in silence.

"Of course you do. But you may be saying to yourself, well, Allen, you're divorced, so of course the house feels empty." He wagged a finger at him. "But to that I say, bullshit! The divorce was not my choice, and she left without my permission, taking something from me, which in and of itself is…you guessed it…unacceptable."

Tito leaned forward and deposited the empty tumbler on the glass coffee table. Beyond them, just outside the floor to ceiling windows, the pool light glowed in the growing darkness, turning from aqua to green to purple, making Allen look like a small ogre sitting there in his chair.

"You sure you wouldn't like another?" Tito shook his head and Allen leaned forward. He slid a large envelope toward him and encouraged him to open it. "For your trouble."

Tito snatched up the envelope and opened it to eye the contents. He looked at Allen and stood. Allen stood along with him and extended his hand. "When you find her, and I know you will, call the number in the envelope. I trust you won't let her know she's been found. And Tito, I don't just want her found. I have other things in mind for her if you know what I mean."

Tito took his hand and purposely crushed it in his massive paw. Allen looked like he was trying not to wince before Tito released him and walked slowly to the door.

"Thanks, Tito. It was good to see you."

Tito opened the door and walked out.

## CHAPTER FOURTEEN

The day started off with a nice crispness to the air, with temperatures a little below normal for the time of year. Vaughn was enjoying it, not sweating nearly as much as she usually would have doing her morning chores. She'd already mucked the stalls and laid down new straw, and now she was inspecting the horses' feet for infection or other issues.

She inhaled the cool air and wondered whether or not they were going to get that rain that was promised later as she placed her hand on Holly, one of her broodmare's shoulders, and ran it down her leg to her foot. She gently lifted it to examine the hoof. She checked the frog, made sure it was intact and no foul odors were coming from the hoof itself, and ran the hoof pick along the sides of the frog to scrape along the edge of the shoe. When she was satisfied that the hoof looked good, she gently lowered the foot, ran her hand along Holly's body to her back leg and lifted the back foot, careful to keep the hoof along the inside of her body so she wouldn't get kicked. She was busy examining the hoof when Gram walked up, clearing her throat loudly to let Vaughn know she was present.

Just when the morning was going so well.

"Yeah?" Vaughn said, cleaning Holly's hoof with the pick.

"You tell me. You're the one who's been avoiding me."

"I've been busy, Gram."

"Bullarkey. You tell me we need to talk and you do nothing of the sort for the next week. So, what is it? Have you let it go, or do you have something to say to me?"

Vaughn lowered Holly's foot and straightened to walk to her other side, heading back up to her head, careful to avoid Gram's gaze. She wasn't in the mood to talk and hadn't been since she'd nearly lost her temper over Gram's telling Natalie about Jeanie. She'd calmed since then, her temper tamed, but she was still right mad and she didn't want to get into with her at the moment.

"Well?" Gram said.

Vaughn trailed her hand down Holly's shoulder and leg to her foot and lifted it carefully. "You know why I'm upset."

"I've got a good suspicion."

"Then what have you got to say?"

"I don't rightly know, Vaughn. Do you want an apology? Fine. I'm sorry. But you know, Natalie knew something was wrong. The way you were acting. She worried she might say something wrong. So what was I supposed to tell her?"

"I don't know. Tell her it's none of her business."

"After all the help she's given us?"

"Well, it isn't. It isn't any of her business, regardless of what she's done or hasn't done." She scraped Holly's hoof, set her foot down, and moved on to the back leg. She trailed her hand down her hip to her leg and lifted her foot. She heard Gram sigh.

"Child, you're unbelievable."

"I'm right though."

"No, you're not. Not in your behavior over the whole thing or your behavior now. And why is it exactly that you didn't want Natalie to know? You don't seem to mind if anyone else knows, the boys and the folks in town included. Is it because you have feelings for her?"

Vaughn nearly dropped Holly's foot. But she refocused and noticed a smell. She examined her frog and set her foot down.

"Well?" Gram said again.

Vaughn stood. She slid the hoof pick into her back pocket. "Holly's got thrush."

Gram crossed her arms. "I'll call the farrier."

"I can do it."

"Are you going to answer me?"

Vaughn stroked Holly's neck. "I'm not going to respond to such a ludicrous question."

"Ludicrous?" She laughed. "You're going to be the death of me, do you know it, Vaughn Marie?"

"Just don't tell her anything else, alright? She doesn't need to know our business."

"No, she's only running the website and learning all the ins and outs of the ranch."

"Exactly my point. It could be dangerous."

"If you're worried then you need to step up and do it yourself. Get over this whole thing with Jeanie. You know we have to have a presence on that inter web or whatever you call it."

Vaughn narrowed her eyes. "Don't tell me to get over it or anything else."

Gram threw up her arms. "Fine. Don't. But don't come crying to me when people question your behavior and I have to tell them something so they don't take it personal and run off when we need them the most."

Vaughn wanted to argue with her, to tell her she was being ridiculous, but she couldn't. Gram was making sense and it made her all the more upset. So she chose not to speak, clenching her jaw instead. Movement from down the stable caught her attention and she looked past Gram as Benny walked up, a look of tight concern on his young face.

Now what?

"We got a problem," he said. "The east fence is down."

"What?" Impossible, she'd just checked it yesterday evening.

"And it's not just down. It's been cut."

Vaughn bunched her fists, left the stall and Gram behind, and followed Benny out to the Gator. She climbed aboard and he slid in next to her. They took off across the ranch, kicking up dust along the way. They rode in silence until they got to the east fence line where Vaughn slowed at the gaping hole. She climbed out of the Gator and stood looking at the hanging wires with her hat resting against her thigh. She looked up, beyond the fence, and decided to look for tracks. She stepped through the hole and examined the ground. Tire tracks ran back into the desert from the fence line. Big tracks. Like those of a pickup truck. There were also hoofprints.

She turned back to Benny. "How many horses got out?"

"I count four. Maybe more."

"Shit." She crawled back into the Gator and Benny followed. They sped back to the stables.

Greer and Gram were waiting for them. Vaughn started barking orders at the boys as she climbed from the Gator. "You two get on some horses and go track down the ones that got away. I'm going to work on repairing the fence."

"Yes, ma'am," they said in unison.

"What's going on?" Gram asked as Vaughn walked up to her.

"Someone's cut the fence. Left a big hole. Some of the mares got out."

"Someone really cut it?"

"Looks that way."

"You think Ricky and Pedro did it?"

"I don't know who else would've."

"But why?"

"Probably because I threatened to fire them if they didn't take a drug test."

"Well, there's nothing wrong with that," Gram said. "If they was doing drugs. Serves 'em right."

"Yeah, but those two." Vaughn shook her head. "They're bad news. My threats pissed them off. And now they're acting out."

"I should call the police."

"You do what you feel is necessary," Vaughn said, hurrying away. But Gram lightly gripped her arm.

"Take Natalie."

"Gram—"

"She can help. And she needs to know what's going on. She's already asking." She motioned toward the corral where Natalie was standing beside Oliver, lightly petting him.

"She'll slow me down," Vaughn whispered.

"She can help."

Vaughn gritted her teeth and stalked into the corral. She controlled her feelings however, and spoke to Natalie with a calm voice. "You want to come help me repair the east fence?"

Her face lit up and Vaughn was glad she'd asked her politely. What was happening wasn't Natalie's fault and Vaughn knew she had to remember that. "Sure."

"Go ahead and wait in the Gator then."

Vaughn left her to retrieve her supplies. She grabbed an extra set of gloves along with some wire and the stretcher and cutter, and climbed back into the Gator. She slammed on the gas and they took off, tearing through the ranch. Natalie held onto the side rail and ran her hands through her hair as the wind toyed with it. She didn't ask questions and Vaughn was grateful, just wanting to get the job done.

When they reached the hole in the fence, Vaughn killed the engine and hopped out. She tossed Natalie the extra pair of gloves and grabbed her spool of wire and cutters. She walked to the fence with Natalie on her heels.

"Oh my God," she said. "Someone did this on purpose, didn't they?"

"Looks that way," Vaughn said. The surrounding desert was quiet, save for the whisper of the breeze. None of the horses remained out to pasture, so she tried to relax a little and just do the job at hand, when what she really wanted to do was kick those idiots' asses.

"You have to call the police," Natalie said, somewhat worked up herself.

"Gram's going to take care of it."

"Well, don't you think you should wait for them to come out, before you fix the fence?"

Vaughn paused briefly. "I don't want to wait." She was concerned about getting the fence fixed before the predicted storm came through. She didn't have time to wait.

Natalie held out her hand. "Hand me your phone then."

"What for?"

"So I can take pictures for the police."

Vaughn slid out her phone and handed it over, thinking it wasn't such a bad idea for her to take some photos after all. Natalie took the phone and began taking photos of the cut fence, zooming in on the cut wires and then taking broader shots. She walked through the gaping hole and took photos of the ground, kneeling to get closer to the tracks in the dirt.

"You a forensic specialist too?" Vaughn asked.

"I know a thing or two," Natalie said, without breaking her focus. "Like the fact that these tracks won't be here for much longer if the wind picks up or if we get that storm that's expected to roll through later."

"Is there anything you don't know?" Vaughn meant it as a compliment, but Natalie straightened and walked back to her, looking at her like she was offended.

"What's that supposed to mean?" She returned her phone.

"I didn't mean anything bad by it," Vaughn said, sliding her phone back into her pocket. "You just seem to know a little about a lot of things. Like you're well read."

"I do love to read. It's about all I do when I'm not working."

"It shows."

Natalie brushed her bangs away from her eyes and smiled. She seemed pleased at Vaughn's assessment of her. It made Vaughn curious as to just how many times she had heard something nice about herself. She reckoned she hadn't heard too many compliments. It was a shame because she deserved them. She was a bright and beautiful woman and she should be treated accordingly.

Vaughn pulled on her gloves, determined to move on with her thoughts, and encouraged Natalie to put her gloves on too. She grabbed her fence cutter and her fence stretcher and got to work with Natalie by her side. She showed her how to first wrap the wire ends around the fence cutter and then wind the ends back onto the same line. They moved on and Natalie did everything she was instructed to do. She caught on very quickly as she knelt next to Vaughn and helped her work.

"Thank you," she eventually said.

Vaughn glanced up at her. "For what?"

"For the compliment. If it was meant as such."

*She's still thinking about that compliment. I really ought to make sure she hears more of them.* "It was."

Natalie smiled again as the wind carried her long bangs across her eyes. She tucked the strands behind her ears but they refused to stay. So she tugged her glove off with her teeth and ran her hand straight back over her head, finger combing her hair away from her face.

Vaughn caught herself staring for a moment, moved by her beauty and graceful actions. She refocused on the task at hand, tightening the wires.

"Are you still upset with Gram about the things she told me?" Natalie asked softly, grabbing hold of the wire for Vaughn after slipping back on her glove.

Vaughn continued to tighten. She didn't respond. Wasn't sure how to. The question was personal, one she didn't appreciate, but she thought back to what Gram had said, about her behavior leading to assumptions and more questions.

"It's been settled," she said, hoping to drop the matter.

"It wasn't her fault, you know," Natalie said. "I pressed her for an answer. I don't think she wanted to tell me. She seems to respect your privacy."

Vaughn said nothing, taking the statements in. Maybe she'd been too hard on Gram. Maybe she was the one who owed her an apology.

"Thank you for telling me," Vaughn said.

They finished working on the fence in silence and Vaughn was grateful. She enjoyed just sitting in the cool breeze across from Natalie as they worked to repair the fence. It was nice and it brought a peace to her she hadn't experienced in some time. Had it been one of the boys she'd been working with, she knew that she wouldn't have been able to work in such peace. They would've talked up a storm. But Natalie, thankfully, respected her need for quiet.

Vaughn had Natalie join her on her side of the fence as they finished. "That should do it," she said, testing the tautness of the wires. It was a good repair and she appreciated the help. "Thank you."

Natalie pulled off her gloves. "Don't mention it."

They picked up the supplies and headed back to the Gator. Vaughn drove them along the fence line to double-check for more damage. Natalie made small talk, asking a few questions here and there, but overall, it was a nice ride. And thankfully, they hadn't found any more holes or cuts in the fence.

Vaughn steered them back to the stables, thankful, for not only Natalie's help, but for small favors.

## CHAPTER FIFTEEN

Natalie brushed down O'Malley at the edge of the corral as Vaughn and June spoke to the police. Vaughn had warned her against talking to the officer, since the fire inspector had come looking for the driver of the burned out vehicle. She hadn't wanted to give the cops, or any authority, any reason to believe that she may be harboring someone. She also warned Natalie that the police would most likely ask her about her bruises. Though they had almost completely faded, Natalie knew that cops were trained to look for signs of abuse. So she decided to work in the corral like any other employee, straining to hear details of the nearby conversation.

"And you believe you know who cut your fence?" the young officer asked, scrolling through the pictures Natalie had taken on Vaughn's phone.

"I'm pretty damn sure," Vaughn said.

The officer returned the phone and readied his pen. He looked at Vaughn questioningly as he waited.

"Come on, Theo," Vaughn said. "You know as damn well as I do who did this."

"I can't speculate, Vaughn, and I won't."

"Oh, come off it," June said. "You gonna get all professional on us *now*?"

"I'm just doing my job, Mrs. Ruger."

She scoffed and kicked at the dirt with her boot. "Real convenient timing if you ask me."

"Look," Vaughn said. "I know Ricky is your cousin."

"That's got nothing to do with it," Theo said.

"Whatever," Vaughn said, holding up a palm. "I'm not suggesting anything here. I just want whoever did this caught."

Theo made some more notes and flipped his notebook closed. In the near distance Natalie heard footfalls and she saw Greer and Benny on horseback leading three horses back toward the stables.

Vaughn and June spotted them too. "Well, at least I got most of my mares back," Vaughn said.

"Who's gonna pay for the missing one?" June demanded. "That no good cousin of yours gonna cover the cost if we can't find her?"

Theo tucked his notebook and pen away. "If he did it, then yes, the law will hold him accountable."

"He won't have to pay for her if he returns her," Vaughn said.

"You think whoever did this kept her?" Theo asked.

Vaughn nodded. "I got a sneaking suspicion he did. Miracle's worth some money and he always favored her."

Theo rested his hands on his gun belt. "I'll look into it. I promise."

"You damn well better," June said. "And you tell those two, tell 'em if we catch them on this property that we got the right to shoot and shoot we will. Without hesitation."

Theo looked at the ground and lightly kicked a pebble. "Now don't go shooting from the hip just yet, Mrs. Ruger. We haven't got proof of anything."

June spit at the dirt. "I got all the proof I need. Those boys was always trouble. From the word go."

Theo looked to Vaughn as if she were the reasonable one. "Keep the guns at bay. We don't want this to escalate to where people get hurt."

"Then you give those two our warning," Vaughn said.

Theo nodded. "I'll be in touch." He left and walked back to his cruiser.

Greer and Benny led the three horses into the corral where Vaughn inspected them. June leaned on the bars of the pen and watched.

"They look injured?"

Vaughn ran her hands over each horse, carefully examining them. "Nah. They seem to be okay."

Benny lifted hooves for a quick look-see while Greer filled a trough with fresh water. Natalie left O'Malley to join Vaughn.

"They really okay?" she asked, stroking one of the horses.

"This time," Vaughn said. "We were lucky."

"I'm glad the weather has cooled a bit," Natalie said. "I'd hate to think of them out there in one-hundred-fifteen-degree heat with no shade."

Vaughn clenched her jaw as if thinking about it. She looked like she could kill whoever cut the fence. Her horses seemed to be everything to her. They were not just her livelihood, but her heart. She obviously loved them, and when anything bad happened to one of them, she seemed to suffer right alongside them.

Natalie felt for her, already developing feelings for the horses herself. Vaughn must feel so helpless, unable to stop the two men from targeting and tormenting them. She knew exactly how that felt.

She touched Vaughn's arm. "I'm sorry," she said. "I know how this feels."

Vaughn looked as though she didn't believe her. So Natalie explained. "I know what it feels like to be targeted and to have no control or a way to stop it. You're simply at the person's mercy. It's an awful feeling and no way to have to live."

Vaughn's eyes flooded. She glanced away and Natalie dropped her hand. Vaughn cleared her throat and looked back to her.

"I forgot about all that you're going though," Vaughn said. "For that I'm sorry. And I'm sorry you're having to go through it, because you're right, it's no way to live." She led the horse away with a stiff arm and guided her through the open gate of the corral. She passed June and disappeared into the stables.

"I don't know what you said to her," June said. "But you got to her."

Natalie walked up to the bars and leaned on them just like June. "I just told her I understood how she was feeling. It's no fun being the target of someone's harassment."

"No, it's not. And you know all about that, don't you?"

"Unfortunately."

"Vaughn's never had to deal with anything like this before."

"I didn't suspect as much. She's really taking it hard. She really loves those horses, doesn't she?"

June laughed. "If there was a word greater than love, then that wouldn't even come close to how Vaughn feels about these horses. Crazy child used to sleep with them when she was a kid. I'd get up in the middle of the night to find her bed empty and I'd come out here to the stables and there she'd be, all curled up in a stall, next to a horse."

"That's so sweet," Natalie said, touching her heart.

"I've got a picture of it over the mantel," June said. "It's my favorite one."

Natalie made a mental note to check it out. "Say, June? I've been meaning to ask you, who's the woman in the pictures with Vaughn in the guesthouse?"

"That's my daughter, Vivian. Vaughn's mother."

"Oh, I'm so sorry."

June slid her eyes over to her. "For what? She ain't dead, child. She just doesn't live here."

"Oh."

"She lives in Taos. She's an artist there. Paints for a living. Does a damn good job of it too."

"Did she paint that picture of the woman in the red dress? The one hanging in the guesthouse?"

"She did. As well as most of the ones in the main house."

"Wow, she is good."

"That she is."

"Does she come to visit often?"

"She hasn't been here in some time now. What with the pandemic and all. Vaughn's starting to miss her too. I can always tell. She gets quieter than usual. And moody as all get-out."

"Maybe she'll come soon," Natalie said. "After I leave."

"Don't you go thinking you're the reason she ain't coming."

"Well, I am in the guesthouse."

"Yes, and we want you there. As for my daughter, I love her, but she's flighty. Can't ever decide nothing and stick to it. So, don't you worry about being here. She can come anytime, even if you're here, and she knows it."

Natalie nodded and conceded. She moved on to the next thing on her mind.

"Do you really think those ex-employees cut the fence?"

"I do."

"They're just wanting to cause trouble or what?"

"I'd say so. They never did like Vaughn much because she expected them to work and she wasn't shy about getting on their case when she caught them lollygagging. And they didn't like that much."

"I just can't imagine what they must've been like. Benny and Greer are such good workers and they're so good with the horses."

"Benny and Greer is good boys and these days, around these parts, that's hard to find. We were lucky enough to know their families. So we know they was raised right. Whereas we didn't know nothing about them other boys."

"You've been getting some interest from the job postings I listed," Natalie said. She'd seen some of the emails June had received. She'd been excited, hoping that the website and the details in the job listings were helping.

"Yeah, now I just gotta find the time to interview them. Vaughn needs to be in on it and she don't got much free time these days."

"Well, I can fill in for her. You know, do her chores while she takes time to interview. If that helps."

"We might take you up on that. If Vaughn will allow it. She don't like to give up control."

"I can't say I blame her. This ranch, she feels so responsible."

"She's a good girl. But sometimes her head's too big and too stubborn for her own good. She overthinks and she refuses to give in and that don't leave room for much in the way of growth." June waved her hand. "But I've gone and said too much again. She's gonna tan my hide before it's over with."

"You just care about her and worry. I understand. And I promise I won't say anything."

June looked at her. "You seem to be a good girl, too, don't ya? And I can tell you care about this ranch and Vaughn too."

"I do."

"I wish Vaughn could find someone like you. Settle down. Relax a little."

Natalie blushed. She wasn't sure what to say. Just the mere thought of being with Vaughn was nearly overwhelming. She knew she'd think about it the rest of the day and well into the night. She'd imagine her strong body lying down over hers, her able hands skimming over her aching skin, her beautiful mouth capturing her tight, budding—

"I didn't mean to imply anything," June said, interrupting her thoughts.

"You didn't," she said a little too quickly.

June pushed off from the bars. "I better go before I get myself into trouble." She wagged her finger at her. "You be good, ya hear?" She grinned, teasing her.

Natalie smiled in return, though her face was still on fire and her heart was hammering in her chest. "I will," she managed, but her mind went right back to Vaughn lying with her in her bed, late, late at night and Natalie knew she was being anything but good.

## CHAPTER SIXTEEN

I want you to look at this," June said as she pointed at the computer screen.

Vaughn walked over to the desk with her wet, sun-streaked hair combed back from her face and a pair of cotton pajama pants on, along with a threadbare T-shirt. She smelled of a fresh, spicy soap as she knelt down next to June.

June pointed to the bottom of the website screen. "See that? That's how many visitors we've had to the site."

"Oh."

"Oh? Is that all you have to say?"

"What do you want me to say?"

"Well, considering that Natalie says this is already double what we had for all of last year, I'd say you owe this a lot more than just 'oh.'"

"Double?" She stood.

"Yes, double. And it's only been close to two weeks since it went live."

"Wow."

"There we go. That's more like it." June clicked the mouse and closed the page. She leaned back in the office chair and crossed her arms. Darkness had settled in outside and they'd just finished supper and were getting ready to turn in for the night. June was just doing her nightly check of the website and reading over her emails. She'd gotten quite efficient now that Natalie had shown her step by step how to do it. It wasn't as complicated as she'd worked it up to be.

"Have you given any more thought to those job applicants Natalie and I printed out for you? We need to call them in for an interview."

Vaughn sank down onto the couch and ran her hands through her hair. "God, I don't know."

"Well, you better know some time soon. We need new hands around here. You've said so yourself."

"I did."

"So what's the problem?"

Vaughn glanced up at her. "I'm worried we're just going to end up in the same position we are now. With a couple of disrespectful, lazy ranch hands who think they're better than the work at hand."

"Yeah, I'm a bit worried about that too. Which is why I think we ought to interview a bunch rather than a few. We've got seventeen applicants. Natalie says we can even interview them over the computer if we want. Might be more efficient that way."

"It would be," Vaughn said. "But we need to see how they are with the horses before we hire them on."

"Agreed."

"But I suppose we can start by weeding them out virtually first."

June cocked her head, confused.

Vaughn explained. "Over the computer."

"Oh. So you want to get started, then? I can send out the emails tonight, asking for vir—"

"Virtual."

"Virtual interviews for Wednesday and Thursday. Course it's going to take a while, so you'll need to let Natalie take over for you on those days. Best to show her the ropes some more tomorrow."

Vaughn groaned. "You know how I feel about letting someone else do my job."

"I do know, but you're going to have to do it, Vaughn. Sooner rather than later."

"Yeah, I know. Its just that…she's a novice, Gram."

"She can hold her own. She's quite tough. Plus, she'll have Benny and Greer and Suzanne will be here those days."

"I'm not worried about that."

"Then what are you worried about?"

"What if she gets hurt?"

June smiled. "Ah."

"Why are you smiling? I'm being serious."

"I'm smiling because you just told me all I need to know about the situation, dear child."

"Oh, I did not."

"You care about her."

"Well, of course I care. I don't want to see her get hurt."

"You care about her more than you're saying. Don't even try to argue either."

Vaughn stood from the couch. "Fine. I won't. You crazy old woman."

"I'm not that old, and I'm not that crazy."

Vaughn smirked. "Whatever, Gram."

She headed for the hallway. "Go ahead and send those emails."

June moved the mouse and woke the computer. "I'm on it. You have a good sleep, Vaughn Marie."

"You too, Gram." Vaughn disappeared down the hallway and June worked on typing out and sending the emails, marking in her calendar along the way. She hoped most of the applicants would agree to the suggested times. It would make things a lot easier, but she knew it wasn't likely. They'd probably have to run the interviews into Friday. And hopefully have the ones they didn't weed out come for visits to the ranch on Saturday and Sunday.

As she sent the last email, a handful of applicants began to respond, confirming their interview time. She smiled, feeling good about getting things done. She recalled a time when she was the sole one responsible for things like this, working alongside her late husband, Jack. He worked the ranch and the horses and she worked behind the scenes, taking care of the rest. They'd been a good team and she missed him so. But he'd been gone ten years now. Funny how sometimes it felt like yesterday and other times it felt like an eternity.

Jack had been a good man and she knew she'd been lucky in finding such a kind, hardworking soul. He'd been good to their daughter too, and even better to Vaughn. Those two had been like two peas in a pod. Riding together, working the horses, sleeping out under the stars just for the fun of it. She remembered when Jack and her had first discovered Vaughn out sleeping with the horses. She'd said she'd been doing it every night. Sleeping with a different horse each evening, so that they all had a turn at companionship. Jack had been so moved that he'd made her a little bed with a cot, and he'd tucked her in every night next to the horse of her choosing. And she'd slept in the stables for close to a year before she'd announced that the horses all felt better and no longer needed her. That's when Jack had offered to sleep out under the stars with her, whenever she wanted. And Vaughn had wanted to quite frequently.

June could still recall hearing her child-like laughter late at night as they slept on cots in the corral. June would sleep with her window open in late fall and early spring and listen to the two of them giggle and cut up. Until eventually silence would overcome them and they'd fall asleep and sleep peacefully until the rooster crowed. Then they'd get up and start in on their chores until breakfast, with Vaughn following Jack around like a loyal dog, eating up his every word and mimicking his every move.

Needless to say, Vaughn had been devastated at his loss. She stayed at his bedside as much as she could, knowing he'd want her to carry on with the ranch rather than worry about him. So she came and sat with him as he slept, which wasn't a lot at first, but as the cancer progressed, it seemed like all he did was sleep, with the morphine and what not.

She was there when he passed. They all were. It was early evening, around supper time and the home nurse had warned them that it would be soon. She and her daughter Vivian and Vaughn had sat vigil and held his hands until he took his last breath.

Vaughn had stood up and thrown an angry punch. She'd hit the wall and created a small indention. It hadn't fractured her hand or anything, but she'd been right lucky that way. It did slow her in finishing her chores, which upset her a great deal. But she kept on, not missing a second of work on the ranch. She was determined to make her grandpa proud, she was. And proud, well, June knew the man would be more than proud. It was just a shame that Jeanie had had to come into their lives and ruin everything. She'd damaged Vaughn in more ways than Vaughn would like to admit. Child still hasn't fully recovered.

June closed down the computer and stood for a long stretch. As she walked toward the hallway for her own shower, she thought about Natalie and how lucky they were to have her. Maybe Jeanie had come into their life for a reason. Maybe she'd come and broken Vaughn's heart, so that when Natalie came, Vaughn could see just how good she was. She hoped that was the case. Natalie would be good for Vaughn and vice versa. If only the two of them could see it.

"I reckon they will at some point," she said to herself as she entered her room to grab her nightgown and robe to head to the shower. "I just hope they do it before it's too late." She didn't know when too late would come along, but she knew it was quickly approaching.

## CHAPTER SEVENTEEN

Allen slid his AMG GT Mercedes coupe along the curb in front of the small apartment complex in North Phoenix. He sat for a moment, debating his next move. Ahead of him, and across the street, he spotted Tom's red pickup truck. He groaned, his displeasure with the young man growing day by day. Tom had yet to find Natalie and he'd even spoken to her roommate, supposedly, and gotten nowhere. He'd spoken to Nico about him, and he'd assured him he'd turn up the heat on the kid, but so far it didn't seem like anything had been done.

"Never send an idiot to do a job you should do yourself," Allen said as he killed his engine and climbed from the car. He hurriedly walked up to Tom's truck and knocked on the window. Tom lowered it, looking surprised. He flinched when Allen raised his hand to rest it on the door. Allen almost laughed. Good. It was good for him to be a little afraid.

"Do you have any news?" Allen asked, already knowing the answer. He knew Tom would've called him right away had he found anything.

"No, sir," he said. "Sorry, sir."

Allen tapped the door. "No worries, son. No worries."

"Sir?"

"You go on home now," he said. He smiled at him.

Tom looked horrified. "I don't understand."

Allen leaned in, causing Tom to rear back. "Let me put it this way, then. You're fired."

"But, sir—"

"No, no, no. You don't get to argue. You just get to take your sorry little ass and leave."

"But I—"

Allen grabbed him by the collar. "Didn't you hear me, you worthless piece of shit? I said leave!"

Tom blinked rapidly and started his engine. "Okay. I'm going. I'm going."

Allen released him and backed away. He watched as Tom put the truck in gear and sped away. He took a deep breath, straightened the jacket of his suit, and faced the apartments once again. He looked both ways up and down the street and crossed it quickly. Then he made his way through the complex to Natalie's second-story apartment. He took the steps two at a time as he climbed, and when he reached the porch, the overhead light came on and he put on his best smile before he opened the metal screen and knocked.

He heard voices inside, more than one, and he turned his head so that his ear was against the door, trying to make them out. Could Natalie be back home and the idiot Tom had somehow missed her? No. The voice was too deep to be Natalie's.

He knocked softly and waited. The voices came again, one in particular closing in on the door. Allen backed away and the door opened, wide and fully, revealing a tall but gangly young man.

"Yeah?" he said, looking at Allen with disinterest.

"Who the hell are you?" The question just flew out of him, his anger boiling dangerously close to the surface. Was this his replacement? Had Natalie indeed found a new man? Like hell. Not if he had anything to say about it.

"Me? Who the hell are you?"

Allen puffed out his chest. "Where's Natalie?"

"Who?"

"Natalie, you idiot! Where is she?" He tried to push past him to walk inside, but the man blocked him and grabbed his arm. He was surprisingly strong for his slim build. "I want to see her now!"

"Whoa, bro, no way. No way you're coming in here." He pushed Allen backward, almost knocking him off his feet. Allen came at him again, his anger now raging.

"What's going on?" a female voice said from inside the apartment. Allen froze as Natalie's portly roommate, Gayle, came to the door. "Who is this?"

"I don't know. Some crazy dude talking about a Natalie or something."

"She's my wife," Allen seethed, smoothing his clothes. "And I demand to see her. Now!"

"Oh, right," Gayle said. She looked at him with contempt. "She's not here."

"I want to see for myself," he said.

To his surprise, she moved aside. "Fine. Come on in."

Allen looked at her twice to be sure she meant it, then he walked inside, brushing past the gangly man with the large Adam's apple. The apartment smelled strongly of pot and he walked around quickly, finding Natalie's room right away. Once inside, he closed the door behind him and locked it. He rummaged through her things, searching her dresser, nightstand, and closet. He found nothing of significance. Not even a private little diary. "Fuck." He sat down.

He wondered again if perhaps she'd met someone else and they'd come to sweep her away. But Tom had assured him that that wasn't the case.

As if Natalie could find someone else. He laughed at the suggestion. She was too weak, too needy. She had nothing and was nothing. No, she needed him to be anything at all. And she knew it.

Natalie was his, she just needed to accept that. He didn't understand why she fought it. He gave her everything she ever wanted. Money, cars, houses. Himself. What was there to complain about? But complain she did. About nearly everything. Arguing with him about freedom and rights and boundaries. What the fuck? Of course there were rules she had to abide by, whether she liked them or not. That was the price to pay for being his and his alone. Any other woman would've killed to be in her shoes. But Natalie had been ungrateful. Which was a shame. They could've been good together. So very good. Why couldn't she just see that and come home?

"Um, hello?" Gayle knocked on the door and tried the knob. "You can't just stay in there."

Allen stood and crossed to the closet. He slid the hanging clothes across the rack. Not much was missing. Not much at all. He went back to the dresser and searched her underwear. Not much was gone from there either. Could it be that Natalie had really disappeared? As in, something bad had happened to her? It didn't seem as though she'd planned to leave. At least not for a long time. So, where was she? Had she really just decided to take off on a whim and now she was gone?

Tito had told him there was no movement on her credit card or bank account. So maybe she really had met with foul play. If she had, what would that mean for him? Could he handle her being gone, forever?

No. He couldn't. And it wasn't possible. She had to be somewhere. She couldn't just up and vanish.

He opened the bedroom door and shoved his way past Gayle and the man. He left the apartment without another word, not even bothering to question the potheads. He knew more than they did, most likely. So, what was the point? He hurried down the steps and slid back inside his car. With his phone in hand, he dialed Tito. When he answered he kept it short but sweet, saying all he needed to say.

"You find her, or I kill you."

## CHAPTER EIGHTEEN

I knew when you hired them on, that they were gonna be trouble," Kim Babcock said as she positioned herself to trim Holly's frog. Vaughn had called her about Holly's possible thrush, and Kim had come as soon as she'd had an available appointment time.

Vaughn turned over a nearby bucket in Holly's stall and sat, glad Kim was finally there to take a look. "I wish you woulda said something."

"What was there to say? Hey, that hand Pedro of yours keeps asking me out and he's rather persistent about it?"

"Sure, I would've put a stop to that."

"Well, it's over now. He's gone and I haven't heard from him any." She began trimming the frog and Vaughn watched as she worked, always amazed at Kim's calming effect on the horses. Vaughn had been keeping an eye on Holly since she'd first noticed the thrush and Holly hadn't exactly been too keen on her checking her frog a few times a day.

"Wish he would leave us alone," Vaughn said.

"Aw, he will. He's just ticked off at ya. He'll eventually move on."

"I was hoping this business with the police investigation would send him and Ricky in another direction completely, but I haven't heard anything, and the damn officer we reported to is Ricky's cousin."

Kim paused and looked over at her. "You kidding me?"

"No, ma'am, I am not."

"Wow."

"Uh-huh."

"I can see why you're so concerned." She refocused on Holly's foot. "But they haven't done anything since the fence, have they?"

"Other than hang on to my missing mare, Miracle, no."

"Wait, they have Miracle?"

"Best we can figure. Benny and Greer and I followed her tracks well into the desert and they just disappeared as if she'd been loaded up into a trailer."

"Oh my God."

"And like I said, we haven't heard anything from the police since we reported everything."

"Geez, Vaughn, I'm sorry. But if I were you, I'd be calling that police department up and asking some questions."

"Yeah, I'm going to call this afternoon after our midday interview with a potential employee. Gram and I have been interviewing like crazy. My head's spinning with all the applicants we've talked to."

"See anyone promising?" She moved on from the frog and began trimming the hoof itself of bacteria.

"A few. They'll be coming by this weekend to meet the horses."

"Any women in the bunch?"

"One."

"That's it?"

"Uh-huh."

She finished and carefully placed Holly's foot in a chlorine-based solution. Then she cleaned her hands and leaned on the stall to talk to Vaughn.

"So, who's the woman I saw as I was driving in? It wasn't Suzanne."

"Oh, that's Natalie. She's staying with us for a while in the guesthouse."

"She's cute. She single?"

"I don't think you're her type."

She grinned. "Vaughn, honey, I'm everyone's type."

Vaughn couldn't help but laugh. Kim was a looker, she'd give her that. With her shoulder-length flaming red hair and wicked light blue eyes, she definitely turned heads. Not to mention her wild ways. Vaughn had heard stories about her numerous seductions of men and women alike. She'd even tried to get Vaughn's interest at one point. But Vaughn had told her they were better off as friends and Kim had agreed and moved on.

"So, can I meet her?"

"Natalie?" Vaughn felt heat creep up her neck to her cheeks. She didn't like the idea and she was trying to figure out why when Natalie strolled up.

"Hi." She smiled from the entrance of the stall with her hands on the back of her hips.

"Well, hello," Kim said, walking up to her shake her hand. "Natalie, right?"

"Right." Natalie took her hand.

"I'm Kim." She gave her a thousand-watt smile.

"Oh, you must be the farrier," Natalie said.

"That's me."

Natalie looked past her to Holly. "How is she? Is she okay?" She stepped inside the stall and looked at her soaking foot. She carefully stroked her neck.

"She's got a bit of an infection, but it should clear right up." Kim watched her closely. "You like horses?"

"Oh, I love them. I just hope they like me in return."

"Well, what's not to love? I mean, you look pretty good to me."

Vaughn stood, having heard enough. She didn't want Kim hitting on Natalie. She told herself it was because Natalie was dealing with enough already with her ex-husband, but she knew deep down that it was more than that. She just chose not to search, at that moment, deep enough to find out exactly what it was.

"Natalie, will you go see if Gram's ready for that one o'clock interview?"

"Sure." She told Kim it was nice to meet her and she walked out of the stall. Kim watched her go and turned to Vaughn.

"Hey, what gives? She's really cute. Even more beautiful up close."

"Like I said, you're not her type."

"Well, how do you know that?"

"Because I do." Vaughn walked to the entrance of the stall, unwilling to discuss the matter further. "You can bill me for the visit like you usually do."

"Okay, Vaughn." She tilted her head as she stroked Holly down. "I didn't step on your toes, did I? With Natalie? Because if I did, I'm sorry I—"

"Don't worry about it," Vaughn said. "It's all good." She left the stall and headed for the house.

Vaughn walked into the house and saw Natalie standing at the kitchen sink with Gram, cleaning up after their eleven thirty lunch.

"She's not quite ready for the interview," Natalie explained. "So, I thought I'd help her finish up the cleaning."

"Why'd you tell her to come check on me?" Gram asked. "You know I'll be ready. All we have to do is log on to that contraption."

"Just wanted to be sure."

But Gram studied her and Vaughn could almost see the cogs of her mind turning. "It wouldn't have anything to do with that Babcock girl out in the stables, now would it?"

Natalie's face crinkled with question. "Kim? Why would it have anything to do with her?"

Gram smiled. "Yes, Vaughn do tell. Why would it have anything to do with Kim?"

Vaughn opened the fridge and grabbed a can of root beer. She cracked it open and slouched onto a kitchen chair and slurped. "It doesn't."

"No?" Gram said, pulling up the drain and turning to dry her hands on her apron.

"No."

Natalie, too, finished drying the last plate and she turned to dry her hands on the dish towel. She looked so innocent and confused.

"Kim seems nice," she said. "And Holly seems to trust her."

"She's a good farrier," Vaughn said.

"But she gets around," Gram added. Vaughn glared at her, but Gram continued. "What? She does. Everybody north of Phoenix knows it."

"She gets around?" Natalie asked.

"Yes, child. That woman is known not only for her farrier abilities, but for her abilities of seduction as well. Hell, she even tried to bed Vaughn not too long ago."

Natalie appeared shocked. "She did? You mean she's…"

"Oh, she goes both ways," Gram said.

"And you didn't, did you?" Natalie asked, pointing the question to Vaughn. "You didn't sleep with her?"

Vaughn wondered why she was asking. Wondered why she looked so troubled at the thought. "No, I didn't."

"She's not Vaughn's type," Gram said. "She's too wild."

Vaughn sipped her root beer and hoped that would be the end of it. But Gram kept on. "Not that Vaughn hasn't had a wild one or two from town from time to time. But they never last long."

"Gram," Vaughn said.

"What? You have had a wild one or two, haven't you?"

"My personal life is not up for discussion."

"Well, the girl is curious. Aren't you, Natalie? And rightfully so."

Natalie blinked rapidly. "I'm not trying to pry. And you don't have to tell me anymore. Really."

It was clear that Natalie was uncomfortable. And it was also clear that Gram wasn't going to stop. So Vaughn stood and left the room, carrying her root beer into the living room to sit at the desk. She could check on the website and email as she waited for Gram to get her shit together and back off. She didn't know why she was so hell-bent on setting her and Natalie up. Neither one of them had shown any outward interest. Vaughn knew because she hadn't, and because Gram would've told her if Natalie had.

Vaughn logged onto the computer and checked the email. There was nothing new. She sighed as she heard Gram continuing to talk about Kim and some of her local conquests. Natalie didn't seem that interested, staying mostly silent, but Gram kept on. Vaughn slid her phone out from her jeans and made the phone call to Theo. She figured she might as well get it over with and her curiosity was getting the better of her. He answered on the fourth ring, surprising her. She hadn't expected him to pick up.

"Theo, it's Vaughn Ruger."

"Vaughn, hello."

"I'm calling to see if you've made any progress on my case."

"I've got a few leads I'm following up on."

"A few? As in different people?"

"I'd rather not get into it just yet, Vaughn. I still have some investigating to do."

"Well, when should I call again?"

"I'll call you when I have something more."

"My mare, she's still missing. I'm concerned about her well-being."

"I'm sure you are," he said. "And I promise you I'm doing all I can to find her."

Vaughn rubbed her brow, wishing she could believe him and let it go. But she couldn't. She just felt like he wasn't going to do all that he could because of his relationship to the number one suspect.

"I'll check back with you in a couple of days," Vaughn said.

"Now, Vaughn—"

She ended the call. She would be damned if she was going to listen to him. She wasn't going to sit back and wait any longer. No. She was not only going to call when she saw fit, but she was going to do a little investigating of her own. She continued to rub her brow as Natalie entered the room.

"What did he say?" she asked, obviously having overheard some of the conversation.

"Not much. He said he's got some leads but that he's still investigating. So he won't share them with me."

Natalie rested her hip on the desk. "How frustrating."

"It is."

"Do you have a headache?"

Vaughn questioned her with a look but then lowered her hand. "A bit."

Natalie left her and returned a few seconds later with a bottle of Advil. She opened it and poured two tablets into Vaughn's palm. Vaughn thanked her and downed them with her root beer. She hadn't even had to complain about her pain or ask for some painkillers. Natalie just knew and she handled it right away, being so kind and attentive.

"You're worried about your mare," Natalie said softly.

"Yes. She—we would've found her by now if she was out in the desert. Or she would've come back."

"I'm so sorry. Is there anything I can do?"

Vaughn looked at her and fought getting lost in her caring gaze. Oh, how a part of her just wanted to get lost in her. To swim languidly in her kind and caring soul. But she couldn't. Not now and maybe not ever. The thought made her throat tighten and raw tears threatened. *Why am I reacting so strongly to her?*

Gram had been right. Vaughn had had a few women in her lifetime, so she wasn't exactly a novice when it came to attraction. But why Natalie? This stranger from Phoenix who had a crazy ex-husband and a mysterious life to boot? She didn't want to think about it. She didn't have *time* to think about it.

"No. But there's something *I* can do." She stood and headed into the kitchen. She found Gram putting away the dried dishes. "You're going to have to do this next interview on your own or with Natalie."

"Why's that?" she asked, pausing as she lifted a dish to put away in the cupboard.

"I got something I gotta do." Vaughn plucked her car keys off the key rack by the door and walked outside into the bright sun, leaving Gram alone with her questions.

## CHAPTER NINETEEN

"Where is she going?" Natalie asked June as she walked back into the kitchen. They both watched through the kitchen window as Vaughn hurriedly climbed in her truck to speed away down the drive.

"Lord, if I know."

"I think she might be going to go look for the missing mare. She hinted as much back in the living room. Said there was something she could do about it."

"I hope like hell she's not going after those two birdbrains. That will only bring trouble."

"She wouldn't, would she?" Natalie's stomach tightened as she imagined Vaughn confronting the men on her own. Would they hurt her?

"With that child, who knows. When she gets a bee in her bonnet, she does whatever the hell she sees fit. And right now, those boys...well, they're on her radar and that's not a good thing."

"Would they...you know, hurt her?"

June met her gaze. "I don't rightly know, Natalie. I should hope not, not if they know what's good for them. Maybe I'd better go after her." She removed her apron and tossed a dish towel on the counter. Then she crossed to the keyring and removed her set of keys. Natalie followed. "What about the interview?"

"We'll have to reschedule." June looked back at her as she opened the door. "What are you doing?"

"I'm coming with."

June opened her mouth as if she was going to argue, but seemed to change her mind. With a single nod, she headed out to their other, older truck, and unlocked the doors. Natalie followed, climbing into the passenger side. The first thing June did when she got in behind the wheel was to reach back and grab the shotgun from the gun rack. She popped it open, checked to make sure it was loaded, and returned it to the rack.

"Do you think we'll need that?" Natalie asked, her tightening stomach now feeling downright sick, making her feel like she was going to throw up.

"I hope not. But you never can be too careful." She started the old grumbling engine and they took off after Vaughn, following her trail of dust. Ahead, to the south, dark clouds were beginning to build, and Natalie hoped it wasn't an ominous sign of things to come.

"Do you know where she may be headed?" She saw Vaughn's truck leave the drive to the ranch and turn onto the private dirt road. But there was no telling if they'd be able to keep up with her. Especially once she noticed she was being followed. Natalie got the sense that Vaughn wanted to do this on her own.

"I don't. But I've got this." She tossed a cell phone onto Natalie's lap. "Vaughn bought it for me last week. Said there's something on it where we can always find our phones if needed. I can see hers and vice versa. Maybe you can figure it out."

Natalie woke the phone and found the appropriate app. Sure enough, she could see Vaughn's movement. "Got it," she said.

June slowed a little. "Good. We'll just fall a ways back then." They rode in silence and lost sight of Vaughn quickly. Natalie watched the phone and told June which way to turn when needed, and soon they were back in town, back in north Phoenix and driving through an industrial area.

Natalie pointed as June made a turn off Deer Valley Road and slowed. "She's come to a stop over there, behind that building." There weren't many cars around, very few in the parking spaces. The area seemed to be quiet, desolate, the buildings warehouse-style structures and vacant office spaces.

June slowly drove the truck to the side of the long, one-story building. She crept along the edge, easing the truck forward until they could peek down the other side of the building. They spotted Vaughn's truck parked along the side and Vaughn was walking up to a closed garage door. They watched her try to lift it again and again with no luck.

"I wonder why she wants in there," Natalie said.

"I don't know, but it must be important." June turned the wheel and drove the truck toward Vaughn. Natalie said nothing, not even when Vaughn spotted them and walked up to the window.

"You followed me?" she said.

"Looks like you could use some help," June answered.

"How are you going to help me?"

"I gotta jack in the back. That's how."

Vaughn raised a brow. She walked to the rear of the truck and lifted out the heavy looking jack. She carried it to the closed garage door as Natalie and June climbed from the truck to join her.

"What is this place?" Natalie asked, glancing around.

"Pedro, one of the idiots, mentioned this garage one day when we were talking about auto repairs. He said his father had a garage he was letting him lease for free to work on his truck. And I happened to remember where it was today."

She managed to lift the door up a couple of inches, enough for June to slide the jack under. Vaughn cranked the jack and the door began to lift. She got it up about a foot and a half and went down on all fours to look beneath it.

She came back up in a flash. "She's in there," she said. "Goddamnit."

June looked to Natalie. "Call the police."

Natalie did as instructed and June took the phone from her to speak to the operator. Vaughn got down on her back to slide under the door. "It's warm in here. She's probably in bad shape."

"Oh, no," Natalie said, getting down on her back with her.

"No, you stay out here," Vaughn said to her as she slid inside. "This could be dangerous. Besides, I need someone to flag down the police with June."

"But you might get hurt," Natalie said as Vaughn made it all the way inside and pushed to a stand.

"I might. But no sense in you getting hurt too." She looked down at her. "Please. Go."

Natalie maneuvered back out and stood. June was on the phone but lowered it as a truck came barreling toward them, loud engine revving. June quickly handed the phone to Natalie and climbed inside her truck to retrieve her shotgun. She stood next to her vehicle with it aimed at the oncoming truck. Natalie reported what was going on to the operator, terrified that this was not going to end well. The operator told her to take cover and to stay on the phone. Natalie kept her on the line, but she didn't take cover. She didn't have time.

When the truck pulled up next to them, it slowed, and the two men inside gave them a hard look, saw June with the gun and the partially opened garage, and then sped off.

June lowered the gun and sighed.

"Was that them?" Natalie asked as she put the operator on hold.

June nodded. "They know they's in trouble now."

Natalie gave an update to the operator and heard oncoming sirens. Vaughn opened the garage door from the inside as two cop cars pulled into the complex and sped toward them.

"She's in bad shape," Vaughn said, waving June inside.

Natalie ended the call with the operator and pointed into the garage as the cops exited their vehicles, guns drawn. "The men are gone," she said. "But the horse is in there, along with the owners."

The cops nodded and quickly went inside to assess the situation. Natalie heard them all talking. She stayed outside, trying to be respectful. June's voice raised and she came out cursing.

"Go and get them!" she yelled back into the garage.

She wiped a tear as she leaned on the hood of the truck. Natalie walked up to her and laid a gentle hand on her shoulder.

June gripped it. "They're gonna pay," she said, wiping another tear. "They're gonna pay. One way or another."

Vaughn emerged, leading the horse out of the garage. The mare was moving slowly and had obviously gone without food. She squinted in the sunlight as Vaughn rubbed her and cooed to her. Natalie's own eyes filled with tears.

"Will she be okay?" she asked.

"I hope so," Vaughn said. "For their sake, I hope so."

The cops walked into the light as well, and one of them began taking photos of the horse. June and Vaughn gave them all the information they had on the two men. And Natalie helped where she could, describing the truck they were driving along with some of the license plate number. She'd also given it to the 911 operator. She hoped that it was enough to catch the guys. She could still see their beady eyes as they'd slowly driven by. The two men had looked young but grimy, their clothes greasy. They'd also had a full gun rack in their back window and Natalie knew they were all lucky that they hadn't stopped to confront them.

She returned the phone to June with a shaky hand.

"You okay, child?"

Natalie gave a nervous laugh, but wiped away tears as they began to fall. "I guess I don't do well with the threat of violence." She wasn't sure why she was so shook up, only that her adrenaline had shot nearly sky high, like it had with Allen anytime he got confrontational.

June pulled her into her arms. "There, there. It's all over now."

Natalie clung to her for a moment, but she spied Vaughn, standing there all alone with her horse, tears flooding her eyes. Natalie drew away from June and walked up to her. And without a word, she embraced her and held her tight.

Vaughn was stiff at first. Ramrod straight. But Natalie felt her body melt and soon Vaughn was gripping her in return, her body silently shaking as she quietly sobbed.

"I'm so sorry," Natalie whispered.

Vaughn didn't say anything in return. She just pulled away and wiped her cheeks with the back of her hand. She nodded, letting Natalie know that she heard her.

Natalie stood with her and loved on the horse by her side, with not another word spoken.

## CHAPTER TWENTY

Natalie heated a cup of water and opened a tea bag to bob inside the mug. She opened her front door and stepped outside. The night air was cool and crisp, and she inhaled the fresh scent of the desert and the wildflowers that were coming back into bloom in the garden. She also smelled rain and looked up at the dark sky. Lightning ricocheted from cloud to cloud in the near distance and thunder growled, letting her know it was on its way.

The storm had been building all evening and it seemed as though it was finally time for it to show its strength. She eased down on the front step and sipped her tea, keen on watching the storm move in. There was something elemental about storms that she loved. They made her feel alive and at one with Mother Earth. They were beautiful.

She blew on her drink before she took another sip. As she did so, she heard the crunch of footfalls coming from around the side of the house. She lowered her mug and waited, and to her surprise, Vaughn appeared.

"Didn't think I'd see you till morning," Natalie said with a smile. She noticed that Vaughn still had on the same clothes she had on earlier, having spent all her time with the recovering mare once they'd arrived home.

Vaughn motioned to sit next to her.

"Please," Natalie said, and Vaughn slowly sat with a groan.

"How's your back?" Natalie asked. It seemed that every evening poor Vaughn was walking nearly hunched over with her hand on her lower back. How she got up and worked the ranch every day with pain like that, Natalie didn't know.

"Oh, it's cranking at me."

"It must be awful," Natalie said. "Having to work so physically hard with a bad back."

"It's an adventure," Vaughn said. "I'll say that much."

"Would you like a cup of tea?" She looked as though she could use a good cup. That and a massage. But Natalie wasn't about to offer that. Just the thought of rubbing Vaughn's muscular back caused her heart to flip-flop in her chest. She fanned her face, suddenly feeling hot. She stopped when she saw that Vaughn was watching her curiously.

"You know, I think I would like a cup. It smells delicious."

Natalie handed Vaughn her mug and pushed herself to a stand. "I'll be right back. Don't go anywhere."

"I'll be right here."

Natalie hurried inside and made Vaughn a cup of tea. It felt good to be doing something nice for her, even if it was something as simple as a hot drink on a stormy fall evening. She made her way back outside and traded mugs with Vaughn, who took the cup carefully, wrapping her hands around it like a hug. They sat and sipped quietly before Vaughn spoke.

"What kind of tea is this? It's really good. Kind of spicy."

"It's a sweet and spicy blend with cinnamon and orange, along with notes of other flavors. I love having it when the weather starts to cool."

"I can see why."

Natalie smiled over at her. "Well, there's more where that came from." She immediately regretted voicing that out loud. She almost smacked her forehead in disbelief. *There's more where that came from? Can I sound anymore cheesy?*

"I mean, well, you know. Anytime."

Vaughn returned the smile. "Thanks."

Natalie searched her mind for something to say. Something that wouldn't make her seem like a total idiot. "How's Miracle? She doing okay?" It wasn't exactly a lighthearted topic, but it was better than telling her there's more where that came from.

"She's doing as well as can be expected."

"And the vet? What did he say?"

"He thinks she'll make a full recovery."

"That's wonderful, Vaughn."

Vaughn stared into her steaming tea. "Yeah, but I just can't get over it. The way I found her, what she'd gone through." She shook her head. "If I ever get my hands on those two I'll ring their necks. I swear I will."

"Not if June gets to them first. She seemed pretty pissed as well."

"She is. And you're right, she's more of a threat than I am. You do not want to piss off June Ruger, that's for sure. She handles things the old-fashioned way. Back when ranchers took the law into their own hands. Back when your guns spoke for you."

"Then they better stay away. If they know what's good for them," Natalie said, looking off into the flashing lightning. Thunder rumbled again, this time louder, closer.

"I don't think they're that smart," Vaughn said, sipping her drink. "They haven't proven to be so far."

"I can't believe you found the horse before the police. Why didn't he know about that place? Isn't the guy his cousin?"

"No. This was Pedro's place. And he wasn't legally leasing the building, so it would've been difficult to learn about unless the police heard it firsthand."

"Still. A little detective work would've gone a long way."

"Very true."

"Did they end up finding the guys? Have you heard?"

"Last I heard they couldn't locate them. And that was..." She checked her watch. "Two hours ago."

"Geez maybe you'll have to do that for them too. I bet you know where they like to hang out."

"I do. And I've shared my knowledge, trust me. What they'll do with that knowledge, I can't say."

"Well, hopefully they'll give the case to someone other than the cousin."

"One can hope."

"Is that even ethical? To investigate a relative?"

"I don't know. But it didn't seem to scare him away from the case."

"I would complain, Vaughn. That just doesn't sound right."

"I did."

"Good."

"But now I fear I've got another man upset with me. A man who has influence in these parts. I might end up regretting complaining."

"Let's hope not."

Thunder boomed loudly and Natalie startled. "Maybe we'd better go inside." She stood and lightning flashed directly overhead and another crack of thunder came, along with a downpour of cold rain. She and Vaughn hurried into the bungalow, closing the door behind them.

"Is it me or did that come really quickly?" Vaughn asked. "Or was I just too preoccupied today to notice all the buildup?"

"You had a lot on your plate."

"I did, didn't I?"

Natalie set her mug on the kitchen counter. "You most definitely did." She welcomed Vaughn farther inside. "I'll go get us some towels." She breezed into the bathroom and returned with two towels. She handed one to Vaughn and busied drying herself with the other. Then she grabbed her cup of tea and led the way into the cozy living room. "Please, have a seat."

Natalie sat in the leather armchair as Vaughn stood awkwardly next to the couch, holding her mug as well as her towel and her hat. "I don't know. I should probably get back to Miracle. I don't want her to be alone tonight. Not after all she's been through."

Natalie stood, placing her mug on the small side table. She felt panicked and spoke quickly. "No, don't go. Not yet."

Vaughn looked confused. Natalie explained.

"You always…leave. We never really get a chance to talk."

"I have things to do. A ranch to run."

"I know," Natalie said as she walked to her. "But it seems like it's more than that. It seems like you avoid me."

Vaughn stared at her in silence, her hands going slack by her side. She noticed that she was spilling her tea onto the dark tile and she hurriedly righted the mug and apologized. "I'm sorry. Here, I'll clean it up." She knelt to dry up the spill with her towel, pushing her hat aside on the tile, but Natalie knelt too, stopping her.

"It's okay," she said.

"No, it's not. I should've been paying more attention." She wiped at the spill as if she'd spilled nuclear waste. Natalie, this time, stopped her by gripping her hand securely in her own.

"Vaughn. It's okay. Really. It's just tea."

Vaughn stopped and looked into her eyes. Natalie felt her breath catch as she searched the windows of her soul. What she saw there both awed and fascinated her. Love, loss, desire, all of it brimming and swirling together in a hurricane of fear and confusion. She reached out, wanting to quell that inner storm. She grazed her cheek with her fingertips. Whispered to her.

"Vaughn. It's okay." She drew closer. Touched her lips, shared her breath. She closed her eyes, pressed into her, against her, their lips caressing. Lightly, deftly, like the touch of a feather, both of them so tentative, like they were afraid to even breathe.

Natalie grew dizzy, both from the feel of Vaughn's warm lips, and from the lack of oxygen from holding her breath. She trembled as she reached up and held Vaughn's face. Trembled again as she felt Vaughn shake and inhale a quick, shaky breath.

"Natalie," she whispered and the kiss deepened, Vaughn parting her lips to tug on Natalie's. Natalie responded by doing the same, tasting Vaughn fervently, feverishly, clinging to her shirt with her hands. They stood, fused together, feeding, dying of thirst for one another. Vaughn pulled her closer, tightly against her and moaned into her. "Natalie," she said again.

"Oh, Vaughn," Natalie breathed as Vaughn attached herself to the sensitive skin of her neck. Natalie leaned back in offering, giving herself completely, melting beneath her hot and hungry mouth. Vaughn grabbed her hips and lifted her with ease and led them onto the couch, where she lay Natalie down and crawled atop her.

"Vaughn," Natalie said. "Oh, Vaughn I've dreamt of this."

Vaughn nibbled her neck, came back up to her ear and whispered, "For how long?"

"For a while now," she said, running her hands along the strong planes of her back. "I've thought of you for a while now."

Vaughn positioned her firm thigh between Natalie's legs. "Yeah?"

"Oh, yes."

"I've been fighting it," she said. "For a while now."

Natalie sighed, clawing at her back as the pressure from her thigh rubbed against her throbbing center. "Oh, Vaughn. Don't fight it. Don't fight me."

Vaughn paused and hovered above her. She stared deep into her eyes. She looked as though she was willing to confess her soul to Natalie, to confess all her deepest feelings, but a short knock came from the door and a split second later it opened and June walked in beneath an umbrella, staring at a sheet of paper as she moved.

"Natalie, I've been looking over this interview schedule and I'm not sure if Vaughn will have the time tomorrow—" She froze as she finally looked up and spotted them on the couch. Vaughn jumped up and tried to straighten her clothes. Natalie sat up and absently touched her lips.

"I'm sorry," June said, truly surprised. She turned away from them as if to give them some privacy. "I'll come back later."

But Vaughn beat her to the door, scooping up her hat along the way. "No, you stay," she said, placing her hat on her head to pull open the door. "I need to get back to the horse."

June seemed as frazzled as Natalie felt.

"But—"

"It's fine," Vaughn said. "You and Natalie talk business." She looked to Natalie and gave a little wave. An awkward wave. One that said, I have no idea what to do. "I'll see you later."

Natalie said the only thing she could say. "Okay." And Vaughn was out the door as thunder clapped again loudly overhead, followed by a bright flash of lightning, illuminating the empty doorframe.

## CHAPTER TWENTY-ONE

June watched as Vaughn disappeared into the dark, rainy night. She blinked, as if she had rain in her eyes, and lowered her umbrella, unsure she'd seen what she thought she'd seen. Slowly, she turned and faced Natalie, who was sitting looking as shell-shocked as June felt. She knew then, that what she'd seen was real.

"I'm so sorry," she said as Natalie caressed her own lips, as if they still stung.

Natalie swallowed and shook her head. "It's okay."

"No it's not. I shouldn't have barged in like that."

"June. It's fine."

June leaned her umbrella against the wall next to the door and walked in to set the piece of paper on the coffee table. "I just wanted to go over this darn schedule and I guess I got carried away. I just really had no notion that Vaughn would be here." She rubbed her forehead. "Lord, I've been so stupid. Here I've been trying to get the two of you together and you two were already well on your way."

Natalie rubbed her hands on her denim-clad thighs. "No, June, not exactly." She laughed a little, her nerves showing. "That was—impromptu."

"You mean that was the first time you two…"

Natalie chewed her lip and nodded.

"Oh, lord. I really am sorry. I ruined it, didn't I?"

"Don't be so hard on yourself," Natalie said.

June eased down next to her on the couch. "I'm afraid you don't understand. Vaughn…she'll be scared away now. She… well, for one she's embarrassed. She's a very private person. And for another, it's very difficult for her to confess her feelings. Or to show them for that matter. Since Jeanie that is. So, I'm worried she won't…come back to you."

"Ever?" Natalie said, incredulous.

"I don't know, child. I don't know. She hasn't, to my knowledge, been with anyone since Jeanie. So, your guess is as good as mine."

Natalie stood and began to pace. June tried to comfort her. "But you seem to be different. She obviously has feelings for you. So maybe she'll come around."

"I'm not so sure. She…" She stared off in thought. "She seemed so confused, so, I don't know, tentative and trepidatious. And yet… so passionate." She touched her mouth again, as if remembering.

June blushed and got up and excused herself. "Well, I've intruded enough for one night. I reckon I ought to go find Vaughn and apologize again." She grabbed her umbrella and opened the door. Natalie stood still, watching her in a dreamlike state.

"I'll see you tomorrow." She nodded toward the schedule. "I revised that. Have a look see when you see fit."

Natalie absently nodded.

June bid her a good night and stepped out of the house and back into the cool rain. She propped open her umbrella and hurried toward the stables. Puddles were already pooling in the desert landscaping around the bungalow and even more were pooling in the hard, clay dirt on the way to the stables. Thunder growled again and lightning flashed, though both seemed more distant now. June slowed as she cowered beneath the shelter of the stables and closed her umbrella. She set it aside and walked down the row of horses to the next to the last stall where Miracle was kept. She found Vaughn in there, resting on a blanket next to the horse. She was stroking her, talking softly.

June felt bad for interrupting, but she needed to say her piece.

"You don't have anything to apologize for, Gram," Vaughn said, keeping her eyes on the horse, who lay next to her.

"Oh, but I do, child. I interrupted a very private, intimate moment. One of possible great significance and I'm so very sorry."

"Like I said, it's no big deal."

"It is, Vaughn. And it pains me to hear you say it isn't."

Vaughn continued to pet Miracle, soothing her with her soft coos. "I'm sure Natalie understands."

"She does. But do you?"

"Of course."

"It won't scare you away from her, will it?"

Vaughn didn't answer. She just kept rubbing on Miracle.

"Vaughn?"

"Turn off the lights on your way out, will you?"

June stared at her. Vaughn didn't say anything more and June's heart sank. Vaughn was gone, the moment with Natalie, however significant and passionate, gone, carried away with the retreating storm. She'd feared as much. And she'd been right. Vaughn was just too fearful, too damaged to really admit to her feelings and allow herself to feel and experience them. And what was worse, was that June had no idea how to help her.

"She's finally calmed," Vaughn said, referring to the horse. "Since she first arrived home. Guess it just takes time."

June closed her eyes, thinking of more than the horse. "I guess it does." She left her and walked down the long row of horses to the entrance to the stables. Once there, she switched off the lights and retrieved her umbrella. But instead of opening it, she stepped outside into the falling rain and allowed the drops to penetrate her skin. She looked up into the sky and thought of Vaughn. Her strong-headed, strong-willed, strong-hearted granddaughter. Maybe she was just like a traumatized horse. Maybe it was going to just take a lot of time, love, and patience before she was her old self again.

But as June walked back toward the house, she wondered just how much time it would take and if Natalie would stick around long enough to find out?

## CHAPTER TWENTY-TWO

Tito pounded on the door and waited for Allen to pull it open, acting like he'd been interrupted. He was breathing hard and he laughed a little, as if unnerved at the unannounced visit. Tito's continued silence only seemed to make him all the more nervous.

"What brings you by?" he finally asked.

Tito balled his fists. "You called."

The last time he'd called Tito he'd threatened him, and Tito responded by hanging up. Now it seemed to dawn on him that maybe that hadn't been such a good idea. Especially considering that Tito knew Allen was home alone and that Tito was easily strong enough to snap his neck if he saw fit.

Allen laughed again and offered him entry, obviously trying to play it cool. "Come on in. Have a drink. You look like you could use one." Allen went to the wet bar and began pouring the expensive tequila. Tito stood quietly just inside the living room. Allen brought him his tequila and motioned for him to sit.

But Tito remained standing, tumbler of tequila in his hand.

Allen sipped on his drink and nervously eased down into an armchair. He crossed his legs, probably hoping to come across as relaxed. He was still in his business attire, no doubt because he hadn't been home long enough yet to change into his more casual wear. Tito had interrupted his usual routine and that gave him some satisfaction.

"How can I help you, Tito?" Again, he sipped his drink. In the background, a Debussy song played over the speakers. And just outside the dark window, the pool light once again glowed as it changed colors.

"I got your message," Tito said. "Loud and clear."

"Oh, that?" Allen waved him off. "I was frustrated."

"You were serious."

"I was upset. But rest assured, all is well. Have you found anything new?" He offered a smile. One that probably worked well on his clients. But it didn't faze Tito, who remained standing in silence.

"Her car," Tito finally said. "It's been impounded."

"Impounded?" Allen placed both feet on the floor and leaned forward.

"It was found burned out. In the desert. She wasn't with it."

Red heat rushed to Allen's face. "She burned her car? Where?" he asked.

"North. Just off I-17."

"Anything else?"

"No."

Allen stood and downed the rest of his drink. "I take it the police couldn't find her?" No, they couldn't have. His contact there would've notified him.

"No one knows where she is."

"Well, I'm sure you'll remedy that situation, won't you, big guy?"

Tito held out his drink. He didn't want it. Allen walked to him and took it.

"My name is Tito."

Allen backed away. "Right. Of course it is."

Tito turned and headed toward the door. Allen followed him, hurriedly speaking. "Let me know when you get something."

Tito stopped as he pulled open the door. "You will hear from me when I'm ready."

Allen laughed again with nerves. "Sure. Okay. Have a nice evening."

Tito gave him a look over his shoulder as he angled past the two women waiting at the door. "Yeah," was all he said.

## CHAPTER TWENTY-THREE

*Vaughn ran down the stable to Miracle's stall but found it empty. Heart racing, she turned and bolted back to the stable entrance, running out into the overcast sky, searching the corral and the pasture for her mare. There, as thunder boomed overhead and lightning charged the air around her, she saw Miracle galloping toward her with a rider on her back. Vaughn hurried closer, trying to make out who the rider was, and as Miracle drew closer, she saw that the rider was Natalie, her short black hair whipping around her face in the wind. Her sparkling green eyes glinted against the flashes of lightning. She was seemingly transfixed on Vaughn as Miracle approached, galloping gracefully, with Natalie riding atop her in a dance-like state.*

*She looked so beautiful riding Miracle in the approaching storm, so electric, as if the lightning itself was coursing through her lively veins. She left Vaughn breathless, and as Miracle slowed and came to a stop before her, Vaughn whispered her name, whispered it into the blowing storm.*

*"Natalie."*

*She slid off Miracle and into her arms, staring deep into her eyes, whispering in return, "Vaughn." Breathless, she pressed her lips to Vaughn's, capturing them with hers, tugging and tasting. Vaughn warmed from head to toe, unable to get enough of her. She lifted her into her arms painlessly, effortlessly, and carried her away from Miracle, who trotted knowingly toward the stables as thunder once again rumbled overhead.*

*"I've dreamt of this," Natalie said, breaking their heated kiss. "I've dreamt of you, Vaughn Ruger."*

*Vaughn closed her eyes as rain drops began to fall, their cool taps a rhythm that felt foreign and yet familiar. They played her skin expertly and she fell away, falling, falling, falling.*

When Vaughn opened her eyes again, she had to blink to focus. It took her a moment to realize where she was, and when she did, her heart clenched, making her chest ache with disappointment. She sat up in bed and glanced at the clock. It was nearing five a.m. Her alarm was about to sound, so she switched it off.

She pulled back the covers and went into the bathroom to turn on the shower. As she bathed, she tried to wash the remnants of the dream away. It had moved her deeply, soulfully. She'd wanted it so badly to be real. She still couldn't believe it wasn't.

"It almost was," she said as she stood under the hot spray of the shower. Her mind went back to the night before, when she'd tasted Natalie for real, stared into her green eyes, and felt her body pressed against her own. She recalled lying down atop her, taking her in her arms and feeling the heat of her center against her thigh.

"Jesus," she whispered as she traced her hand down her taut abdomen to her own center. She glided over the pressure she felt there, and her knees nearly buckled with instant release as the sudden climax rocked her. She leaned against the shower wall and breathed deeply, trying to recover. The stitches of pain in her back caused her to wince, but she didn't care. The release had felt incredible and she felt like she could breathe better and see clearer. The fog of her mind had also vaporized.

She turned off the water and dried, thinking of Natalie, wondering how she felt about the night before. Was she still thinking of her? Was she still aching for her touch? Was she dreaming of her?

Vaughn climbed from the shower, wrapped her towel around herself, and walked into the bedroom to dress. After she pulled on a pair of worn jeans and slid into a thin flannel shirt, she stared at herself in the dresser mirror, combing back her long mane. She noted the dark crescents beneath her eyes, the sharpness to her cheekbones. She was tired and losing weight, the pain in her back almost too much to bear at the end of the day. She'd probably hurt it more lifting Natalie in her arms, but it had been a moment of passion, one she didn't regret. Not even knowing that it probably shouldn't happen again.

She pushed away from the dresser and switched off the light before making her way to the living room to slip into her boots at the couch. Once she did, she started the coffee maker for Gram, grabbed her own bottle of cold water, and stepped outside. It was still dark out and the air was heavy with moisture from another recent downpour. She walked to the stables, intent on seeing Miracle. She'd stayed most of the night with her, trying to sleep by her side. But sleep had been elusive and she hadn't wanted to keep Miracle from resting, so she'd gone into the house to bed.

She walked past the guesthouse and snuck a look. The house was still dark, and she breathed a sigh of relief. She didn't know what she was going to say to Natalie, or how she was going to behave. How could she tell her that what had happened was a mistake? That she wasn't ready for anything, especially a relationship? And that Natalie had enough to deal with with her ex-husband? They were both in no position to forge ahead together. Right? *Or am I just looking for excuses?*

Either way, the timing was wrong, she could feel it.

*But I also feel fear.*

She shook the realization away and carried on, entering the stables and hurrying down to Miracle's stall. She found the horse standing and she breathed a sigh of relief seeing that she was indeed okay.

"Hey, you," she said, stroking her nose. "Did you rest well?" She walked to the nearby shelves where she retrieved a small bucket of soaked alfalfa cubes. She dug some out and brought them to her to eat. "Hungry, aren't you?" She rested her forehead against Miracle's neck as she chewed. "I was so worried about you, girl. You have no idea. But I'm so glad you're home safe." She stroked her and inhaled her earthy scent. Outside, more rain began to fall, ticking off the roof of the stable.

"Looks like another rainy day. You gonna be okay with that?" Miracle snorted and Vaughn chuckled. "I thought as much. We'll keep you right here, all snug like a bug in a rug. How's that sound?"

"Sounds pretty good to me," a voice said from behind.

Startled, Vaughn turned to see Natalie. She was standing near the stall with her hands in her jeans pockets, a thick green hoodie covering her upper body, setting off her mesmerizing gaze.

"Morning," she said, giving a small smile.

"Morning," Vaughn said, a lump already forming in her throat. "You're up early."

"Mm, a little. I saw you come in here so I thought I'd come out to say hello."

"Oh. Hello."

"Hi." She rocked back on her heels. "How are you?"

"I'm okay." Vaughn refocused on Miracle.

"How is she?"

"She seems to be alright."

"That's good."

"Yeah."

"She's lucky. Guess the name suits her."

Vaughn rubbed Miracle's snout. "Guess so."

"So, you got a minute?"

"What for?"

"I was hoping we could talk about last night while we still had some privacy."

Vaughn's stomach tightened. "What about it?"

"I don't know. I guess I'd like to know how you're feeling. What you're thinking."

"I'm not really feeling much of anything." She swallowed against a painful lump and nearly closed her eyes, knowing she was delivering an awful blow. But it had to be done. For both their sakes.

"Oh."

"And as for what I'm thinking, I'm thinking it was a mistake. A one-time error in judgment. On both our parts." *I can't be hurt again, Natalie.*

Knowing that Jeanie had been seeing another woman nearly the whole time they'd been together had damn near killed her. How could she have been so stupid? Not seen the signs? Well, there were signs with Natalie. Maybe not signs that she would cheat, but there were red flags, things that could and probably would cause trouble. Her ex-husband for starters. And what if, pray tell, she did up and decide to go back to him? Women in domestic violence patterns often did return to their abusers. And that, if she did it, would shatter Vaughn's heart so badly she'd probably never recover.

"I see," Natalie said.

Vaughn looked at her and nearly gasped at the pain she saw in her. She was tearing her heart out and she knew it, yet she kept on, trying to protect her own heart, and delivered the final blow. "We got carried away, swept up in a moment. That's all. I mean, neither of us is in any position for it to be anything more, right?"

Natalie blinked at her. She withdrew her hands from her pockets and crossed them over her chest, as if they were cold and she had to warm them beneath her arms. "Right," she said softly.

"It just wouldn't be a good idea."

"No, you're right. It wouldn't." But her body language told another story. One of differing feelings and thoughts, but Vaughn didn't question her. She didn't want to know. Couldn't handle hearing. She looked back to Miracle and continued to love on her. Natalie seemed to get the message. She kicked some at the ground with her hiking boot and spoke.

"I better go get those eggs before Diablo gets cranky."

Vaughn nodded. "Yeah. Good idea."

"I'll see you around?"

"Sure."

Natalie turned and walked away, and Vaughn once again nuzzled Miracle, burying her face in her neck, unable to watch as Natalie disappeared into the awakening dawn.

## CHAPTER TWENTY-FOUR

Natalie entered the chicken coop quietly, using a small handheld flashlight that June had given her, and plucked the eggs to place in the basket. Some were still warm in her palm, making her feel grounded, like she was connecting with the earth and her creatures. She walked back to the house, leaving Diablo, who seemed confused as to why she was there so early, behind, sitting on the fence, waiting for the first hint of daybreak to make his morning call.

She turned toward the house, unsure if she should go inside if June wasn't up yet, but she saw a light coming from the back of the house, so she chose to enter. June wasn't in the kitchen, much to her relief. She didn't know if she could face her yet, not with what had just happened with Vaughn. So she tiptoed to the counter and set the basket down like Little Red Riding Hood trying not to wake the wolf. She turned on her heel to head back out, but a voice stopped her.

"Where do you think you're going without a hello and a good morning?" June said as she flicked on the light and walked into the kitchen, buttoning up her denim shirt. Her usually wild white hair was wet and twisted into a long braid that ran down her shoulder, leaving a damp patch on her shirt. She smelled of honey and lavender, and though her weathered face was pinched in disappointment, Natalie nearly broke down and cried into her arms, needing her strong comfort. But she managed to refrain, swallowing back her tears.

"Sorry, I wasn't sure if you were awake."

"Well, now you know. So, good morning to ya." She grabbed her apron and tied it on, taking a look out the window over the sink. "Still dark as sin out there."

"It is."

Natalie stood by the door, wanting to retreat. Wanting to run back to the guesthouse and collapse in tears, the conversation with Vaughn ripping at the chambers of her heart. She willed more tears back, hoping, praying, that June wouldn't notice.

But June took one quick look at her, then another, and locked onto her face. "What's wrong with you, child?"

Natalie felt her lips tingle and tremble as she tried like hell to hold her emotions at bay. But Vaughn's words kept replaying and she analyzed them again and again, noting her cold affect, her distance, her adamancy that they weren't in a position for anything to blossom between them.

Her breath hitched as she shook her head and tried to speak. June came toward her, arms outstretched. "Aw, come here. Let us have a look-see." She embraced her and Natalie stiffened, still determined not to break down. But it was no use. June's embrace was firm, yet soft, her words strong, yet welcoming, and Natalie couldn't keep her fences up. The floodgates opened wide, and she fell against her and sobbed.

"Shh." June comforted her, patting her back. "Tell me, what it is, now, huh? Is it your ex-husband? A bad memory?"

Natalie managed to inhale and exhale. "No."

"Then what is it, child?" She drew back and stared into her, rubbing her rough-feeling thumbs over her cheeks to wipe away the damp.

Natalie shook her head. "Nothing. I—I'm okay."

"Like hell." She held her face. "Something's got you all tore up." She stared at her some more and when Natalie shifted her gaze away she seemed to know. She dropped her hands. "Ah," she said. "Vaughn Marie."

Natalie brushed away her tears, unable to deny it. Her breath hitched some more as she tried to compose herself.

"I told you I was afraid of this." She moved to the sink, rinsed the eggs under the faucet, and nestled them in the deep pocket of her apron. She pulled a big mixing bowl from the cupboard and plucked a whisk from a drawer. She got to work cracking the eggs and scrambling them with some half-and-half from the fridge, seasoning them with salt and black pepper. Natalie noticed that June liked to busy her hands while she tried to work through something. Seemed to be a family trait, as Vaughn liked to stay busy as well. She wondered how hard she was working in the stables right now after their brief but telling talk. Was she mucking out those stalls as hard as she could? Forking that fresh straw into each clean stall till her heart was pounding and her sore back thrumming?

*Maybe that's what I should do. I should stay busy. Pretend it all isn't happening. None of it. Not Allen and his harassment and pursuance, not my financial situation, and not Vaughn and her casual but firm brush-off.*

"I'm gonna go back to the bungalow to shower."

"Will I see you at breakfast?" June asked, somehow knowing that she preferred to skip it this morning.

"Maybe tomorrow," she said. "I don't really have an appetite this morning."

June simply nodded when she'd thought she'd argue and insist on her coming. "I understand." She wagged a finger at her. "But you still need to eat. So I'll bring breakfast by in a short while."

"June, that's really not—"

"No arguing now."

Natalie conceded. "Okay."

"You go on now. Go take care of you."

Natalie thanked her and said a soft good-bye. She walked out of the house and toward the bungalow. Dawn was finally breaking and Diablo seemed to take in a huge breath before he let out his first crow of the morning. She ducked inside the guesthouse and muffled his cry as she closed the door behind her. She considered showering but thought against it, needing some hot tea first.

She filled a cup with water and placed it in the microwave to heat. As she waited, she glanced out the front window and saw Vaughn exiting the stables, wiping the sweat from her brow with the back of her arm. She bent to rest her hands on her knees and then palmed her back as if in pain. Her face contorted as she straightened, and Natalie's heart lurched. Everything in her told her to go to her, to help comfort her somehow. But she couldn't. Not anymore. Vaughn had made it clear that what had happened between them was a mistake.

A mistake.

Those were her words.

She teared up again and looked back to the microwave. The timer beeped and she got her mug and bobbed her tea bag into the steaming water. She sat at the kitchen table with her back to the living room and the front window. She couldn't bear to see Vaughn and she wondered how she was going to cope. Dealing with Allen was so much easier. She knew to steer clear and far away from him. He was maniacal and dangerous. An easy read.

But Vaughn was so drastically different. She was deep and kind and strong. And so damned appealing with her quiet way. And the way she kissed, so fervent, so passionate, like she couldn't get enough of her. Natalie knew that it would be impossible to get over her. To just move on like nothing had ever happened. She sipped her tea and focused on her troubled thoughts, conceding to one solution in particular.

It wouldn't be pleasant and it definitely wasn't smart or even feasible, but she felt she had no choice. It was what was best for her, and June had said to go and take care of herself.

Would June understand? For that matter, would Vaughn? Did it even matter at this point?

She finished her tea and went into the bedroom. She stripped down and showered, crying under the cascade of water. Crying like she'd never cried before. Until it hurt, until her ribs ached, and her raw throat begged for mercy. She cried for her troubled past, for her lost childhood, for her mistrust in Allen and the abuse she suffered at his hand, and for her heartbreak with Vaughn, a soul she really thought she'd truly connected with.

She cried for it all.

And when she emerged from the shower, once the water ran cold, she felt better. Could think clearer. And that's when she began to put her new plan into motion.

## CHAPTER TWENTY-FIVE

June wrapped her knuckles on the door and waited. Behind her, the day was beginning, the sun trying to break through some morning clouds. Diablo was on the fence of the coop, on his last crows, and she was grateful. She had a hell of a headache and the little banty rooster crying with all his might was not helping. Breakfast had been relatively peaceful, with Vaughn eating her food in silence as the boys spoke of the day's plans. June didn't say much, though she'd wanted to. But she felt it best to leave the situation between Vaughn and Natalie alone. Even if she wanted desperately to grab Vaughn by the collar and shake some sense into her. But she knew from the past, that that wasn't the way to handle Vaughn. One had to tread carefully and let her think that things were her idea. Easier said than done.

She waited a few more moments and knocked again. The plate in her hands was quickly cooling. What was taking Natalie so long? Was she still showering perhaps?

She knocked again and turned the doorknob and eased the door open. She didn't want a repeat of last night, so she called out.

"Natalie? You there?"

No answer.

She called out again. "Vaughn, you're not in here are you?"

No answer. She pushed the door open farther and stepped inside. The place was quiet, save for the gentle hum of the old refrigerator. She walked into the living room and peeked into the kitchen. Empty. She checked the bedroom. No Natalie.

She set the covered plate of eggs, bacon, and biscuits on the table and looked around. Natalie wasn't there, that was clear. But the place felt different. It felt…hollow. With her mind clicking with panic, she rushed into the bedroom and yanked open the drawers. They were empty. She hurriedly searched the closet and found the same.

"Oh, no. No, no, no."

She ran back into the kitchen and saw it, on the humming refrigerator. A note. June walked up to it and read.

*Dear Vaughn and June,*

*Thank you both so much for all your help. You have no idea how much it meant to me and I'm afraid I'll never be able to repay you for your kindness. Someday I hope to try.*

*Until then, please take care.*

*All my best,*

*Natalie.*

June snatched the paper from the fridge and bolted for the door. She threw it open and ran outside, searching desperately for a glimpse of Natalie. She swept her gaze left and right. Then left again, toward the front drive, beyond the pasture. There, in the distance, was someone walking. A lone figure carrying something on her back.

"Natalie!" But it was no use. She knew she couldn't hear her. She was too far away.

June looked again at the stables and ran as fast as she could to them, bumping into Greer on her way inside.

"Oh, sorry, Miss June. Boy, that was some breakfast," he said, rubbing his stomach.

"Never mind that," June said, brushing past him. "Where's Vaughn?"

"She's back feeding Miracle. Why? Something wrong?"

June continued on down the row of stalls, leaving Greer behind.

"Vaughn! Vaughn!"

"What?" Vaughn whispered harshly at June as she approached. "Keep it down, will ya? She's trying to eat."

"No time," June huffed. She waved Vaughn out of the stall. "Come. Quickly."

"Why? What is it?"

"Come," June said. She tugged on her arm and pulled her down the line to the entrance of the stables. Greer was still standing there looking dumbfounded. Benny came walking up with a horse, grinning from ear to ear until he saw June. His young face fell.

"Something wrong?" he asked.

"Yes, please tell us what's going on," Vaughn said.

June placed a hand on her knee and pointed out toward the front drive. "Look."

Vaughn and the boys followed her demand and squinted off into the distance. Greer spoke.

"There's someone there."

"Yes," June breathed.

"Well, I'll be, there is," Benny said.

"Where?" Vaughn looked harder and reared back. "Who is that?"

"It's Natalie," June said. And she shoved the note at Vaughn's chest. Vaughn opened the crinkled paper and read in silence. She glanced up, took another look at Natalie in the distance, and then back to June.

"She's leaving?"

June nodded.

Vaughn dropped the paper and took the reins for the horse from Benny. She climbed onto Charlie and took off at a trot, soon leading her into a fast gallop, kicking up dust behind her.

June watched with relief as she went, hoping against hope that she would be in time to make a difference.

## CHAPTER TWENTY-SIX

Vaughn steered Charlie down the front drive and rode her as fast as she could go. Natalie steadily grew closer, and Vaughn called out for her as she neared.

"Natalie," she said. "Wait." She tugged on the reins and brought Charlie to a slow trot and then a walk, gliding up next to Natalie who'd stopped and squinted back at her.

She didn't have much of a reaction; her face gave away nothing. Vaughn climbed down off the horse and led Charlie closer as Natalie picked up her pace once again.

"Going somewhere?" Vaughn asked, feeling foolish.

"You could say that." Natalie readjusted the canvas bag on her back.

"Where you going?"

"You really want to know?"

Vaughn sped up, tugging on Charlie. "I do."

Up ahead, a yellow cab slowed and turned down the drive. It was headed right for them.

"That's my ride," Natalie said.

"You called a cab?"

"Didn't have a cell phone for a rideshare. So, I called from the landline in the guesthouse."

The car drew closer.

"You still haven't said where you're going," Vaughn said, now feeling her chest tighten in desperation. What was Natalie thinking? How could she do this? Why was she doing this?

*Because of me. Because of what I said. Shit.*

"I haven't answered you because I have no answer, Vaughn. I don't know where it is that I'm going."

The cab came to a stop as Natalie held up her palm. She walked up to the driver's window.

"You call for a cab?" the driver asked.

"I did."

"Hop in."

Natalie walked to the passenger door. Vaughn hurried after her.

"You can't leave," she said. "If you have no place to go."

"Any place will be better than here," she said, glancing back to meet Vaughn's gaze. "After this morning."

"Look, I—I just meant that we can't—shouldn't—with all that we've got going on—"

"I know, Vaughn. And I think you're right. So I should go."

"But why?"

Natalie was quiet for a moment and Vaughn noticed that the driver, a middle-aged man with a dark, scruffy beard was looking from Vaughn back to Natalie, as if he were following the conversation.

"Because I can't just forget it and move on, Vaughn. Not like you obviously can."

"I—" She sighed. "I'm sorry. I didn't mean to hurt you, I just—"

"You made your point very clear. And I guess I'm just not like you."

"But you can still stay. I didn't mean to make you feel like you had to leave."

"That was all me," Natalie said. "I made that decision on my own."

"Please," Vaughn said. "Don't go." She stepped closer.

"Why?" Natalie said.

Vaughn hesitated. Struggled to find the words. Struggled to somehow get past what she'd said to her that morning. "Because I don't want you to. And Gram doesn't want you to. And the horses don't want you to."

"I think you'll all get along just fine without me." She opened the passenger door.

"No!" Vaughn let out. Natalie paused and looked back at her again. "I mean, no, we won't." She swallowed. "I won't."

Natalie studied her. Really bored into her. Vaughn came closer, went to reach out her hand. "Please," she said. "Stay. I want you to. I—need you to."

Another moment of silence ensued. Then the driver spoke. "Ladies, I've got a schedule to keep here. Can we hurry this along?"

"Mind your business," Vaughn said, still looking at Natalie, pleading to her with her eyes.

"At the moment, lady, she is my business. Now if you don't mind, she and I need to get going."

"Just shut up a minute," Vaughn snapped. She reached her hand out for Natalie. "I can't promise you anything, Natalie. God knows I wish things were different. But they aren't. I'm not. And I'm sorry. I don't know if I'll ever be. What Jeanie did…the betrayal. All the time behind my back—" She shook her head. "But I still want you to stay. Please. You're safe here. And we love having you. We need you. I need you, Natalie."

Natalie lowered her hand from the door. She pushed the door closed. The man sighed and jerked the car in reverse. "Damn waste of time."

Vaughn dug out her wallet and pulled out a fifty-dollar bill. She tossed it in his car at him. "Go," she said, never taking her eyes off Natalie.

He took the money and backed away, back down the drive. Natalie gripped Vaughn's hand and Vaughn led her to Charlie's side where she helped her up in the saddle. Once she was settled, Vaughn climbed on behind her and wrapped her arms around her with reins in her hand. She inhaled the scent of her hair, closed her eyes, and ticked at Charlie, turning her around. Then, with a gentle kick of her heels, she led them back toward home.

## CHAPTER TWENTY-SEVEN

Allen tied the belt to his satin robe as he descended the stairs. The door chime sounded again as he reached the ground level and he barked, "Hang on a damn minute!" It wasn't even ten a.m. Didn't they have any goddamn manners? He still had guests upstairs. New guests. Ones he was thoroughly enjoying.

He got to the door, unlocked it, and pulled it open. Two men in cheap suits were standing at the threshold. One gave him a practiced but nevertheless awful grin.

"Mr. Beaufort? Mr. Allen Beaufort?"

"Who's asking?"

The one with the grin flipped open his identification, showing a shiny badge. "Detective Hallorin. And this is Detective Marks." He flipped the wallet closed and took on a more serious look. "May we come inside for a moment?"

Cops? What the fuck? Were they here for the girls? No. The agency he used was exclusive and extremely private. They guaranteed complete anonymity. So why were these assholes at his door?

"Well, that depends," Allen said. "On why it is that you're here."

"Mr. Beaufort, we're here to discuss your ex-wife." He peeked at his small notebook. "One Natalie Brewer."

Natalie? What the fuck? Had she'd been found? Was she dead? He hadn't heard from Tito since he'd last seen him and that had been a few days before. If she was dead and Tito hadn't found that out and told him, he really would kill him. He needed to know this shit. Preferably before the cops, in case he needed to clean anything up.

"Oh." He covered his heart, as if he were distressed. "In that case, please, come in." He stepped aside and allowed the men entry. He motioned them into the living room and offered them a seat. The detectives sat on the sofa while he snuck a look back up the stairs, hoping that the girls would remain put. He sat in the armed chair across from his visitors, crossing his legs and adjusting his robe to cover his knees. He was drastically underdressed and unprepared for their visit, but he didn't want to leave them alone to go change. He didn't trust cops as a rule, and he was only doing this to see how much they knew about Natalie, if anything.

"Has something happened?" he asked, feigning innocence.

Hallorin stared at him. "Such as?"

Allen shrugged. "I'm not sure. I just assumed that something must've happened. Otherwise, why would you be here?"

Hallorin let the question hang before he spoke again. "Mr. Beaufort, when did you last see Natalie?"

Allen pretended to think for a moment. "I can't really say. A few months ago maybe? As I'm sure you know, she took out a restraining order against me, so I've had no recent contact with her."

"You're sure about that?"

"I am."

Hallorin looked to Marks.

"Mr. Beaufort, it seems that Natalie is missing," Marks said.

"Missing?"

"Her vehicle was found abandoned and burnt some weeks ago and no one has heard from her since."

"Oh. I wasn't aware." Allen looked at his lap and pretended to be saddened by the news. He wasn't totally bullshitting, he really did feel something. Just not sadness. It was more like disappointment. They weren't telling him anything new.

"And you're saying you haven't had any recent contact with her, correct?"

He glanced up. "That's correct."

"Then why, Mr. Beaufort, did you go to her place of residence recently, demanding to see her?"

Allen made a steeple with his fingers and smiled. "Gentlemen, I can assure you I did no such thing."

"We have two witnesses who claim otherwise."

"And whom, may I ask, are they?"

"One of them is her roommate. Gayle Nelson. She says you demanded entry and locked yourself in Natalie's room."

"Gayle Nelson?" He kept his smile. "Am I mistaken or isn't she known to use illegal substances?"

"Meaning?"

"Well, it's obvious, isn't it? She, for reasons I can attest to, has it out for me. She's lying." Hallorin raised an eyebrow at him and Allen continued. "Ms. Nelson has never liked me. And she partakes in recreational drugs. In other words, she's not all there, not very competent. And she's shaken me down for money, more than once. I refused. She promised I would pay one way or the other."

"So you're saying that she's making this up to what, get some kind of revenge?"

"Precisely." He leaned forward. "Let me ask you this. When you spoke to her, did her apartment reek of marijuana?"

"How would you know that if you hadn't been there?" Marks asked.

Allen rested back in his chair. "I have been there, gentlemen. Just not recently. In fact, I've been there twice, and both times the apartment smelled of pot and Gayle herself was high."

"And why were you at Natalie's place of residence?" Hallorin asked.

"To bring her some of her things. As you know, we recently split and she'd left some of her things here at the house. She asked for them and I brought them to her."

Hallorin flipped through his notes. "Your divorce was contentious, was it not?"

"I didn't want the divorce. If you want to call that contentious then so be it."

"Why didn't you want the divorce?"

"Because I love my wife. We had our problems, but I wanted to try and work through them."

"Mr. Beaufort, were you ever violent with your wife?"

"Absolutely not."

"You never put your hands on her?"

"We had our disagreements, Detective, but no, I never put my hands on her. She, however, did put her hands on me a few times if you'd care to discuss that."

Hallorin again looked to Marks. He closed his notebook and stood. Marks followed suit. "I think we've got all we need for now, Mr. Beaufort."

Allen stood along with them. He waved them toward the door. "Please, let me know if I can be of any more assistance."

"We will."

Marks opened the door. Female voices came from upstairs. Allen plastered on a smile as the detectives looked at him curiously.

"Overnight guest," he said.

The detectives exchanged another glance and walked out the door. Allen bolted it behind them and hurried into the kitchen to pick his phone up off the counter where it was charging. He dialed Tito and seethed into the phone, this time leaving a voice mail.

"You stupid son a bitch, the cops were just here. They're looking for Natalie. You better find her before they do, or I swear I'll bury you up to your head in the desert and let the coyotes and ants devour you."

## CHAPTER TWENTY-EIGHT

Natalie settled back into the guesthouse and picked up where she left off, helping June with the website and emails, and helping out with the ranch chores. Each day ended with muscles she didn't even know she had protesting in pain, but she felt fine nonetheless. She liked how a good hard day's work left her feeling spent but accomplished. Besides, the pain was nothing a long soak in the shower couldn't fix, and she made that one of her nightly habits, along with hot tea and some Advil. A nightly routine, that she knew, was probably very similar to Vaughn's.

She hadn't seen much of her since she'd come to fetch her at the end of the drive a few days before. They'd ridden Charlie back to the stables in silence. Natalie thoroughly enjoyed the feel of Vaughn's arms wrapped securely around her as she steered the horse. She'd tried not to think much of the encounter, knowing that Vaughn had only meant the things she'd said in a general sense, but nevertheless her words had penetrated, as how the way she'd looked at her when she'd said them.

*"I want you to stay."*

*"Please."*

*"I need you."*

The words replayed over and over in her mind, churning, with her trying to figure out what all they meant. Why did Vaughn want her to stay? How did she need her? She desperately wanted to ask, but she feared in doing so that Vaughn would retreat even further within herself. Or worse, she'd again reiterate how they weren't ready for any sort of intimacy or relationship, bringing up not only her problems, but Natalie's as well. Natalie didn't want to think about her problems, even though she knew she needed to. It was just that when she did she ended up feeling anxious and hopeless, especially when it came to Allen. She feared she'd never be able to escape him. Just like he'd said.

She finished scrubbing the troughs, refilled them with fresh water, and got busy setting out hay and supplements for the next feed. The day was closing fast, nightfall coming quicker now that it was late September, which meant less daylight and time to do chores. So she started her days with Vaughn, rising at five to help muck the stalls and feed the horses. Though Vaughn seemed to appreciate the help, she remained mostly quiet, doing her work in silence, and focusing a lot on Miracle and her continued care. The mare was coming along nicely, but she still needed small, frequent feedings and Vaughn was intent on doing those herself.

Natalie finished preparing the feed and stepped back into the setting sun, wiping her brow. Voices carried to her from the house, and she saw a man and a woman walking with Vaughn. They were headed right for her. They must be more potential employees. They'd already had a few to the house to meet with and discuss the horses and the job. But so far, Vaughn hadn't found anyone she was ready to trust.

"And this is Natalie," Vaughn said as the trio approached. "She's helping us out temporarily." She didn't bother to introduce the young cowboy and cowgirl.

Natalie said a polite hello, but the introduction had stung. Temporarily. Is that how Vaughn saw her? As just the temporary help? Had she not meant all the things that she'd previously said?

Natalie watched helplessly as the trio walked into the stables with Vaughn discussing some of the horses, while also showing them where most of the supplies were kept. Natalie followed, curious about the young cowgirl in particular. She was younger than Natalie was, that much was obvious, and she looked to have short, close-cropped hair, but it was difficult to see due to the ball cap she wore. She also had on a pair of tight Wranglers, Roper boots, and a snug fitting T-shirt, showing off a rather trim and athletic body. Her very presence felt like a potential threat and Natalie cringed each time the young woman laughed at something Vaughn said.

Natalie tried to focus on cleaning tack, but it was difficult when it seemed that the young woman was laughing every few seconds.

*Laying it on rather thick, aren't we?*

Surely Vaughn would see through it.

Wouldn't she?

Natalie continued cleaning, rubbing one of the saddles so hard her hands began to hurt. She tossed the lightly dampened sponge back into the bucket of water and rubbed the leather down with glycerin soap, all the while listening to the laughing.

She gritted her teeth and rubbed harder, moving from one saddle to another, squeezing out the sponge and starting the process all over again. First the damp sponge wipe down, then the glycerin soap. Over and over. Until her tortured mind could take no more. At last, she finished and she tossed the bucket and sponge out into the aisle of the stables, where it smashed against the wall and spilled onto the concrete floor. It caused a loud commotion and the trio looked over at her from down the row of horses. Vaughn in particular was giving her a confused look. But Natalie didn't care, she just kept walking, leaving the stables behind.

She crossed to the main house, knowing that if she went into the bungalow she'd do nothing but wallow in self-pity and think about packing up again.

What was going on with her? Why was she so upset and jealous? Vaughn had told her they couldn't be together. So why was she wigging out?

*Because she'd also said she needed me and wanted me to stay.*

But the young woman? There was no reason to be jealous. Vaughn wasn't Natalie's and the young woman was no threat. She was a potential employee. Someone who would work for Vaughn. And Vaughn would keep that professional.

Wouldn't she?

*God, I'm so confused. So distraught. Vaughn's right. I'm too much of a mess to even think about her that way.*

She knocked on the kitchen door and entered when June called out. The kitchen smelled of boiled chicken, a scent that always bothered Natalie's delicate stomach. She tried not to think about it.

"I told you you don't need to knock," June said. "Don't tell me you're gonna be as stubborn as the others are around here." She was scrubbing vegetables at the sink. Natalie stood next to her and washed her hands. Then she took the washed veggies and asked if June wanted them diced.

"I'd appreciate that," she said.

Natalie retrieved a knife and took the vegetables to the cutting board. She began dicing the carrots.

"So what's troubling you?" June said, walking to the stove where the boiled chicken sat on a platter cooling. She grabbed a bowl and began separating the chicken from the bone, placing the shreds into the bowl. She worked quickly and expertly with hands as red as a ripe tomato.

"Nothing."

"That's the biggest bunch of bullarkey I've heard in a while."

"Well, it's the truth."

"Child, if that's the truth, then those pigs Vaughn raised when she was little could fly."

Natalie finished with the carrots and started in on the celery. "What is this for anyway? Chicken soup?"

"Yes, and don't change the subject."

"Isn't it a little late to be cooking soup for dinner?"

"It's for tomorrow, smarty-pants. Supper tonight's leftovers. They're warming in the oven."

Natalie sliced harder. She could feel June's eyes on her.

"Well? Am I gonna have to hang you up by your toenails or are you gonna tell me?"

Natalie stopped chopping. "I was just thinking about the man and woman outside with Vaughn."

"Oh. That's Wyatt and Em."

"Right. Possible employees." Vaughn would move on from them and interview more. She was sure of it. No need to worry.

"No, they're the new hires."

"New hires?" Natalie whipped her head around to look at June. "Since when?"

"Since about an hour ago."

"What happened to having them meet the horses first and all that?"

"They have met the horses. Did that yesterday evening when you was already holed up in the guesthouse."

"But I just saw them. In the stables, talking about the horses."

"That's because they had questions after Vaughn's discussion with them today. And they wanted an extra visit with Miracle."

Natalie felt sick. The stench from the boiled chicken sat in the back of her throat, nearly gagging her as she thought about Vaughn working closely with the young woman.

Em.

What kind of a name was Em?

She dropped the knife and clenched her eyes. It was too much. All of it was too much.

"I've got to go."

"Where you going?" June asked as Natalie hurried to the door.

"For a walk."

"Now?"

"Yes." She opened the door and paused, realizing just how rude she was being. She wiped a stray tear and spoke. "I'm sorry, June. I'm just…having a hard time."

"You're not going to try and leave again are you?"

Natalie laughed. "And go where?"

She felt a soft hand rest on her shoulder. "Child, I hope you're not staying simply because you have nowhere else to go."

Natalie fought back sobs. "I'm—not."

"Then look at me. Look at me, child." She lightly tugged on Natalie's shoulder and Natalie turned to face her. June wiped her tears and pressed her wrinkled lips together in concern. "You are wanted here," she said. "Needed here."

Natalie laughed again. "That's what Vaughn said."

"And it's the truth."

Natalie stared into her eyes, wanting so badly to believe her. But she was having such a hard time. She didn't feel wanted anywhere. Needed by anyone. She knew it stemmed from her childhood, but she didn't know how to make it stop.

"I'll stop by after supper," June said. "We'll talk."

Natalie shook her head and tried to argue. "I just want to be alone."

"Being alone is the worst thing for you right now."

"It doesn't matter—"

June pulled on her, making like she was going to shake her. "Course it does. I'll be by after supper."

She palmed her cheek and smiled at her.

Natalie finally gave in and nodded. "Okay."

June gave her a light pat with her palm. "You go on your walk, now. Before the others see you. There's no telling the questions they'll ask once they get a look at ya."

Natalie turned and walked out the door, grateful to be alone, even if it was the worst thing for her.

## CHAPTER TWENTY-NINE

June once again stood at the door to the guesthouse with a warm plate in her hands. She rapped lightly on the door and glanced around while she waited. Darkness had fallen and the temperature had dropped, the breeze warm. The ranch was quiet, save for the occasional cluck of a chicken or the neigh of a horse. Noises that June found soothing after having been surrounded by them all these years.

The door opened and Natalie welcomed her with a soft smile. Though her hair was wet from a recent shower, she still looked worse for wear. The child appeared gaunt, and her eyes were red-rimmed and swollen. It was obvious she'd been crying some more and June's heart ached for her. The poor child had been through so much and it seemed she was still fighting some sort of demons, if not Vaughn and the situation with her. But June didn't pretend to know, because at this point, with Vaughn's continued silence, she really didn't have any idea what was going on between the two of them.

Natalie welcomed her inside. They walked to the small table in the kitchen where June uncovered the plate of meatloaf and mashed potatoes with steamed vegetables. It was what they'd had last night, but it was still a good, hearty meal and the boys and Vaughn had gobbled it right up. Which was why June had had to make Natalie a plate ahead of time so the boys wouldn't eat it all, leaving Natalie with nothing.

June set the plate down and retrieved a fork from the drawer. She sat and motioned for Natalie to join her. Natalie eyed the plate as if was unappealing, but she didn't argue. But rather she slowly sat and began to pick at the food with her fork.

"That's a good meal now," June said, trying to coax her to at least take a bite.

Natalie forked a bite of meatloaf and brought it to her mouth. June watched as she finally ate it, closing her eyes as she chewed.

"Well?" June said.

Natalie swallowed and opened her eyes. "It's good."

June nudged the plate closer to her. "Well, eat up now. Before it gets cold."

Natalie forked another bite and ate it slowly, carefully, as if she were trying to decipher the taste of each tiny morsel. When she finally swallowed, she set her fork down. "I'm sorry, I just don't have much of an appetite."

"It's not the food?"

"The food is good. I'm just not in the mood, June. I'm sorry."

"It's alright." June rose and plucked her a bottle of Lipton iced tea out of the fridge. She brought it to her and sat once again. "At least drink something, darlin', and stay hydrated. You look like death warmed over."

"Thanks."

June squeezed her shoulder. "I don't mean nothin' by it. I'm just worried about you."

Natalie pushed the plate away, but opened the bottle of lemon-flavored tea. She took a delicate sip, then another, and twisted the cap back on.

"I'm sure you are. The way I've been acting…" She shook her head as tears flooded her eyes. "I've been such an ass."

"Shh," June said. "You have a right to be an ass every now and again. Everyone does."

"But I—it's more than that, June. I can't seem to shake it."

"Well, why don't you tell me what's going on, and I'll see if I can help."

Natalie exhaled and rested her cheek in her hand. "I'm cranky. All the time. And lately…jealous. Like really jealous. And I've never been the jealous type. And on top of that, I'm scared. Terrified that Allen will find me."

"Well, no wonder why you're so torn up inside, child. You've got a lot going on."

"Which is exactly why Vaughn says we can't explore anything together, which saddens me like you wouldn't believe. But she's right, isn't she, June? I'm just too messed up." She stood and paced, hand to forehead. "God, I'm just so overwhelmed."

June remained seated, watching her helplessly. "Why don't we take things one at a time and see if we can get somewhere?" She patted the table, encouraging her to sit once again.

Natalie paused mid stride, seemed to think about it, and then joined her. June rubbed her shoulder.

"Tell me what's bothering you the most."

"Right now?" She looked at June with wide eyes.

"Mm-hm. Right at this moment."

"The jealously."

"Okay. What are you jealous over?"

She glanced away, as if ashamed. "Vaughn," she let out. "And the new girl. Em, or whatever her name is."

June reared back. "Em? Lord, why in the world would you be jealous of her?"

"Because she looks…I don't know, like she could be gay. And she laughs at everything Vaughn says like some lovesick schoolgirl. It just…it…infuriates me."

June lowered her hand. "So you have strong feelings for Vaughn."

"Yes."

"Does she know?"

"I don't think so. I mean, she knows I'm obviously very attracted to her, but as for my feelings…no, I don't think she knows."

"You thought about telling her?"

Natalie shook her head. "No way."

"Why not?"

"Because she made it clear that she doesn't feel the same way. She said what happened between us was a mistake and a one-time thing. That we both have too many problems for it to be anything more."

"Ah."

"Yeah. So, no, I'm not going to tell her how I feel. It would be torturous."

"I still think she ought to know, darlin'. For your own peace of mind and well-being."

Natalie looked at her pleadingly. "I can't, June. I just can't. I'm not strong enough to face the rejection."

"What if she doesn't reject you?"

"She already has, by saying what she did."

"What if she's changed her tune?"

"What do you mean?"

"What if the things she said to you were just a defense mechanism? Ones said with the sole purpose of keeping you at bay?"

"Why would she do that?"

"Fear, Natalie. I guarantee you that Vaughn is just as afraid as you are."

"But—"

"I'm not saying I know exactly how she feels. Lord knows she hasn't shared anything with me. I'm just saying that I've known that child since she was born, and I know how she gets when she's afraid of something. Instead of facing it head-on, she runs. Always has."

June continued as Natalie took her words in. "Now as for Em. She's not a threat to you, Natalie. She's a child. And an employee at that. Vaughn will never see her as anything more. Ever."

"But the way she acts around Vaughn, it's sickening."

"She's young and she probably looks up to Vaughn. Or she may even have a little crush. But I can tell you right here and now, that Vaughn will never take advantage of that. Em is an employee. And not that it matters, but she's not Vaughn's type."

"What is…Vaughn's type?"

June smiled. "I think you know the answer to that, child."

"Me?"

June kept her smile.

"But I'm so weak. Messed up."

"You're wonderful," June said. "Bright, funny, heart of gold. You've got so much going for you, Natalie. And I'm not the only one that sees that."

"I wish I could see it."

"Once you get past your fear, you will."

"My fear. Ha."

"Have you heard from your ex? Has something happened there that I don't know about?"

"No."

"Then why the fear? He hasn't found you so far."

"Because I dread the moment he does. And he will."

"What makes you so sure?"

"Because Allen doesn't give up. He always gets what he wants. And what he wants, ultimately, is me."

Her hands shook and she gripped them tightly together as if to stop them. June rested her hand over them to help calm her.

"Maybe you should go to the police again. Tell them your fears. Tell them you are terrified and why."

"I have told them. I even spelled it out for them. So, I can't. Not again. He'll...hurt me."

"That's exactly why you should go. I'll even go with you and you can continue to stay here, where you're safe, while the justice system does something about him."

But Natalie shook her head. "June, I could never do that. I could never put you and Vaughn in danger."

"But you're staying here. Isn't that the same thing?"

"The second he finds out I'm here, I'm gone. He'll follow me, his interest in you two will leave with me."

"Child," June whispered. "You must do something."

"All I can do is hide."

"You can't hide forever."

Natalie stared off into the distance. "I've thought about it. Thought a lot about it. Maybe I can hide forever. Just start over new somewhere now that he can't find me."

"You really want to do that?"

"It's the best thing I can come up with."

June opened the bottle of tea and handed it to her. "Here, drink some more."

Natalie took the bottle and sipped.

June continued. "I think you should go to the police and face him. But that's just my humble opinion. The decision, of course, is yours. And I'll stand by you either way."

Natalie played with the label on the bottle. "Thanks."

"Just think about it," June said. "That's all I ask."

"I will."

June sighed and covered the plate and placed it in the microwave. "You feel any better?"

Natalie rubbed her eyes. "I think I'm too tired to care."

June returned to her and embraced her from behind. "You look too tired to care. You want to come sleep at the house tonight in the guest room?"

"No. I prefer to crash here. Alone."

"Okay."

"But thanks for the talk. And the advice."

"I wish you would heed it."

"I promise I'll think about it."

"That's enough for me. Your food's in the microwave. Heat it up if you get hungry sometime soon."

"Thanks, I will."

June kissed the top of her head and walked to the door. "I'll see you at breakfast tomorrow, yes?"

Natalie nodded.

"You sure you're gonna be okay tonight?" She hesitated at the door, wondering if she should offer to stay the night with her. "I could...stay. If you need me to."

"I'm okay, June. Really."

June blew her a kiss. "Alright then. Night, Natalie."

"Night."

June walked out the door, trying to believe Natalie when she said she felt better, but in no way feeling better about things herself.

## CHAPTER THIRTY

Tito pulled into the paved lot and parked in front of an office door with the business name sprawled across it in fancy font. To his right sat dozens of yellow cabs, all lined up like little bees behind a fence, waiting to swarm, waiting to tell him what he needed to know.

All he had was a hunch, but he'd found out more on a whim than most people with good, solid leads. So he was willing to take a chance.

He popped an apple-flavored Jolly Rancher into his mouth and climbed from his SUV. He lumbered up to the glass door and pulled it open with ease. He heard an overhead bell jingle as he stepped inside. The office was cold, so much so that he thought he might be able to see his breath. He coughed into his fist, both to check and to garner attention. A man behind the counter shoved a wedge of sandwich into his mouth and got to his feet, wiping his hands together to rid them of crumbs. A paper napkin hung from his collar, a makeshift bib.

"Help you?"

Tito tucked his Jolly Rancher into his cheek and slid a photo across the counter to him.

"What's this?" asked the man, whose name tag said Tony. He stroked his mustache as he examined the photo.

"You seen her?"

He shook his head, still looking at it. "No."

"I need to ask your drivers."

The man glanced up at him. "And who are you?"

Tito pulled his wallet out from his back pocket. He flipped it open and showed his private investigator ID. He leaned on the counter, edging closer to the man, who drew away, obviously uncomfortable.

"Okay, buddy. But what's this about? She in some kind of trouble?"

"She could be. She's missing. From the Canyon City area off I-17. I was told you serve that area."

"We do. But I'd need a warrant to check."

Tito leaned in closer to him and stared him down. "You don't want to make me come back."

Tony visibly swallowed and looked at the photo again. "You gotta name?"

"Natalie Brewer. It would've been back in August."

The man side stepped to his computer and typed. After a long moment, he shook his head. "I don't have any clients with that name in August. No cards charged to that name either."

"Check again."

He blinked. Tito leaned farther forward. The man complied, typing again. But again he shook his head. "Sorry, man. Nothing."

Tito swiped the photo and started to walk behind the counter. The man held up his palms. "Hey, whoa. Where you going?"

"To ask your drivers. She could've used a false name. Paid cash."

"None of my guys picked anyone up in Canyon City on that day. I checked."

"I want them to see the photo." Natalie had to have gotten a ride somehow with someone and he was determined to find out with whom. He'd already had one of his contacts check Uber and Lyft. No dice. She had to have used a cab company or been picked up by a private citizen.

The man hurried to him, trying halfheartedly to block him. "Okay, okay. Follow me. I'll take you back." He led the way into the office, through cluttered desks covered in files, paperwork, and older model computers. The scent of food wafted through and grew stronger as they neared a room with an open door. Tony walked through and Tito followed. A handful of men sat at a folding table, drinking and eating while playing a hand of cards. They looked over at Tito and grew quiet.

Tony spoke. "This private detective here has a photo he wants you to look at. The woman would've been picked up in August out at the Rock Springs area."

Tito tossed down the photo. One man slid it over for all of them to see.

Tony continued to talk. "I checked the system. We had no pickups in Canyon City then. But he wanted to show you guys to be sure."

The first two men shook their heads. But the third man, who swiped the photo from across the table, stared at it a long while before he nodded.

"I seen her. But it wasn't in August."

"When?" Tito asked.

"I don't know. A week ago, maybe."

"Where?"

"Some damn ranch out past Rock Springs."

"Where did you take her?"

"Nowhere. She wouldn't get in the car. Some lesbo talked her out of it."

"Lesbo?"

"Some dyke cowgirl. Didn't want her to leave. Sounded like some sappy love shit to me. So, I left. The cowgirl gave me a fifty though, for my time."

Tito snatched the photo, grilling the bearded man with his eyes. "What ranch?"

"I don't know. Midnight something or other."

Tito took the photo and walked out.

## CHAPTER THIRTY-ONE

Vaughn tipped her hat back to scratch her forehead. Then she readjusted it and looked back down at her clipboard. She was doing inventory, waiting for her new stallion to be delivered. Behind her, she could hear Em cleaning the stallion's new stall, while Wyatt continued cleaning on down the line. The two new hands were helping a lot, but Vaughn was finding that they still weren't enough, especially with the new business they were drawing, thanks to the updated website.

She'd sold four horses since the website had been up and she had two more people showing serious interest.

"You want straw alone in here, boss lady?" Em asked her.

Vaughn turned and examined the cleaned area, then looked at Em who was leaning on a broom brush.

"Or do you want a mix of pellets and shavings to welcome him in?"

"You've done your homework," Vaughn said, impressed.

"I asked June. I know how important it is to surround a new horse with things he's familiar with. And June said he's used to sleeping on wood pellets and shavings."

"Nice work. And yes, to answer your question, go ahead and use the pellets and shavings."

"Will do." She propped the broom brush up against the wall. "I could also make up a sweet mix for him to munch on. Might make the welcome a little sweeter."

"Go ahead," Vaughn said. "But don't give him too much. We don't want to upset his stomach."

Em nodded and left the stall. She walked down the line of shelves and hoisted up a bag of wood pellets and carried it back to the stall. Vaughn watched as she slit the bag open with a small knife she pulled from her back pocket. Next she spread the pellets along the rubber mat on the floor, making a nice bed for their new stallion.

Em seemed to be getting along wonderfully. She was a farm kid, had grown up with horses on her family's farm in Wyoming. She'd just recently moved to the Valley and she'd been looking for work similar to what she'd had back home. Vaughn had been impressed by her detailed résumé as well as her references. For a young woman of twenty, she had ten references singing her praises about her work ethic and know how. And from what Vaughn could see so far, those references had known what they spoke of.

"What's his name?" Em asked as she walked down the line of shelves again, looking for shavings.

"Midnight," Vaughn said.

Em chuckled. "Seems fitting, doesn't it?"

"For this ranch? It sure does."

"Well, maybe it's a sign," she said as she lifted two bags of shavings onto her shoulder. "That he's meant to be here."

"Maybe," Vaughn said. Em slit open the bag of shavings. But before she spread them with the fork, she stood and unbuttoned her shirt. She peeled it off and tossed it along the stall wall. Wearing only a form-fitting white tank top, she began spreading the shavings on top of the wood pellets.

For a petite thing she sure was strong. And she had the defined muscles to prove it. Vaughn recalled being that young and boisterous, able to do almost anything without the stab of pain. But those were times long ago.

"Hey," a voice said. Vaughn glanced over to see Natalie slowly leading O'Malley into the stables.

"Hey."

She walked up and joined her, her gaze going from Vaughn to Em, where it lingered. "She's working hard," she said. But it didn't sound like a compliment or an innocent observation. It sounded more like an accusatory statement, like Em was doing something wrong.

It confused Vaughn, but she shook it off, sure she'd just misunderstood her tone. Natalie had, after all, been acting a little differently lately. Vaughn had tried to read into her mood swings, but it had done her little good, because she still hadn't been able to figure out what was wrong.

"Yes, she is," Vaughn responded. "She's a good worker."

"Mm. I suppose."

Vaughn raised her eyebrow, but Natalie moved on.

"I hear you bought a stallion."

"I did. He should arrive here soon as a matter of fact." She looked beyond Natalie and out into the ranch, searching for a truck pulling a horse trailer. She saw nothing but Greer in the corral grooming a horse.

"That must be exciting," Natalie said.

"It is," Em said. "A new horse is always exciting."

"Mm," Natalie said. She looked back to Vaughn. "If you need any help with him, I'm available."

"So am I," Em chimed in. She walked back to the shelves and grabbed a couple more bags of shavings and got busy spreading them with the fork.

Natalie watched her closely and gave her a suspicious look before she focused on Vaughn once again. "Like I said, I'm available. Unless you would like for me to feed Miracle for you."

"Oh, I can do that too," Em said. She finished making Midnight's bed and leaned over the wall of the stall, sweat glistening on her neck and chest. She looked like a young, vibrant tomboy in her ball cap and tank top and her attitude was infectious.

Vaughn smiled and lowered her clipboard. She glanced at her watch. The stallion should be there already. "Why don't you go ahead and do that, Em. That would help me a lot."

"Sure thing." She snatched her shirt and left the stall, tying the shirt around her waist as she went.

Natalie huffed.

"Something wrong?" Vaughn asked, once again perplexed by her mood.

"I'm just trying to figure out why you're letting her, this new kid, feed Miracle when you've yet to let anyone else do it. You said you didn't trust anyone else to get it right."

Vaughn stammered, more confused than ever. Was Natalie... jealous?

"I asked her to do that so you could help me with the stallion. But if you don't want to then—"

"What makes her qualified to feed Miracle, when I wasn't?"

"She has experience with nursing malnourished horses, Natalie. Her aunt runs a rescue ranch."

Natalie led O'Malley into the neighboring stall and crossed her arms over her chest.

"I'm confused," Vaughn said. "Do you want to help me with the stallion, or not?"

"That's fine," Natalie said as she brushed by her. "As long as I'm good enough."

"Natalie," Vaughn said, causing her to stop. "You are good enough."

"Doesn't seem like it."

"Well, you are."

"Then why does Em seem to be getting special treatment? I mean, she's always following you around, jumping up to do every job you mention. It's—" She shook her head. "Maddening."

"She's just learning the ropes around here. And she's highly motivated. Nothing wrong with that."

"Unless it's something more than that," Natalie said.

"Like what?"

"Like maybe she has another reason for going above and beyond for you."

"Such as?"

"I think she likes you, Vaughn."

Vaughn was dumbfounded. "Excuse me?"

"She has a crush. It's more than obvious."

Vaughn shook her head, truly rattled. "Natalie, are you jealous of Em?" For more reasons than one?

Natalie scoffed. "I'm just stating the obvious."

*Could* Em have a crush on her? Was it possible she wasn't seeing it?

"And as for being jealous," Natalie continued. "Maybe I am, Vaughn."

"But why? Surely you know that I'd never…" she shook her head, unable to even contemplate doing anything with Em. "She's my employee."

"So am I, aren't I?"

Again, Vaughn shook her head. "No, Natalie, you aren't. You're a friend and you're helping out. We're helping each other out. And our relationship…." She wasn't sure what to say. "It's completely different."

"Our relationship?" Natalie said softly.

"Yes."

"What is our relationship?"

Vaughn stared into her pain-filled eyes as she searched for words. "Natalie…"

But Natalie turned, tears brimming. "Let me know when the stallion arrives and I'll come help." She started walking away.

Vaughn took a step to go after her. "Natalie. Wait. Let's talk this through." She was surprised at her own words, as she was the one who usually avoided heavy conversation about emotions and feelings. But she was willing and able to discuss this. She didn't want Natalie feeling confused and jealous over something so ridiculous. She didn't want Natalie to feel upset at all.

"I can't," Natalie said. "Not right now. Not when I don't even know what it is I'm feeling myself." She hurried out of the stables and into the corral.

Vaughn watched her go, feeling helpless. Natalie was torn up inside, she could see it, and Gram had also brought it up on more than one occasion. But Gram had also been tight-lipped as to the reasons why, wanting to keep Natalie's confidence, which Vaughn understood and could appreciate. Vaughn just wished she knew what was bothering her so badly. She wanted to fix it, whatever it was. She was a fixer. Whether it came to Gram, the ranch, or anything else, she was driven to make things right.

*Unless it's me personally.*

She walked out into the late afternoon sun and set her clipboard in the back of the Gator. Natalie was loving on Oliver as she wiped her own tears from her eyes. Vaughn leaned on the bars and watched, curious, with her heart bleeding for her. If it was something as simple as jealousy, she'd pretty much just put that to rest. So why was Natalie still so upset?

Maybe she really didn't know. Like she'd said.

If that was the case, there was no way Vaughn could fix it. Nothing she could do, other than to be kind and offer to lend an ear. But she very seriously doubted that Natalie would take her up on that. Things had been different between them since that night in the guesthouse, and consequently the discussion at the end of the drive. Things just weren't the same, and Vaughn blamed herself for that. She hadn't exactly handled things in the best way.

In fact, she'd pretty much screwed everything up.

But how could she make it right when she knew that giving in to her attraction to Natalie right now wouldn't be good for either one of them? Not when Natalie still had her ex-husband to contend with. That was going to have to be handled, one way or the other. And Vaughn still feared that when that did happen, Natalie might turn tail and run back to him. She'd seen it before with her aunt and it hadn't been a pretty picture. Her aunt had paid the price for it with bruises and fear that seemed to last a lifetime. She didn't want to see that happen to Natalie, but she also had herself to think about. She was trying to do what was best for both of them. Until they worked out their issues, things couldn't possibly work. Could they?

*I can't.*

She sighed and tipped her hat back to scratch her forehead again. Then she rested her arms on the bars and rested her chin on her hands. Natalie was speaking softly to Oliver, stroking him down, nuzzling his neck. Natalie's dark hair was glinting in the sun, her eyes blazing in the rays as she looked over at Vaughn. She was damn near breathtaking as she stood there in her jeans and snug henley top, loving on that horse in the late afternoon sunlight.

*I may not be able to fix things right now, Natalie. But I'm still here. And I still want you here. I just hope that I can continue to convince you of that.*

## CHAPTER THIRTY-TWO

Natalie finished grooming Oliver and walked him back inside the stables. Em grinned at her as she fed Miracle, and Natalie wanted to smack the grin right off her face.

*God, what is wrong with me? Why am I feeling so inadequate and combative when it comes to this girl?*

Natalie led Oliver into his stall, closed him in, and returned to the corral as Greer led another horse inside. There were only a handful of horses left in the pen, but they weren't Natalie's current concern. She was looking for Vaughn and wondering if the young stallion had arrived yet. A quick glance at her watch showed that another half hour had passed. So where was the horse?

Had he arrived and Vaughn had changed her mind about having her help?

*I shouldn't have behaved the way I did. I really need to get a grip.*

She stared out over the pasture searching for any sign of Vaughn or the new horse, but she saw nothing. Just another handful of horses grazing out in the pasture. Natalie walked toward the main house, determined to find Vaughn so she could apologize. But just as she reached the side door to the kitchen, Vaughn came rushing out, colliding into her.

"Shit, I'm sorry," Vaughn said, hurrying by her.

"No, I'm sorry. And I'm sorry I was such a jerk back in the stables. I just—"

"We can discuss it later. Right now, I have to go." She headed for her truck, nearly breathless.

Natalie followed. "What's going on?"

Vaughn opened the door and climbed inside. "There's been an accident on the private road. The stallion's involved."

"Oh, no." Natalie rounded the truck and yanked open the passenger door. Vaughn didn't protest when she crawled in and slammed the door. Instead, she cranked the engine and peeled out in the dirt, leaving the house behind, pulling a horse trailer behind them.

"What happened?" Natalie asked.

Vaughn rang her hands on the steering wheel. "I'm not sure. I just got a call from the guy delivering him saying he was in trouble, saying he'd been in some sort of accident."

"God, I hope it's nothing serious."

"Me, too."

They sped down the drive and turned quickly onto the private road. "Vaughn, I know you're worried, but don't kill us before we get there."

"Sorry." She slowed a little and they continued down the dirt road. It didn't take long before Natalie could see a vehicle and what looked like a horse trailer. The vehicle, a white dually truck and the matching trailer were jackknifed just off the side of the road. Natalie leaned forward and gripped the dash.

"Oh my God."

"Yeah, it doesn't look good."

Vaughn pulled in close to the trailer and braked. She and Vaughn climbed from the truck. An older man came around the side of the dually, dabbing his forehead with a blood-stained handkerchief.

"You alright?" Vaughn asked, immediately going to the trailer to peer inside.

"I've been better," the man said. He joined Natalie and they too peered inside the trailer.

The black stallion was standing, but he was all the way to one side. He was snorting and anxious to move.

"He seems to be okay, but we won't know for sure until we get him out of there," the man said.

Natalie turned to him and examined his head. He had what looked to be a small cut up near his hairline. It was still bleeding.

"We should call an ambulance," Natalie thought out loud.

But Vaughn looked at her quickly and Natalie realized that she probably shouldn't be there if they did.

"I'm fine," the man said.

"Are you sure?" Even if she had to leave, it didn't matter. She wanted the man to be okay.

"I'm sure." He extended his hand. "I'm Marv." He motioned toward the stallion in the trailer. "And that's Midnight."

"Natalie," she said taking his hand. "And that's Vaughn."

"Nice to meet you," Marv said. "Just wish it was under better circumstances."

Vaughn glanced back at Marv. "I'm going to open the trailer and get him out."

"Go right ahead," Marv said. "You'll have to take him the rest of the way in anyway. My tires are flat."

"How did that happen?" Natalie asked as Vaughn carefully opened the trailer.

"Come here, I'll show you." He led the way back down the road and pointed at the ground. A black strip was lying haphazardly across the road with large roofing type nails on it, sticking up like spikes. "I couldn't stop in time," he said. "And I honestly didn't know what the hell it was."

Natalie knelt and touched the strip. She tried to maneuver one of the nails, but it was glued heavily to the rubber material of the strip. It appeared to be some sort of homemade tire spike device, staked into the road. Similar to what the police use when trying to stop a runaway suspect. She stood and turned slowly in a circle, looking for a nearby vehicle or a person watching them. She saw nothing but the surrounding desert.

"You're lucky you're okay," Natalie said. She once again studied his wound. "I really think you should have someone look at that."

"I'll take care of it later. Right now, I want to get Midnight to his new home and make sure he's okay."

Vaughn opened the trailer and slipped a rope halter onto Midnight who snorted at her. Vaughn spoke softly to him and carefully tried to lead him out of the trailer, but it was obvious he was scared. Vaughn spoke to him again and stroked his snout. Then she lightly tugged on his lead again and backed up as he began taking tentative steps toward her.

"That's it," she said. "Good boy. What a good boy."

Marv was right there when he emerged, praising him as well. Midnight staggered a bit, as if he needed to regain his bearings, but he followed Vaughn farther out, walking just fine. He bobbed his head and neighed, as if letting them know.

"Good boy," Vaughn said. She petted him and smiled. "I think he's okay."

"Thank Christ," Marv said, holding the handkerchief to his head. "I thought we were done for."

"Vaughn," Natalie said, waving her over. "You need to see this."

Vaughn walked with Natalie back down the road to the makeshift tire strip. She stood looking at it for a moment before she knelt and carefully touched a spike.

"Are you the only one who uses this road?" Natalie asked, already getting a painful lump in her gut.

"Going this way, yes. My ranch is the only place out this way."

Vaughn stared out over the vast desert just as Natalie had done moments before. When she seemed to find no answers, she stood. "We need to get back to the ranch. It's not safe out here."

Natalie hugged herself and rubbed her arms from the cold chill bumps that had erupted on her skin. "You think it was those boys?"

Vaughn adjusted her hat and kicked at the dirt. "I don't know who else it would be."

Marv stood with Midnight. "If I was you, I'd call the police," he said. "Someone coulda been killed."

Vaughn walked back to the horse and gently took his lead. She walked him to her trailer and loaded him up. Thankfully, he didn't fight her. Natalie watched as she closed and secured the door.

"Let's go." Vaughn opened the driver's side door and climbed in. Natalie went in through the passenger side and slid over next to Vaughn so Marv could ride with them. When they were all three set, Vaughn turned around and drove back toward the ranch.

They sat in silence with Marv examining his blood-stained cloth from time to time and Natalie trying not to notice the feel of Vaughn's leg occasionally touching hers. Vaughn seemed to be somewhat aware herself, because each time it happened, she shifted and cleared her throat. Natalie wanted to reach over and place her hand on her leg, to calm her, to let her know it was alright, but she refrained, fearing it would send the wrong signal. But the memory of Vaughn's strong thigh pressed against her body kept infiltrating her mind, making the ride and the close proximity all the more difficult. She briefly closed her eyes and centered herself, focusing instead on the problem at hand. Someone had placed that tire strip in the middle of the road. And the target seemed to be Vaughn and those going to and from her ranch. But who would do such a thing?

It had to be the former ranch hands, Ricky and Pedro. They were the only ones with the grudge. She opened her eyes.

Unless…

No. It couldn't be Allen. He would've made himself known. He would've barged in and demanded Natalie back, voicing all kinds of insults and threats to everyone he saw. And even if he would've taken the more low-key approach, he would've done a lot more than use a homemade tire strip. The whole thing seemed rather juvenile which was why she thought of the former ranch hands.

Marv took a last look at his handkerchief and folded it nicely to put in his shirt pocket. He spoke. "Looks like you've got yourself a bit of a troublemaker here, Vaughn." He glanced over at them as he dug a tin of dip out of his front pocket. He opened it, plucked out a pouch of tobacco, and tucked it in his lower lip. "You got any idea who it could be?"

"I got some idea," Vaughn said.

"Well, you ought to tan their damn hides."

"Oh, I plan on doing more than that."

"You going to get the law involved?"

"I am."

"Good. A little time in the local jail outta do 'em some good."

"I agree."

"They caused you any trouble before?"

Vaughn breathed deeply and made the turn up the ranch drive. They drove through the gate and past the mounted cameras. "They cut my fence and stole one of my best mares."

"Christ almighty." He turned to look behind them. "Is that why you got the cameras?"

"Yes, sir."

"Well, I'll be goddamned. You've got more trouble than I thought."

"It will be remedied. I can guarantee you that," Vaughn said and clenched her jaw. Natalie could feel the barely harbored anger coming off her and this time she did place her hand on her leg. Vaughn glanced at her, and Natalie gave her a soft pat.

"Yes, it will," Natalie said, removing her hand. "Rest assured."

Vaughn's stone-like face softened at that and she pulled the trailer around to the stables and parked. Marv opened his door and climbed out with a grunt, but Natalie remained, looking at Vaughn.

"You okay?" she asked.

Vaughn narrowed her eyes as she stared through the windshield. "I don't know."

"We'll get it sorted." She touched her leg again.

"We?" Vaughn asked.

Natalie nodded.

"You aren't still upset with me?" Vaughn asked.

"No."

"Thank God. I don't think I can handle much more at the moment."

"I'm sorry, Vaughn," Natalie said. "About this and about the way I've been behaving."

Vaughn looked at her. "I just want to make sure you're okay."

Natalie withdrew her hand, feeling way too much emotion toward her. She wanted to respect their boundaries, the ones Vaughn had put into place, regardless of how hard it was for her.

"I'm not," she said, being honest. "But I'm hoping I will be."

Voices came from the stables as Benny and Greer and Wyatt and Em came running out. Vaughn switched off the engine and opened the door. But before she climbed out she looked again at Natalie.

"Let me know if I can help."

Natalie smiled wistfully at her. "I will."

Vaughn emerged from the truck and the group gathered around her, asking questions and staring back at the horse trailer. Natalie sat and watched for a moment, content on remaining inside where it was relatively peaceful. It wasn't until June came out and poked her head in, that she snapped out her trance.

"You okay, darlin'?"

Natalie scooted toward her and climbed out of the truck. She once again smiled, this time feeling more certain than she had only moments ago. "I am."

## CHAPTER THIRTY-THREE

Allen gripped his desk as the line rang and the automated voice mail played. When it finished and he heard the beep, the signal to leave a message, he seethed. "I'm paying you good money. Very good money. And you don't answer your phone when I need to talk to you? Well, that had better change if you know what's good for you, Tito. You hear me?" He slammed the receiver down and leaned back in his office chair, still fuming.

How could Tito not answer his damn phone? He needed to talk to him. Jesus, he was beginning to think he'd made a mistake in hiring him. He was beginning to think the big man was as incompetent as Tom. The little runt bastard. It was his fault he was in this mess. He was the one who'd lost Natalie to begin with.

Goddammit. Why did he hire anyone?

*Because I don't have the time to do it myself.*

He couldn't go searching for Natalie and run a business. It was impossible. Someone had to keep an eye on the employees and the transactions. Otherwise, there would be no money. And money... well, that was the most important thing. Finding Natalie being a close second.

He lifted the receiver again to call his secretary, but the line beeped before he could.

"Mr. Beaufort?" his secretary said as she came on over the speaker.

"What?"

"There are two detectives here to see you."

Allen rubbed his forehead and sighed. The day was just getting better and better.

"Very well."

The secretary disconnected and a knock came from his door.

"In!"

The two detectives he'd met before walked into his office, looking very no-nonsense in their cheap suits. Christ, where did they get those horrible things?

"Mr. Beaufort. Nice to see you again."

"Make it fast, gentlemen. I have a tight schedule to keep."

The detectives sat in the chairs across from his desk. "Well, now is that any way to greet us? You'd think your first question would be in regard to Natalie and whether or not we had any news. And yet…it wasn't." He raised an eyebrow and Allen glanced away, wanting to pummel the asshole. Detective Hallorin. Yes, that was his name. Motherfucker.

When Allen said nothing, Hallorin continued. "In case you're interested, we haven't located her yet. But we've got some good leads to follow up on. One of them being you, Mr. Beaufort."

"Me?" He knew he looked disgusted. He felt it.

"Yes, sir. You're the one." He flipped open his notebook and searched the inside pocket of his suit for a pen. He found it and clicked it, ready to write.

"I can assure you that I had nothing to do with her disappearance," Allen said, trying not to talk through clenched teeth.

"Well, I'm beginning to think otherwise, Mr. Beaufort. Especially in talking to those who know Natalie best. Seems you have been in contact with her, because you've been harassing her. Is that correct?"

"I have no idea what you're talking about."

"No? See, that surprises me because her roommate, tells us that you've been having her followed."

Allen scoffed. "This is a waste of time," he said. "I've already told you—"

"Have you been having her tailed, Allen? And—" He checked his notes. "Harassing and threatening her? Despite the restraining order?"

"No."

Hallorin shifted, cleared his throat, and looked to his partner, Marks, who stood, with his phone outstretched. He showed Allen the pic on the screen, and Allen nearly cringed.

"Is that you in the photo, Mr. Beaufort?"

"It's hard to say. It's grainy."

Hallorin smiled. "It was taken from a doorbell cam from one of Natalie's neighbors. Seems you were there the day Gayle and her boyfriend claimed you were. And more than a few times before that, lurking. One time even forcing your way into the apartment. Care to fill me in on that?"

Allen didn't speak.

"Are you still unsure? Because we have more photos. A handful in fact, from all the different dates."

"What do you want?" Allen asked.

"The truth, Mr. Beaufort. If you can manage it."

Allen met his steely gaze. "Look, I may have gone to see Natalie, but I only wanted to talk to her, to beg her to come home."

"So, you forced your way in?"

"She wouldn't listen, I was desperate for her to just listen."

"And that's why you've gotten rid of her, isn't it, Mr. Beaufort?"

"No. I didn't. I—love her. She's my wife. I only want her to come home."

"And yet you have overnight guests at your house. Doesn't sound like you're missing her too much to me."

Allen narrowed his eyes. "I may have had some fun. But that's to be expected when your wife leaves you and you haven't had sex in months."

"Fun, you say?"

"That's all it was."

"Well, Mr. Beaufort, I also have a problem with that claim as well. You see, we waited outside your home when we last paid you a visit and we questioned your overnight guests. They paint a very different picture."

"Oh?"

"It seems that your idea of fun is a little different from theirs. Your idea of fun seems to be a little rougher than what they were expecting."

"I like a little bondage. So what?"

"You're a sadist, Mr. Beaufort, that goes well beyond what you refer to as a little bondage."

"I didn't do anything illegal. Those girls, they complied."

"Because you paid them. Handsomely. Which in and of itself is illegal."

"Oh, come on. Are you really here to bust my balls over some overly sensitive hookers?"

The detectives exchanged a glance. "No, we're here to find Natalie. And we believe you know where she is."

"Like I already told you, I don't."

"Then you wouldn't mind if we search your home and office?"

Allen clenched his fists, trying very hard to control his temper. "What for?"

"To search for clues, of course."

"You'll need a warrant."

Marks held up some folded papers. "We have one."

Allen stood. "You've got no right."

"Actually, we do."

"You won't find anything." He stood, so angry he could punch right through the wall. He was right though, they wouldn't find anything. At least he hoped he was right. He was usually very careful about his business dealings, as well as his personal dealings. He had to admit he'd gotten a little sloppy with the hookers, but they were just that, hookers. No one would take their word over his.

Allen stalked toward the door.

"Where are you going, Mr. Beaufort?"

"I'm seeing you out." He yanked open the door and waited. The detectives slowly stood and walked toward him. Marks handed him the warrant.

"We'll start here, at the office, while another team searches your home."

"Where am I supposed to go?"

"I'm sure you'll find someplace, Mr. Beaufort. A man of your means."

Allen fished his car keys out of his pants pocket and walked out of the office. He didn't bother to stop when his secretary asked him what was going on. He just kept walking, making his way to the elevator, wondering what in the hell he was going to do next.

## CHAPTER THIRTY-FOUR

Y ou had better do something, Theo," June said as she rose from the table to walk him to the kitchen door. "Because this time around someone got hurt and could've been killed."

Theo opened the door and placed his hat on his head. He motioned at the other officer who stood out by the cruiser that it was time to go.

"I always do my best, Mrs. Ruger. You know that."

"I don't know that, Theo. Not anymore."

He pressed his lips together in a frown. "I'm sorry you feel that way."

"Well, go and change my mind then. Punish these boys for what they done."

"They'll be punished, Mrs. Ruger."

"Right. You've just got to find them first." She shooed him out and closed the door behind him. The police had been there for a good hour or so, filling out a report and going out with Vaughn to inspect the tire contraption and to look at Marv's truck and trailer. EMS came for Marv, though he protested, and took him to the hospital to check his head. The whole afternoon into evening had been shot and she had to quickly rustle up something for supper.

She opened the fridge and grabbed a container of pork chops, glad she'd thought to thaw them. She retrieved the barbecue sauce and brought it all to the counter. She was washing her hands in the sink as she spoke to Vaughn, who was sitting behind her at the kitchen table with her head in her hands.

"I don't know why those boys are targeting us so badly," June said, checking the oven. She'd already set it to preheat. "You'd think with the law looking for them that they'd be hiding, not still coming around here making trouble."

"They're not the brightest bulbs in the bunch, Gram. And Ricky, he's vengeful. I gathered that much just from hearing things about him around town. And I reckon they've got it in for me because of my threats and because now the law is after them. Since I'm the one that set that in motion."

"Well, they'd be smart to steer clear of here."

"They would be. But like I said, they aren't exactly smart."

June sighed, wishing Ricky and Pedro would grow a brain, but realizing that would probably never happen. Not in this lifetime anyway. "You should go shower. It'll make you feel better," she said to Vaughn.

"I'm not sure anything will make me feel better right now, Gram."

June looked out the window. "Well, how about Natalie? Will she make you feel better? Because she's coming."

June turned from the sink to dry her hands as Natalie lightly knocked and stepped inside.

"Hey," she said, looking from June to Vaughn. "Saw the cops leave. Just wanted to make sure all is well."

"It's the best it can be, I suppose," June said stripping open the package of pork chops.

Natalie slowly approached Vaughn and placed a gentle hand on her shoulder. "Anything I can do? I already fed and watered Midnight and Em took care of Miracle."

"Thank you," Vaughn said, dropping her hands. She gave Natalie a tired-looking smile.

"No problem." She looked to June. "Want some help with dinner?"

"I'm not going to tell you no," June said as she placed the pork chops into a casserole dish. She walked back to the sink and washed her hands again, returned, and opened the barbecue sauce. "You can grab a bunch of potatoes and scrub them and get them ready to bake."

"On it." Natalie opened the pantry door and retrieved several baking potatoes and carried them to the sink. Vaughn stood from the table as June grabbed the sauce brush and began lathering the pork chops in sauce.

"I'm gonna go double-check on Midnight and Miracle," Vaughn said, walking to the door. She was once again moving like she was in pain and June felt as helpless as ever.

"Don't you go doing anymore work," she said. "You let them kids handle the rest of it."

"Yes, ma'am," she said as she set her hat on her head and walked out the door.

"That child," June said. "She's going to kill herself working like she does."

Natalie was scrubbing the potatoes. "I thought the new hires would lessen her load."

"I thought so too. But I think we're going to have to hire some more and even then you know she won't stop."

"She's going to have to slow down," Natalie said. "And have a doctor look at her back."

June laughed. "Hell will freeze over first."

"She can hardly walk, June. I think it's time."

"Well, maybe she'll listen to you. You seem to have an effect on her."

Natalie turned off the faucet and brought the potatoes to the counter. She took a knife and stabbed slits in them for better cooking.

"You ain't gonna say nothing to that?" June asked, readying the pork chops for the oven.

"What should I say? I haven't exactly had a good effect on her here lately."

"Well, you've been down. Hell, I think we've all been down with all that's going on." She carried the dish to the oven, opened the hinged door and slid it in. She turned back to Natalie.

"We can cook those in the microwave," she said. "Put them in for five-minute increments, turning them every time you check them."

"Yes, ma'am." Natalie took the potatoes to the microwave and set some of them inside before starting it up. "Anything else?"

June pointed to the fridge. "We need to steam some vegetables."

Natalie opened the fridge and got out two heads of broccoli and some carrots. She carried them to the sink to clean them.

In the meantime, June got the yeast rolls from the freezer and readied them for the oven by spreading a little butter on top. "How you been feeling, darlin'?" she asked. "Any better? I haven't been seeing much of you."

"I've been busy with chores and working my other online jobs."

"They must be taking up a lot of your time."

"I haven't blogged in quite some time, worried Allen would find me somehow. But I'm almost through what little savings I had, so I really need the money."

"I don't know how the whole online tracking thing works, sugar, but I doubt he'll find you if he doesn't know about the blogs. Is that what they're called?"

Natalie finished cleaning the veggies and brought them over to the counter where she began pulling the broccoli apart and snapping off the lower portion of the stems. June got her a bowl to put the pieces in.

"Mm-hm. Blogs."

"Does he know about them?"

"I'm sure he does. He's had private investigators on me and I'm sure they've discovered my income. But I don't think they can trace me here."

"Is that why you prefer to give us cash for rent?"

"Yes. I give you the cash I brought with me. Thankfully, I thought to withdraw a big amount before I took off. I've been doing that for a while now because I don't like him knowing what all I spend my money on. Just in case he has someone checking."

"What an awful way to live."

She sighed. "You get used to it."

"I've said it once and I'll say it again, I think you should go back to the police."

"I know you feel that way, June. And I hear you, I do. I'm considering all my options."

"That's good."

"And as for how I'm feeling..." She shrugged. "I'm a little better after having apologized to Vaughn. But I'm still not my usual self."

"Why do you think that is?" June grabbed a carrot and began slicing it.

"My childhood."

June glanced at her. "Oh?"

"I've been thinking a lot about the past and I didn't exactly have what you would call a standard childhood." She paused as if gathering her strength. "My father died suddenly when I was thirteen and I was put into foster care."

June stopped chopping. "Oh, child, I'm so sorry."

Natalie reached for a carrot. But she didn't start slicing. "It was rough."

"Do you mind if I ask where your mother was?"

Natalie laughed. "Mother? As far as I'm concerned I never had one. She left us when I was two, ran off with some druggie. I haven't seen her since."

June touched her arm. Natalie continued. "It doesn't matter though. It never did. My father was all I ever needed. And then he got sick and it happened quick. He was gone within six weeks of diagnosis."

"And you had no one else to take you in?"

"I did not." She finally began chopping the carrot. "So I was carted off to foster care where I suffered some more. At least at first." She stopped and stared off into space. "I just couldn't seem to do anything right. Not a thing. I was never good enough. Ever. And they let me know it." She started chopping again. "But the second house wasn't so bad. They were decent people. Unfortunately, the damage had been done and it was hard for me to overcome. I had trouble settling in, with trusting people, with school. It wasn't a fun time."

"How long were you at the second house?"

"About a year. They let me go because I kept getting suspended from school. They didn't know what to do with me."

"That's awful."

"I can't really blame them. I was lost and damaged goods and I wouldn't stop fighting at school. Wouldn't allow the bullies to get their way."

"Good for you."

She laughed. "It wasn't so good, trust me."

"And house number three?"

"House number three was not good. The man, he liked me a little too much and I wouldn't have it. So I hit him one night when he came in my room. I broke his nose and that was the end of house number three."

"Oh, no."

"Yeah," she nodded and scooped up the bit of carrots to place in the bowl.

The kitchen began to smell of barbecue and June carried the pan of yeast rolls to the oven where she slid them in on the lower rack. Natalie opened the beeping microwave and checked the potatoes, turning them over before cooking them for another five minutes.

"I managed to stay in house number four until I graduated high school and turned eighteen. But then I was out and that meant I had nowhere to go so I really struggled for a while and I…met the wrong people and got mixed up in drugs."

"Natalie, no."

"'Fraid so." She handed June the bowl of veggies and June put a pot on to boil, inserting a collapsable vegetable steamer into the pot. She poured the veggies in and put the lid on.

"But I met a really nice woman. A social worker, and she honestly saved my life. She got me into a rehab and I got cleaned up. But…that's where I met Allen. My ex-husband."

June opened the oven and checked the rolls. They weren't quite done. The pork chops, however, smelled delicious.

"Tell me about him," she said as she closed the oven door.

"There isn't much to say. He totally swept me off my feet, June. He was handsome and successful business-wise, and he seemed to really love me. Said he wanted to give me the life I'd always deserved, full of love and acceptance and security. But it was all a farce. He wasn't real. That person wasn't real. The real Allen, as I soon found out, is…your worst nightmare."

"It took me a while, but I finally managed to leave him. I had to give up everything though. Friends, finances, you name it. I was on my own once again. I slowly rebuilt a small existence, but he wouldn't let me go. He's never going to let me go."

She sat at the table and stared off into space again. June came and sat next to her. She tilted her chin toward her.

"You listen here. You will have a life again. And he will leave you alone. You just have to keep fighting."

Natalie's gaze shifted over to hers. "I don't know if I can, June. I feel so defeated. So unimportant in this world."

"That's your past haunting you. You've got to tell it to get lost, that you've already lived through it and you've moved on."

"How?"

"By doing what you just did. By talking about it and facing it. By exposing it to the sunshine, instead of letting it grow and fester in the dark."

Natalie wiped away a stray tear. "You really think that'll work?"

"I know it will."

The door opened and Vaughn came back in, removing her hat. She took one look at Natalie and June and asked, "Am I interrupting?"

"No." Natalie said. "Not at all." She smiled and wiped her eyes again.

"We're just finishing up supper," June said. "So have a seat."

Vaughn hung her hat on the back of the chair and sat, keeping her eyes on Natalie. June stood to check on the rolls again and when she glanced back at the table, she saw Vaughn and Natalie holding hands.

## CHAPTER THIRTY-FIVE

Vaughn sat on the end of her bed, putting on her cotton pajama pants and soft Wrangler T-shirt. When she was dressed, she stood at her dresser and combed her wet hair. Her day had been long, beginning at five and going well past six. She was so exhausted that she could hardly keep her head up at dinner. Thankfully, June had poured her a glass of iced tea and the caffeine in it had seemed to help. But now it was nearing nine o'clock and exhaustion was plaguing her once again. She set down her comb and examined the dark marks beneath her eyes. She looked as tired as she felt. If not more so.

She headed for the door and winced, her back tightening in pain once again. When was it going to let up?

She reached the living room and sat to slip on her sneakers. June was sitting at the desk working at the computer, her wild mane piled into a loose bun.

"Going somewhere?" she asked, peering at her over her reading glasses.

"I'm going to go check on Midnight."

"You just did that before supper."

"I need to do it again. He's anxious."

"You're not going to start sleeping out there with the horses again, are you?"

"I hope it doesn't come to that."

"Vaughn, I was kidding."

"Oh." She stood. "I'll be back in a few."

"Alright. Go, if you must."

Vaughn walked out the kitchen door into the cooling evening air. The sky was black with a few clusters of stars, the city lights too close for an exceptional view. She enjoyed looking skyward nonetheless, and she was doing so when she nearly ran into Natalie.

"Sorry, didn't mean to scare you," Natalie said, carrying her laptop. She seemed out of breath. She, too, was in her pajamas, hers a matching set of dark green satin pants and a button up shirt. Vaughn wondered if the color set off her eyes in the light.

"You didn't," Vaughn said. "What's up?"

"A lot. I'm a little panicked." She glanced around, as if to check her surroundings. "I got an email. It's—strange and I'm not sure if it's authentic."

"Okay," Vaughn said, drawing out the word.

Natalie opened her laptop like she was going to show Vaughn, but seemed to change her mind. She closed it and breathed deep. "It says it's from a detective. A Detective Marks. It says they've been looking for me for some time and that they've noticed my recent posts to my blogs."

"You've been working?"

"I have to. I need the money."

"Why didn't you tell me? We could've worked something out."

"Like what? You're already helping me out by letting me stay here."

"I don't know. I could've paid you for managing the website and posting the job listings. Or for doing the chores. Something. We could've worked something out."

"Well, I didn't want to put you out, Vaughn." She shook her head. "Anyway, this detective, he seems to have found me. Or at least seen that I've been posting. But I'm not sure it's really a detective. I mean, what if it's Allen or one of his cronies?"

"You didn't respond, did you?"

"No."

"Don't. Not until we check this out somehow."

"I've already done a search for Detective Marks. He's a real person, a real detective. And the email address looks authentic, but

I'm afraid. Even it it's really the police, I don't know if I should respond. Then someone will know where I am."

Vaughn's mind raced, searching for a solution. "Tomorrow, I'll take you into town, to an Internet cafe. You can log on there and send an email. Tell him you're fine but you don't wish to disclose your location."

"Think he'll buy it?"

"I don't see why not. It's the truth."

Natalie seemed to think it over. "I don't know, maybe I should just remain silent."

"If you do that, they may keep looking for you to confirm it's you and that you're okay."

Natalie sighed. "Shit. I'm so scared, Vaughn."

"I know. But I think this can be a good thing. Maybe you could open up a dialogue with this detective about Allen and your fears."

"Not you, too. June keeps telling me I should talk to the police."

"It's not a bad idea."

"If you knew Allen, you'd understand why I don't want to take that risk."

"But, Natalie, you're safe here. No one—"

A sharp cone of headlights shone on them as a vehicle pulled in from the drive.

Natalie stiffened. "Oh, no. It's him. He's found me."

"It's not him," Vaughn said. "It can't be."

They both watched, frozen in shock, as the vehicle pulled up and the back passenger door opened. A woman stepped out into the dim lighting of the porch light and came toward them.

"Vaughn Marie, is that you, my darlin'?"

Vaughn stared, dumbfounded. "Mom?"

"Hey, sweetie!" She hurried up to her and threw her arms around her, hanging off her neck. Vaughn grimaced as her back spasmed, but she was careful not to make a noise.

"What are you doing here?" Vaughn asked, drawing away. Her mother released her, much to her relief, and smiled up at her.

"Surprise!"

Vaughn blinked in disbelief. "Are you really here?"

"I am." She pinched Vaughn's cheek.

"But—how?"

"It's magic," she said with a laugh. She squeezed Vaughn's cheek again and spoke to the Uber driver who had retrieved her bags from the back hatch of the vehicle. Her mother took her two rolling suitcases and wheeled them toward the guesthouse, her gaze still on Vaughn.

"Are you surprised? I knew you would be." She stopped mid stride as she finally noticed Natalie. "Who's this?"

"This is Natalie. She's—"

"I'm—"

"She's a good friend who's staying in the guesthouse," Vaughn quickly said.

Her mother appeared confused for a second, but then seemed to recognize her somehow. "Oh, right. So you're Natalie."

"There's room in the main house for you," Vaughn explained. "You can have the spare bedroom."

"It's okay, Vaughn," Natalie said. "She can have the guesthouse. I can go get my things."

"No, absolutely not," her mother said. She stepped forward and shook Natalie's hand. "You're fine right where you are. And I'm Vivian, by the way."

"Natalie."

"Hello, Natalie. My, aren't you a cute little thing."

Vaughn wasn't sure if Natalie was blushing, but Vaughn sure was. Natalie was cute. Beyond cute. She was downright stunning, even in the dim light of night and it seemed her mother had noticed just as much as she had.

How Natalie could think that Em would ever turn her head was crazy. The cowgirl was attractive, in a young tomboy kind of way, but that was just it. She was young. Too young. And she was her employee. How could she get Natalie to see that?

Vaughn tried to take her mother's suitcases from her. But she caught one look at the way Vaughn was walking and refused.

"Huh-uh, little miss. You look like you've done enough lifting already."

"I'm fine," Vaughn said, trying again to take the cases. But her mother shooed her away.

"Here, allow me," Natalie said, stepping up to take the bags. She rolled them up onto the porch and opened the door. Vaughn watched as her mother smiled and joined Natalie at the door, touching her shoulder as she walked inside ahead of her. "And you're an angel too."

Vaughn followed them inside and called out for Gram. "Gram, we have a surprise for you."

She came into to the kitchen and her eyes widened at Vivian. "Well, my goodness. I didn't think you would get here as soon as today!" The two embraced and Vaughn eased into a chair, her back now in constant pain, whereas before the pain came in stabbing attacks. She stared them down.

"Wait a minute, you knew she was coming?" Vaughn asked.

Gram shrugged. "Maybe."

"She told me all about what's going on around here and I just had to come," her mother said.

"As they say, wild horses couldn't keep her away," Gram said with a grin. She brushed Vivian's graying hair away from her face and kissed her cheek. Soon, Vaughn thought, her mother's hair would be entirely white, just like Gram's. The two were so much alike, even in looks. The only difference, other than the age gap, was their creativity. Gram had a fondness for cooking and landscaping, whereas her mother had a passion for painting and sculpting. Both were incredible talents and Vaughn knew she'd inherited her own creativity with photography from both of them.

Natalie spotted her brief cringe from the pain in her back and came to her side.

"Are you okay?"

Vaughn gripped her lower back. "Don't say anything, but I think it's getting worse."

"What can I do?"

"Get me that ice pack from the freezer if you would."

Natalie gave Vaughn's shoulder a squeeze and waited a moment for Gram and Vivian to head off toward the bedroom. She opened the freezer and dug out the blue ice pack, wrapped a dish towel around it, and brought it to Vaughn. "Do you want to sit in the living room? Maybe lie on the couch?"

"Can't. I still need to check on Midnight."

"I can do it."

"Would you mind?"

"Not at all."

"I really appreciate it." Vaughn tried to stand, but she cried out at the immense pain. Natalie gripped her arm and helped her straighten.

"Holy shit, that hurt," Vaughn said, finally able to move.

"Come on, let's get you to bed."

"I'm not ready for bed."

"Too bad. I'm making the call and I say you're going to bed."

Vaughn gritted her teeth as she moved, one foot slowly in front of the other. "I'm hurting too damn bad to argue with you. Just get me there."

They headed through the living room and down the hallway. They were just about to enter Vaughn's bedroom when Gram and her mother emerged from the spare room. They immediately noticed Vaughn's stature.

"Your back?" Gram said, coming to her side.

"I'm fine," Vaughn tried, not wanting to worry them.

"She's far from fine," Natalie said.

Vaughn gave her a look. Natalie didn't back down. "Vaughn, you're not okay."

"Tell me how bad it is," her mother said, walking up to her to touch her face.

Vaughn winced as she tried to turn to go into the bedroom. "It's pretty bad."

"She needs a doctor," Natalie said. "But first, let's get her to the bed." The three of them helped guide Vaughn into her room and onto her bed. Natalie knelt and removed her sneakers, gently lifting and swinging her legs over onto the mattress. She waited while Vaughn rolled onto her side, then she placed the ice pack behind her and Vaughn eased back over. Natalie draped the covers over her and adjusted her pillows.

"I'm going to go get her some Aleve," Natalie said, leaving the room.

Her mother came to her and took her by the hand. "Looks like you've got a pretty good friend there."

"Natalie's...special."

"I can see that."

"She's heaven-sent is what she is," Gram said, adjusting the ceiling fan speed with the remote. "You want it higher?"

"Low is fine." She didn't want to wake up cold. It was hard telling if she'd be able to reach for another blanket. "No need to fuss," she said as she looked at the both of them.

"Nonsense," her mother said. "Let us fuss. It's our job, as your mother and grandmother."

Vaughn closed her eyes, absolutely exhausted and overwhelmed by the pain. "Like I told Natalie, I'm in too much pain to argue."

"I'm going to call the doctor's office first thing tomorrow morning," Gram said.

"I'm sure I'll be fine come morning," Vaughn said.

"Bullarkey. You're going in and that's that. No getting out of it this time."

"You really should go," her mother said. "Gram's told me how bad it's been."

Natalie entered the room carrying two frosted bottles of water and a bottle of Aleve. She handed one water to Vaughn and dispensed an Aleve into her palm. "You want another? You can take two."

"I don't know if I should." She didn't like taking medicine. Didn't like anything foreign in her body. She'd had to convince herself to take Advil on the regular, otherwise she couldn't work. So, one Aleve was stretching it.

"You can hardly move. I think you better take two," Natalie said.

"Listen to her," Gram said.

Vaughn finally agreed, knowing she probably needed it, but also feeling ridiculous for all the fuss. She swallowed the pills with the water and returned the water bottle back to Natalie who set everything on the nightstand. "It's all right here if you need it."

"Okay. Thanks. And thanks for checking on Midnight. You'll do that right now, won't you?"

"On my way."

"If he's acting anxious, his calming supplements are on the shelf in front of his stall.

"Got it."

"And maybe some of his sweet mix."

"Of course."

"And, Natalie? He likes it when you sing to him."

Natalie smiled. "I can't carry a tune."

"I don't think he cares. And will you come back and give me an update?"

"Sure." She smiled again and left the room. Once again, her mother spoke.

"She really is an angel. Please tell me she's more than a friend."

Vaughn's eyes began to feel heavy in the low lamplight. She blinked slowly, her mother going in and out of focus. "No." She licked her dry lips. "Not yet."

## CHAPTER THIRTY-SIX

Natalie hummed to Midnight as she massaged his neck while watching him eat a little of his sweet mix. The stallion had calmed considerably since she'd arrived, and she could tell they were both getting sleepy. It was time to rest.

She removed the feed bucket, gave him one last pat, and left the stall. He watched her with his large, liquid black eyes. She blew him a kiss. "Good night, sweet boy." She secured the door and walked away, still humming. When she reached the entrance to the stables, she switched off the main lights and headed for the house. She was still in her pajamas and slippers, deciding to visit Midnight without changing first. A few horse hairs never hurt anyone and her slippers, well, a little dirt never hurt anyone either.

She knocked softly on the kitchen door and entered the house. It was quiet, the kitchen lit by the light over the stove. She moved silently, and crept through the living room back to Vaughn's room, where she again gave a soft rap and opened the door. Vaughn lay asleep on the bed, snuggled in her soft blue blanket and bedsheet, lit by the bedside lamp. Her snores were soft and almost inaudible. Natalie smiled, amused, and approached the bed. She reached out to switch off the bedside lamp, but Vaughn stirred and her eyes flitted open.

"Natalie," she said. And it sounded soft and raspy, very much like it had on the night of their first kiss. Natalie warmed from head to toe, wanting to kiss her once again. To hold her and cradle her from the pain. But doing so would probably only cause more pain, in more ways than one, at least for the time being.

"I'm here," she said, brushing her hair away from her face. Her cheeks were tinged red from the heat of sleep, her sun-streaked hair mussed. She looked adorable and so enticing. If she could just lie down next to her and snuggle.

No.

*I can't.*

She chided herself for allowing her mind to go there again.

"Midnight?" Vaughn asked, her eyes looking incredibly heavy.

"He's sleeping tight."

"You?" she asked, surprising her.

"I will be soon, too."

"You, want to…. stay?"

Natalie wasn't sure she'd heard her right. Vaughn spoke again.

"Sleep here. Next to me. Where it's safe."

"Vaughn, I—" God, she wanted to. More than anything. But she knew she wouldn't be able to sleep being so close to her. She'd only keep her awake as she tossed and turned, trying to settle her anxious mind and her yearning body. It just wasn't a good time. For either of them.

"Please. I'm…worried."

Natalie took her hand. It was warm, the palm rough in spots from callouses. It stirred her nevertheless and she struggled to speak, to decline her invitation. "I'll stay on the couch. How's that?"

Vaughn's eyes fell closed and stayed that way. "'Kay."

Natalie lightly brushed her lips across the back of her hand and switched off the bedside lamp. Then she carefully pulled the door closed and walked into the living room. She sat on the couch, slid out of her slippers, and lay down, pulling the throw off the back of the sofa to cover her body. She stared up at the ceiling in the quiet house for what felt like hours before her eyes grew heavy. But when she glanced at the clock above the desk it read ten thirty. It had only been a few minutes.

With a deep breath, she rolled onto her side, closed her eyes, and fell asleep.

When she woke, she was confused as to where she was. But a quick look around grounded her and she sat up. It was still dark out. The clock read three thirty. She wasn't sure what had woken her. She sat very still, listening. A rustling sound came from outside. And what sounded like whispers. She went rigid with fear. Had she locked the kitchen door? She hadn't. Oh, no.

It was Allen. He'd found her and he was there.

She wanted to bolt, to run to Vaughn's room, but she couldn't bring herself to move. The only thing she could do was reach over and turn on the living room lamp. She sat there, heart thudding, mind on fire with thoughts of fear and doom. More rustling, hurried whispers, then in the near distance, the sound of an engine. She looked toward the window, through the sheer drapes. She saw the flash of headlights as a vehicle turned around and started down the drive, disappearing into the early morning darkness.

Whoever it was, was gone.

She exhaled and nearly fell over with relief. When she'd regained her bearings and her courage, she rose and walked to the kitchen door. The first thing she did was lock it, and the second thing she did was peek outside through the window. But she saw nothing and no one in the dim light. Only the vacant front yard and the two trucks. Beyond that, in the darkness, sat the rest of the ranch, quietly sleeping.

But someone had been there. She was sure of it.

She walked back through the living room and down the hallway, choosing to stop at June's door where she knocked softly before cracking it open.

"June," she whispered. "June, wake up."

"Natalie?" she rasped.

"I think someone was just here."

June switched on her bedside lamp and swung her legs over the bed. She eased into her slippers and stood to slip into her robe. She followed Natalie down the hallway, Natalie whispering along the way. "I was asleep on the couch and I woke and heard someone out front. I saw headlights as they turned and drove away."

"Did you see who it was?"

"No. I was—too afraid to get up and look. But I switched on the lamp, and I think it scared them away."

"You did good." June patted her shoulder and went to the gun cabinet nestled in the far corner near the back door. She pulled out a rifle, made sure it was loaded, and grabbed a flashlight to walk into the kitchen. Natalie followed her.

"Should I wake Vaughn?"

"Not yet." June stood sideways against the door and peered outside through the window. She unlocked the door, pulled it open, and stepped outside. Natalie once again followed and they stepped out onto the porch.

The early morning had a pleasant chill to it and Natalie hugged herself as they searched the property, taking a tentative step off the porch. June switched on the flashlight and swung the beam of light around.

Natalie held her breath as the light fell upon the front landscaping and the vehicles. She was certain someone was going to jump out and attack. Certain it would be Allen.

"I don't see nothing," June said. "They must be gone."

"I saw them drive away." But she wasn't absolutely certain someone hadn't remained behind. "But still, we should look."

June walked closer to the vehicles and stopped dead in her tracks, pointing the beam of light at the tires on Vaughn's truck. "Look," she said.

"Oh my God." The tires were slashed. June aimed the light on her truck. It seemed to be fine. Maybe Natalie really had scared them away before they could damage June's tires.

"Sons a bitches," June said, furious. She marched back up to the house and killed the flashlight beam. Natalie hurried after her and they walked back inside. June closed the door behind them and Natalie made sure to bolt it. June saw her.

"Let 'em come in. They can meet the end of my rifle." She shook the rifle briefly as she spoke and leaned it against the counter before switching on the coffee pot. Then she collapsed into a chair at the table and motioned for Natalie to join her.

"What are we going to do?" Natalie asked.

"Other than buy Vaughn new tires? I don't rightly know."

"Do you think it was those boys?" She had to know. Because if June was certain it was them, it couldn't be Allen and she could at least take some comfort in that.

"I don't know. Probably. You said you heard whispers. As in more than one?"

"I think so."

"It's probably those two jackasses. Theo probably hasn't caught them yet and they're lashing out, having some fun with us."

But Natalie still wasn't sure. The email had really shaken her up. June seemed to notice her doubt.

"You don't think so?" she asked.

Natalie hesitated. "I don't know, June. I—" She told June about the email and about her fears. June listened quietly and rose to pour them both some coffee.

"I doubt it was him, hon," she said, taking a sip from her mug as she handed Natalie hers. "He sounds like the type of man that would make more of an entrance. Not slash some tires in the night and run away."

"You're probably right." But was she? It would be like Allen to toy with her, to frighten her and make her second-guess her every move. He'd gotten pretty good at it.

"You still don't seem convinced," June said.

Natalie wrapped her hands around the hot cup. "I probably won't ever relax until he's behind bars or out of the country or..." She shook her head, not wanting to go there.

"Dead?"

"I would never wish him dead."

"No, you wouldn't. But it sounds like he's wished you dead more than a few times. He strangled you, for God's sake."

"He wanted to scare me."

"And he did. But, Natalie, someone like that...they will do it again and they will escalate. It's not safe for you."

Natalie cocked her head. "You sound like you volunteered at a women's shelter or something?"

"Darlin' I *was* the women's shelter. As I told you briefly before, my sister, God bless her, went through something very similar amidst her divorce. And I tell ya, she's never been the same and that man hasn't bothered her for a decade or more now."

"He hasn't? What made him stop?"

"Prison."

"Oh."

"Yeah, he got put away for what he did to Sissy. But still, she's never been the same."

"I'm sorry."

June waved her off. "No need to be sorry. Just want you know so you can make the best decision for you."

"But it's why you want me to go to the police, isn't it?"

"So, you don't end up like her, being afraid to go out, being afraid of everyone you meet? Yes. It would be a shame for you to end up like that, Natalie. It would break my heart. Or worse you could get hurt. Hurt real bad. And I'd…never get over it."

Natalie teared up. She reached for June's hand and held it. "I know you care. And I thank you." They locked eyes for a moment and then withdrew their hands to sip their coffee.

"Don't thank me, just listen to me."

Natalie chuckled and grew serious once again. "What do you think Vaughn's going to do about the tires?"

"Well, she'll be madder than a hornet, that's for sure. But other than that, there's not much she can do considering her back."

"Yeah, I think she's going to be down for a while and that's going to really upset her."

"It will. But we've got to get her better."

Natalie nodded and took another sip. "You're going to call Theo, right?"

"No. I'm going above Theo this time. That little runt can just get over it. It's his cousin doing this, and he's got no business handling it."

"I agree."

June mumbled to herself as she continued to drink. From behind June, Natalie saw Vaughn walk slowly into the kitchen. She was holding her back and bent forward at the waist. "What's going on? Why are you two up?"

June looked to Natalie and then back to Vaughn. She exhaled. "We got a problem." She stood and took Vaughn outside.

## CHAPTER THIRTY-SEVEN

June climbed out of the Gator and came around to help Vaughn. They walked slowly to the front gate where they stopped and stared. Dawn had broken and the sky was a pale gray, light enough for them to see. In the distance, Diablo crowed his morning tune, waking the rest of the ranch.

She and Vaughn had already examined the tires on Vaughn's truck and discovered they'd indeed been slashed with a sharp object. And now they stood at the gate, which hung open at an angle where it had obviously been tampered with, the two cameras that had been posted, dangling in the breeze, hung by the wires that had helped to secure them.

"You get any feed from those cameras?" June asked.

Vaughn looked pale, sick with disgust and pain. She staggered a little as she dug her phone out from her back pocket. She brought up the feed from the cameras and stood closer to June so she could see. They watched as a small pickup truck approached the gate and someone climbed out, dressed head to toe in black, and sprayed something on the lens. They weren't able to see anything, then the feed flashed and went off as the cameras were destroyed.

"Look like one of the boys?" June asked.

"I can't tell."

"Me neither."

Vaughn put her phone away and pulled on the gate. It swung haphazardly and squeaked in protest.

"I understand the cameras," Vaughn said. "But did they really have to destroy the gate too?"

June kicked at the dirt. "Come on, let's get back to the house. You need to get off your feet."

"Getting me off my feet ain't gonna do anybody any good."

"It'll do you good. Now come on."

June helped her walk back to the Gator where they both climbed in. June drove the long way back to the house so they could check the fence line for possible damage. Thankfully, they found nothing else amiss.

June pulled to a stop in front of the house, but Vaughn didn't move to get out. "We need to check the horses," she said.

"Natalie and Vivian already did, remember? They did that right away."

"I want to see for myself."

"Vaughn, they're fine."

"Gram, you either drive me over there or I walk."

June sighed. "Child, I don't know who you're gonna kill first. You or me." She drove the Gator over to the stables and climbed out to help Vaughn inside. They checked each stall, made sure each horse was okay before June could talk her back outside and get her back to the house. Once there, Vivian helped June get Vaughn onto the couch, boots off, and an ice pack secured at her lower back. June then handed her the remote control.

"What's this for?" Vaughn asked.

"The television, what else?"

Vaughn tossed it aside.

"You gonna pout all day?"

"Maybe."

"Lord help us all, Vaughn's pouting." June walked away as Vivian passed her with a mug of black coffee for Vaughn. "Careful, she's being difficult," June said. She entered the kitchen, switched on the oven to preheat, and pulled her bowl of flour out from under the sink for biscuits. She got the milk, poured some in the bowl, opened the container of Crisco, and dipped her hand in, scooping out a couple of dollops to mix into the flour as well. She stood there mixing with her hands until she had herself a good dough and then she scooped out small handfuls to put on a greased pan. When she finished, she slid the pan in the oven and washed her hands. Natalie walked in, holding the basket of fresh eggs, which she set on the counter. She smelled of the earth and the morning chill, her face flushed with it. She took off her ball cap, one June recognized as one of Vaughn's, and ran her hands through her short dark hair before returning the hat to her head.

"Well, how are things? Was anything else damaged?"

June restarted the coffee pot and took the eggs to wash them. "The front gate and cameras. They're a total loss."

"The cameras? Shit, I had forgotten about those. Were they able to pick up anything before they were damaged?"

"Just some man climbing out of a little pickup. He was covered in black. Couldn't make out nothing."

"Damn."

June turned, placing the eggs in her apron. "Your man, he doesn't drive a little pickup, does he?" She didn't think it was Natalie's ex, but she wanted to be sure and she wanted Natalie to be sure. Maybe it would help to put her mind at ease.

"Allen? Gosh no. He drives a black Mercedes. Among other luxury cars."

"Oh, right. Well, see then? It's not him."

"Allen would never bring his Mercedes out here on the dirt roads."

"I don't think it was him, Natalie. He would've tried to do something to you, wouldn't he?"

"I wasn't in the guesthouse though. I was in here."

June grew quiet. She knew she couldn't convince her. She stood at the island and cracked the eggs into the mixing bowl as the kitchen began to smell like fresh biscuits. Natalie came to her side. "Want some help?"

"You can get the bacon out."

Natalie opened the fridge and got out the bacon. Next she retrieved two frying pans. One for the eggs, one for the bacon. "Thank you, darlin'," June said. "Why don't you go check on Vaughn? She might like a refill on her coffee."

"Where is she?"

"I'm in the living room," Vaughn called. "And I can hear you, so don't say anything bad about me."

"Wouldn't dream of it," June said, laughing.

Natalie disappeared into the living room as Vivian entered the kitchen.

"Need any help, Mama?"

"You can put that bacon on to fry."

"How much?"

"Enough to feed an army. Benny and Greer will be here."

"Say no more." She got busy turning on the stovetop and frying up the bacon. "You call the doctor yet?" she asked softly. June stood next to her at the stove and readied the eggs for the pan.

"Too early still."

"How are we gonna get her to go?"

"Knock her out if we have to. But she's going."

Vivian laughed. "I dread the fight already." She shook her head. "She doesn't look good, Mama. I think you're right. She's overwhelmed."

"She is."

"I should've come sooner."

"What could you have done? She won't listen to no one."

Vivian turned to look behind them. "She seems to listen to Natalie pretty well."

"That's because she's got a soft spot for her."

"She likes her? I knew it!" she whispered.

"She just doesn't know what to do about it yet. She's fighting it some I think."

"That's Vaughn. Always the stubborn one."

"Well, after Jeanie and that mess, I can't say as I blame her."

June waited while the bacon snapped and fried before she poured her egg mixture into her pan.

Vivian glanced over at her. "So, what's Natalie's story?"

June hesitated. "I'll fill you in later."

"Uh-oh. That bad?"

"It's not her. It's her ex-husband. Think Sissy all over again."

"Oh, no. Poor thing."

"She's having a time of it."

"He's not coming around here, is he? You don't think last night was him do you?"

"No, no. It was those boys, I'd bet on it. No, Natalie's husband doesn't know she's here. She's sort of hiding out."

"Ah. Gotcha. Probably smart if he's anything like Aunt Sissy's ex."

"What are you two gabbing about?" Natalie asked as she walked back into the kitchen.

"We're talking about you," June let out, causing Vivian to guffaw.

"Well, don't let me stop you," Natalie said with a smile.

"We were just saying that you seem to have an effect on Vaughn. A positive effect."

Natalie glanced back toward the living room. "You hear that, Vaughn?"

"Yeah."

"I have a positive effect on you, so that means you've got to listen to me."

"Not a chance."

Natalie laughed. "So much for that positive effect." She refilled the coffee mug and returned to the living room.

"She's adorable," Vivian said, turning the bacon. "I hope Vaughn can see that."

"Oh, I think she does. She just needs time to work it out. They both do."

"Well, let's hope that time comes sooner rather than later."

"From your lips to God's ears, honey."

## CHAPTER THIRTY-EIGHT

Tito pulled his SUV over on the dirt road near the Midnight Mine Ranch and killed the engine. He removed his binoculars from the case and put them up to his eyes and adjusted the lenses. In the distance, he saw movement on the ranch near the stables. Two men and one woman. He focused in on the woman. It was Natalie Brewer. He could tell by the short dark hair and petite build. She was leading a chestnut horse into a corral.

He continued to watch her and study her surroundings. He knew the ranch was relatively small by ranch standards, with only a few employees. He also knew that the ranch was only barely able to make ends meet, with its owners, Vaughn and June Ruger, doing all they could to save it. And it seemed that Natalie was doing her best to help. She seemed to know her way around the horses and the ranch, helping quite a bit, something he hadn't expected, based on the things Allen Beaufort had told him about her. According to Allen, Natalie was a spoiled brat who only appreciated stature and wealth and she'd stolen from him when she left him. But in watching her these past few days, he was beginning to doubt that story. He was beginning to doubt a lot of things about Allen.

As if on cue, his phone rang, announcing Allen as the caller. He held the phone, looking at the screen, debating whether or not to answer. But he knew if he didn't that Allen would just keep calling, harassing him to no end.

"Yeah," he answered.

Allen immediately started in on him. "Where have you been? What's going on?"

"I'm doing the job you paid me for."

"Well, how am I supposed to know that when I can't get a hold of you, you fucking moron?"

"I'm working."

"What about Natalie?"

"What about her?"

"Are you really doing your job?"

"Yes."

"Not good enough."

"You're allowed your opinion."

Allen groaned. "Listen, you fucking moron of a giant, I'm going to do things from here on out, you got me? I'm not happy with you or the job you're doing."

"Fine."

"Fine?" He continued to yell at him and cuss him. Tito pulled the phone away from his ear and ended the call. He tossed the phone into the passenger seat as it rang again, announcing Allen as the caller. He ignored it.

He brought the binoculars back up to his face and found Natalie once again. Now she was walking with one of the owners, Vaughn Ruger. Vaughn appeared to be in great pain, struggling to walk as she held her back. Natalie helped her, guiding her to a nearby truck as the other ranch owner emerged, June Ruger. The two of them helped Vaughn into the truck. Then June climbed behind the wheel as another woman, one he didn't recognize, also climbed into the vehicle.

He shifted in his seat as the truck began to drive away, leaving the ranch behind. He set down his binoculars and started his engine. It was time to move.

He turned the vehicle around and drove to the back side of the ranch, intent on getting some more work done with Vaughn and June now gone, whether Allen Beaufort liked it or not.

## CHAPTER THIRTY-NINE

The ride to the doctor's office was awful and Vaughn was grateful when they finally arrived and she could stand, freeing herself from the uncomfortable seat of the truck. Her legs were wobbly as she carefully emerged and stood on the pavement. Her mother was instantly at her side, gripping her arm as Gram locked up the vehicle.

"I can do it," she managed to say as the two of them tried to lead her inside the doctor's office. She was tired and cranky and in horrible pain. And she was sick of all the fuss everyone was making over her. But more than that, she was worried about the two idiots who were targeting her and the ranch. What would they do next? Hurt someone? Steal another horse? Her ranch, her employees, and her loved ones were in danger, and the cops were doing jack shit about it. She didn't know what she was going to do, but she knew she needed to do something. The police just weren't cutting it.

She made it into the medical building and all the way up to the elevator before Gram started talking about going to get her a wheelchair. "Absolutely not," Vaughn said. "I can make it."

"Vaughn, you can hardly move," Gram said.

"It will hurt worse to sit in a wheelchair." It was true, she knew that from sitting on the car ride over. But it was more than that and she knew it. She pushed her pride from her mind and left it at that. It would just be too uncomfortable, and thankfully, her mother and Gram seemed to accept it. So she forged on, rode the elevator up to the second floor, and staggered all the way down the long hallway to her doctor's office.

Unfortunately, she had to sit in the waiting area after checking in, but it soon became too painful so she vacillated between sitting and standing as she waited. When she finally went back and saw the doctor, she didn't receive great news. Her doctor referred her to a neuro-spinal center for a consultation and told her to rest. She argued with her, telling her about the ranch and all that needed to be done, but her doctor held firm. Vaughn walked out with her paperwork, too upset to talk. So her mother and Gram helped her back to the truck in silence. They made it halfway home before they couldn't contain themselves any longer.

"Well, you gonna tell us what's going on?" Gram asked as she drove.

Vaughn stared out the window, feeling trapped by pain and overzealous fussing from her mother and Gram. She wanted to jump out of the truck.

"I have to see another doctor. A neurosurgeon."

"A neurosurgeon?" Vivian asked.

"Yes. She said I should consult a neurosurgeon because it involves my nerves. So she referred me to the Barrow Brain and Spine Center."

"She thinks it's that bad?" Gram asked, looking over at her.

"She suspects. And no, I don't know anything else."

Her mother placed her hand on her leg. "I know you're in pain, Vaughn, and you're upset, but you're going to have to talk to us. We need to know what's going on."

Vaughn sighed and rubbed her forehead. Her mother was right. "I'm sorry, I'm just…"

"You don't have to apologize for feeling crummy," Gram said. "Just fill us in."

"Well, I can't work," Vaughn said, her voice cracking with emotion. She'd never said those words before and they nearly tore her throat as they fought their way out. "She said I have to rest." Even if she tried to work she knew she wouldn't be able to. She was hurting too damn bad now.

"I'm sorry," her mother said. "I know this is hard on you."

"I've never not worked."

"I know. But it's only temporary. And I'm here, I'll help."

"It won't be enough," Vaughn said. "I mean, it's appreciated, but it won't be enough. Not with all the new business."

"We'll hire a couple more hands," Gram said. "I know things will continue to be tight if we do, but we got no other choice."

Vaughn closed her eyes and massaged her brow. "You're right," she finally said, opening her eyes to stare out into the passing desert.

"We'll get on that with Natalie first thing when we get home."

"Natalie? She helps with the hiring?" her mother asked.

"She posts the job listings for us on numerous websites," Vaughn said. "She also made us a whole new website for the ranch. She did a really good job."

"Did she? Wow. The more I hear about her, the more I like her, and I didn't think it was possible to like her any more than I already did."

"She's a little trouper," Gram said. "You don't know the half of it."

"I know she sounds like a keeper," her mother said, smiling over at Vaughn. She patted her leg. "What do you think?"

"I think I'd rather not discuss my romantic life with my mother and grandmother right now." Mainly because she didn't know what to say in response to her mother's question. She had too many other things on her mind at the moment. Maybe when all this chaos slowed down she could take the time to reevaluate and go from there.

"Oh, alright. I guess I can understand that," her mother said. "I never did like discussing your father with your gram and gran. It just felt weird."

"Thank you," Vaughn said, grabbing her mother's hand to hold. "I appreciate you understanding."

"You know, I've been thinking…" her mother said.

"Uh-oh," Gram said. "That's always a frightening statement."

"Funny, Mama." Her mother continued. "I'm selling my place in Taos."

"You are?" Gram asked, turning to look at her.

"I've wanted to for a while now."

"Why?" Vaughn asked. Her mother, as far as she knew, loved living in Taos and selling her art. This was definitely news.

"Well, because I miss home. I miss you," she said, squeezing Vaughn's hand. "And you, Mama. And well, I think it's time to come back home. Especially now with all the help that's needed."

Gram smiled and patted her leg. "Well, I'm just thrilled! I'll have both my girls. Doesn't get much better than that."

Vaughn smiled at her as well. "That's great news, Mom. I've really missed you."

"Thank you, sweetie."

"Will you still paint?"

"Oh, I'll always paint. I just might not do it full-time. At least not until you and the ranch get back on your feet."

"Just think," Gram said. "The three Ruger women all under one roof again." But her face clouded. "Unless Natalie leaves. Then you'd be in the guesthouse I suppose."

"Natalie's leaving?" her mother asked.

"At some point I reckon she will," Gram said.

Her mother looked over at Vaughn. "Why would she leave? I thought she was happy at the ranch and with you."

"She is," Vaughn said. "But it was only a temporary arrangement." She leaned forward to look over at Gram. "Has she said she's leaving, Gram?"

"She's talking about it again. Talking about her future and looking for a place online. I don't think she wants to stay in Phoenix. She's still too worried about her ex-husband."

Vaughn's stomach clenched. "I wish I could fix that situation."

"Don't we all."

"Maybe you could talk to her," Gram said. "See what she's thinking."

"Yes, please do," her mother said. "I'd hate to see her go. I'd really like to get to know her better."

Vaughn nodded and stared out through the windshield. *Natalie's thinking about leaving Phoenix?* While she understood why, she didn't like the idea. In fact, it made her feel sick inside and panicked. Her heart was racing. She had to talk to her. Had to stop her. She couldn't leave. Not the ranch, nor Phoenix.

"I'll talk to her when we get home." This was something that could not wait. She didn't want Natalie taking off like she did last time. And knowing Natalie and the way she feared confrontation and her ex-husband, she just might try to pack up and sneak off, thinking it was the safest way to do it.

God, were any of them safe right now? What with Ricky and Pedro roaming free and doing as they pleased to make their life hell, and Natalie's ex-husband lurking somewhere, none of them were safe and it was an awful feeling.

Her head hurt just thinking about it all. And her back was damn near killing her from sitting so long. Thankfully, they were almost back at the ranch.

Gram exited I-17 and turned off onto the private road. They drove for a few minutes before they passed an oncoming vehicle. Gram slowed and pulled over as the SUV drove by, not bothering to slow for them at all. Vaughn turned and tried to get a good look at the driver, but he'd blown by them, kicking up dirt along the way.

His tag said Arizona, so he was local.

"Who was that?" her mother asked, looking behind them as well.

"Some asshole," Gram said, pulling back onto the dirt road.

"I don't know," Vaughn said. "I hope it wasn't Natalie's ex."

"She said he drives a fancy Mercedes," Gram said.

Vaughn glanced behind them once again, not having a good feeling about the mysterious SUV. Where was he going so fast and more importantly, where was he coming from?

"Do you think it was those ranch hands who've been bothering you?" her mother asked.

"No. They don't have the money for a nice SUV like that. And the driver looked to be alone," Vaughn said. "Whoever it was had to be coming from the ranch, so I guess we'll soon find out who it was from the others."

"I guess so," Gram said as she slowed to turn onto the drive.

But Vaughn still had a bad feeling. And she hoped, as they drove up to the damaged gate and cameras, that she wouldn't find more chaos ahead.

## CHAPTER FORTY

Natalie stood in the corral rubbing down O'Malley and trying her best not to pace when she saw Vaughn's truck pulling up the drive. She made herself wait patiently, until they'd parked in front of the house before she left the corral and walked over to meet them, swallowing the rising ball in her throat as she did.

Vaughn crawled slowly from the truck and Natalie hurried to her side as Vivian slid out and gripped her other arm. June went ahead and opened the kitchen door as they led her inside.

"Who was here?" Vaughn asked, while wincing in pain.

Natalie didn't answer. She didn't want to upset her until she was safely lying down, either on her bed or the couch. But Vaughn didn't let up.

"We passed him on the way in. He was speeding. Driving like a madman in some expensive SUV."

Natalie silently prayed as her heart about beat out of her chest. It was happening. Right now. Her time at the ranch had finally come to an end. Oh, God. What would happen next? No matter what, she wouldn't let anything happen to Vaughn, June or Vivian. Even if that meant she had to take off again, this time for good.

"Natalie?" Vaughn said as they entered the house.

"Do you want to lie on the couch or your bed?" Natalie asked, still trying to put her off.

"I want you to answer me," Vaughn said. She stopped her progress and looked at Natalie. Natalie motioned toward the couch.

"On the sofa first."

Vaughn grimaced but listened, walking to the couch where she slowly sat and allowed Natalie to remove her shoes to put her feet up. Once she was settled, she grabbed her hand, not allowing her to walk away.

"Tell me," she said. "Who was here?"

Vivian and June were looking at her too, with questions in their eyes. Natalie trembled as she removed the paper from her jeans pocket. Still shaking, she managed to open it and hand it to Vaughn, who read it quietly.

"Where did you get this?"

"It was on the door to the guesthouse. I didn't see it in the dark when I went to change earlier this morning. So, I didn't find it until after you left."

Natalie reread the note as Vaughn looked at it. It read: LEAVE OR ELSE.

"So, the man we saw? He did this?" Vaughn asked.

"I don't know," Natalie said. "If the man was Allen, I guess so."

"Wait," June said. "It was probably whoever slashed the tires. Don't you reckon?"

"Then who was the man and why didn't he come to the ranch? He was driving away from it," Vaughn said. "Like a crazy man."

Natalie shook her head. "It's Allen. All of it. That note proves it."

Vaughn chewed her lip, handing the note back to Natalie. "Not necessarily."

"Vaughn, come on!" Natalie said. She refolded the note and shoved it in her pocket. She wanted to burn the damn thing, but she held on to it, afraid to destroy it. She might need it to show to the police, if she decided to call them.

"It doesn't necessarily mean it's Allen," Vaughn said softly. "It could be Ricky and Pedro."

"But why? They don't even know me."

"No, they don't. But they've seen you. When we found Miracle. So they know you're here and they may be trying to scare you."

"I don't know," Natalie said.

"Look, I know you're scared," Vaughn said, but let's not jump to any conclusions."

Natalie disagreed. "This was a warning, Vaughn. This was serious. I—"

"I don't want you to go," Vaughn said adamantly. She rubbed her brow as if her head hurt, but then calmed. "Please, Natalie, promise me you won't do anything rash."

Natalie looked from Vivian to June, and they quietly excused themselves, obviously sensing that she and Vaughn needed a private moment. "I will do what I think is best."

Vaughn cursed under her breath. "Don't do what you think is best for me. Or June or Mom. Okay? Let us worry about ourselves. We're fine. And we're gonna be fine. Allen isn't going to hurt us."

"You don't know that."

Vaughn reached out for her hand. Natalie took it and Vaughn pulled her closer. "I don't want you to go," she said. "Please. Promise you'll stay."

"I'm scared, Vaughn. Scared he will hurt you and this ranch. You don't know him. He's—crazy."

"Then I'll tell the police. I need to call them anyway to follow up on the tires and gate and cameras."

Natalie thought about arguing but changed her mind. Maybe it was time to talk to them. For everyone's safety. "Okay," she said. "I'll stay. But only if you continue to rest and let me help you. Let all of us help you."

Vaughn groaned. "If it keeps you here, fine." She kissed her hand and Natalie exhaled a shaky breath.

"Tell me about your back."

"I'm probably going to need surgery."

Natalie's mouth fell open. "Really?"

"Really."

"Gosh, Vaughn."

"I know. So I'm going to be out of it for a good while. Which is why we need you to post the job listing again, if you don't mind."

"Of course not."

"Can you do it today?"

"Sure. I'll do it right now." She started to head toward the door to go get her laptop, but paused. She didn't want to admit it but she feared going into the guesthouse alone again. She feared that Allen would be lurking there in the shadows.

"What's wrong?" Vaughn asked, watching her closely.

"Nothing."

"Liar."

"It's just—I'm a little nervous about being alone in the guesthouse. I know it's silly but—"

"Stay here," Vaughn said. "I think that's the best plan for now. Us all being under one roof."

"You sure?"

"Absolutely."

Natalie nodded. "I'll go get my things."

"You want someone to go with you?"

She considered it but knew she was being ridiculous. "No, I'm fine."

"Okay. See you soon."

Natalie gave her hand a squeeze and released it to go. She bypassed June and Vivian on her way out. "Just going to go get my things," she said. They both smiled over cups of coffee. They'd already started lunch, which Natalie could smell cooking on the stove.

"Okay, darlin'" Vivian said with a wink.

"We're glad to have you," June said. They'd obviously overheard the conversation with Vaughn.

Natalie returned the smile and walked out the door, already feeling much better.

## CHAPTER FORTY-ONE

June shook the young man's hand. "It was nice to meet you too, Collin. I look forward to working with you." He was a young cowboy of twenty-five, had some experience wrangling cattle, and seemed willing and able to do the job. He also had manners, which only impressed her all the more.

"Ma'am," he said, tipping his cowboy hat. "I'll see you Monday." He walked away, heading back toward his pickup.

June sighed, feeling relieved. Collin was the second and final new ranch hand. They could always hire more if needed in the future. But she and Vaughn seemed to think they had enough for now. Especially with Vivian and Natalie continuing to help out. She walked back toward the house to check on Vaughn, who had sat in on the virtual interview but hadn't met Collin or the other new hire, Jason, in person. She was laid up on the couch and having a tough time accepting her immediate future. So June had been the one to meet the new hands and show them around.

She entered the house as dusk was settling in. She'd sent supper home with the others in some Tupperware, knowing she'd be too busy to serve it with the two new hires stopping by to tour the ranch and meet the horses. So, the house was quiet, save for Vaughn who was in the living room cursing.

June grabbed her a cold can of root beer from the fridge and walked into the living room to find her lying on the couch, looking at her phone and cussing up a storm.

"What's wrong with you?" June asked, handing her the root beer.

Vaughn frowned but took it, and did her best to sit up. She moaned in pain and June felt for her, unsure what to do. It was going to be like this until her surgery in two weeks, and then for some time after as she healed. They were all just going to have to get used to it.

"Damn tech guy can't come out to replace the cameras until next week. This is the second time he's put me off."

Thankfully, the gate had been fixed. But it wasn't foolproof. Someone could still get in, if they drove through fast enough or had bolt cutters. But it was the best they could do considering they couldn't afford an electric one. So Benny locked it up every evening as he left, following the other ranch hands out. Which, he should've just done, June realized as she glanced out the window to see all the vehicles gone, save for hers and Vaughn's.

"It's been over a week. He should've already had it taken care of," June said.

"I know." She cursed again and cracked open her drink, then sipped it slowly. "Thanks for this, by the way," she said, gesturing with the can.

"You're welcome."

"So, how did it go with the new hires? They pass the final test?"

"They did. They both start Monday."

"Great." She took another sip but seemed less than thrilled. June watched her closely, concerned. She'd lost weight and her usual sun-kissed skin was paler now, due to being indoors. And her mood had changed. She was solemn where she was once feisty and determined. June had noticed it after her appointment at the brain and spine center and her meeting with the neurosurgeon. Vaughn had learned that she had stenosis. Her spinal cord was compressed, causing unbearable pain. The surgeon wanted to do surgery to relieve the pressure and he wanted to do it sooner rather than later. So now the waiting game. And in the meantime, Vaughn had to rest and suffer on the couch or in her bed. Unfortunately, all the resting was getting to her.

June glanced at the stack of magazines and books that Natalie kept bringing her and the easel Vivian had set up for her to experiment with painting if she wanted to. But Vaughn had little interest in either, preferring to play on her phone and text everyone at the ranch about their jobs, checking in and letting them know what all needed to be done. She was about to drive everyone crazy. June included. She also, for as long as she could tolerate it, sat at the computer and learned all about the website and studied the finances. While doing both was going to help a lot in the long run, June was growing weary of the constant questioning. She wished Vaughn would do what she was supposed to do and actually rest and *relax*. But it didn't seem it was in her to do so.

"That's one more worry off your plate," June said, hoping it would calm her some. But Vaughn had seemed to have already moved past it. She was looking at her phone again.

"How does he expect me to monitor the drive when I have no cameras?" Her thumbs were flying as she texted. "I'm sending him another message. I'm going to go with someone else. I don't care if they do cost more."

"You're worried about those assholes doing something else, aren't you?"

Vaughn glanced up. "Well, yes. Aren't you? It's been too quiet around here."

"Maybe the cops are finally close on their tail so they're laying low."

"Yeah, right. The cops who refuse to keep us updated?"

"You never know."

"They won't stop, Gram. Not until they get caught and put away. I expect they'll strike again here soon."

"Let's hope not." June eyed the TV tray she'd set up for Vaughn. Her supper was still on it, growing cold. "You not going to eat?"

"I had a few bites."

"Vaughn, you have to keep up your strength."

"What for? I'm not doing anything."

"For your upcoming surgery."

She didn't say anything to that. Just absently stared down at her phone.

"Will you put that thing away and talk to me?"

Vaughn sighed and tossed the phone aside. "Fine. What would you like to talk about? My horrible MRI results? Or the risks of the surgery? Or how about the fact that I'll be laid up for at least a few more weeks? Take your pick."

"How about Natalie? How are things going there?"

Natalie had taken her supper to the guesthouse to work on her laptop in the quiet. As far as June knew, she'd finally reached out to the detective who had sent her the email, telling him her location and insisting on some sort of protection for her and the ranch, but he'd offered little in the way of help, telling her that Allen had disappeared as of two weeks ago. Just up and vanished once they served a search warrant on his residence and business. Apparently, the man was on the run. June hoped he ran far and wide and never returned.

Natalie feared that he would still come after her. She was thinking like Vaughn. Worried that things were too quiet. She was still sleeping in the main house every night. Making herself a little bed on the couch, while Vaughn moved to her bedroom to retire. She only went to the guesthouse to work on her blogs when she needed the quiet. But even doing that, here lately, seemed to frighten her. So when she was there, she left the door open wide while she worked, convinced it was somehow safer to do things that way. That at least she could see outside and call for help if needed. Thankfully, the weather was now nice enough for her to be able to do that.

"What do you mean?" Vaughn looked surprised at the question and frankly, a little worried.

"Nothing." It was obvious she still didn't want to talk about it and she didn't want to keep bugging her about it. The last thing she wanted to do was to scare her away from Natalie. But she did wonder about the two of them and what their future held, if anything. She'd sure hate to see Natalie go.

"No, what did you mean by that? Has Natalie said something?"

"Like what, Vaughn?"

"Like maybe how she wants to leave. I don't know. I'm not exactly a catch anymore, am I? And the way I've put her off...I wouldn't blame her if she wanted to leave again."

"Vaughn, she's not going to go because you've hurt your back. You ought to know her better than that."

"But maybe it would be better for her if she did. I don't want her to feel like she has to take care of me."

"I don't," Natalie said, entering the room. She'd come in through the kitchen without them noticing. "I like taking care of you."

Vaughn clamped her mouth shut. Then, tentatively, said, "You do?"

"Can't you tell?" She sat down next to her and gripped her hand. "Nothing makes me feel warmer inside than helping you."

"But I'm...useless."

Natalie shook her head. "No, Vaughn. You're everything."

June smiled, moved by her words. Vaughn kept flushing. June stood, aiming to give them some privacy. "See if you can get her to eat. She won't do it for me."

Natalie looked at the plate on the tray. "Vaughn, you finish eating while I run back to the guesthouse to shower and change. Then we'll watch a movie together or something. How's that sound?"

Natalie did this every night with Vaughn. She either put on a movie, having signed them up for something called Netflix, or she worked a puzzle with her or played a board game. It was really quite sweet and Vaughn seemed eternally grateful and liked having her near.

Vaughn grumbled but Natalie pulled her close and kissed her on the forehead, shutting her up. "Fine, I'll eat," Vaughn finally said.

"Good. I'll heat it up for you." She took the plate and carried it into the kitchen to put into the microwave.

June was still smiling in the doorway. Vaughn caught sight of her.

"What?"

"Just enjoying watching you give in. It's a sight I've rarely seen."

"Oh, be quiet."

June laughed and left her alone, bypassing Natalie on the way back into the kitchen. She worked at washing the dishes as she heard Natalie return Vaughn's plate to her and leave.

It sure was nice to have Natalie around.

## CHAPTER FORTY-TWO

Goddamn fucking Tito. He'd really screwed him. He'd paid him good money, real good money to do one thing. Find Natalie. And did he do it? No. Or at least he wouldn't know if he had because the asshole wouldn't answer his phone. So he'd said good riddance to him, just like he had that little fucker Tom. Christ, was everyone out to screw him over? Did he have sucker written on his forehead?

He pressed on the gas pedal and cursed at the weak horsepower the little car had. No good fucking car. Couldn't Nico do better than this? Better than a fucking used little piece of shit? He'd said it would keep him incognito. Ha. That might be the only thing it was good for.

He drove faster, gripping the worn steering wheel tightly, and squinted ahead. Even the headlights seemed to be weak. Christ, it was dark. He took his foot off the pedal and coasted, uncomfortable with the unfamiliar terrain. But that had been his life lately. Uncomfortable. Nico had put him up in some Godforsaken house in the west valley, out near Surprise. A small tract home with weeds growing in the backyard and scorpions around every damn corner. This morning he'd gotten out of the shower to find one crawling up the bedroom curtain like it owned the damn place. He'd called Nico furious and he'd promised to send someone out, but he'd yet to follow through. And of course Allen couldn't be there when the guy came, because it would blow his cover, so he'd gone for a drive.

The drive had continued though once he'd received the phone call. The phone call he'd been waiting for from his contact at the police department.

"Fuck you, Tito, you giant bastard." He pressed on the gas again and sped onward, thinking things over. "Fuck you, Tito, and fuck you, Detectives. None of you will get the best of me." He laughed.

He'd heard the cops had come looking for him after the search warrant had been executed. Maybe they'd found something after all. Maybe it had something to do with his business dealings. Or maybe it was all the info on Natalie he had stored on his home computer, something he'd forgotten he'd had. He wasn't sure, he just knew they were after him. That's where Nico Fitz came in. The two of them went way back. In fact, Nico had been the one to give him his start at a real business venture. He'd believed in him and given him the capital needed to get things rolling. He'd trusted Allen after Allen worked for him for a couple years making deliveries and collecting fees. Allen had been good at his job. He'd been a real ball buster and he always got results. He'd gained respect for that.

So now Nico was helping him once again. Hiding him, supporting him, funneling him news. The cops, they'd never catch on. Nico was too good and had too many connections. Allen was home free if he wanted it. He was being offered a safe place in South America, all the women he wanted, and a new business to boot. All he had to do was say yes and Nico would send over the new passports and wire him the cash he needed. But there was one thing he needed to do first.

One thing he had to do. The one thing that was a long time coming.

## Chapter Forty-three

Natalie hummed as she dressed and combed her hair after her long shower. The hot spray had massaged her tired shoulders and calmed her weary mind. She had so much on her mind lately, it was a miracle she could even still form the words to write when it came to her blogs and promoting products. But luckily, she'd been able to pull it off, enough to bring a paycheck or two so she could at least keep paying Vaughn rent. Vaughn had told her not to worry about it so much, but she did. She knew the ranch was still struggling even though business was picking up. It would be a while before things started to noticeably improve on the financial front, and in the meantime, she wanted to keep up her end of the bargain.

She didn't know how much longer she'd be able to stay at the ranch, so she needed to make sure she paid her dues. Vaughn and June had helped her a lot in allowing her to stay and she wanted to do right by them. But doing so didn't give her the answers she was seeking where Vaughn was concerned. She knew Vaughn didn't want her to leave, but she couldn't stay there forever. At some point she'd have to go, especially if Vaughn decided she didn't want to pursue a relationship with her. It would just be too painful for her stay at that point, regardless of how much she loved the ranch and spending time with Vaughn and June. And then there was Allen. What was going to happen there? Detective Marks had told her he'd disappeared, but what did that mean for her?

Was he gone for good? Did he skip town? Was he finally in trouble for all his shady business dealings? Or worse, could he be coming for her?

"I'm being ridiculous. He wouldn't come for me. Not with the cops looking so hard for him. It would be a crazy move."

She switched off the bedroom light and walked into the kitchen to grab the box of vanilla tea from the cupboard. She wanted to make some for her and Vaughn tonight as they watched a movie together. It would pair nicely with the cinnamon rolls Vaughn had declared she wanted. Natalie had laughed, but agreed to make her some just as soon as she got back to the house. At least Vaughn was eating. And she hoped she'd eaten her dinner as well, but she wasn't going to expect much there. Vaughn's appetite had shrunk dramatically since she'd stopped doing all the physical work, and now, with her low moods, they were lucky to get her to eat at all.

Natalie reached for the tea and turned around, humming once again.

A soft knock came from the front door. She'd forgotten that she'd closed and locked it before her shower. It must be June wondering what was taking her so long. She walked to the door and unbolted it and opened it.

"Sorry, June, I—"

"Hello, Natalie," Allen said, pointing a gun straight at her. He shoved her back inside before she even had a chance to let out a scream. When she tried, he struck her across the face and sent her sprawling.

"I wouldn't make any noise if I was you."

She touched her cheek where he'd hit her, the sting turning to a throb. She scrambled to get up, backing away from him, but not as afraid as she was angry. She stared at him, confused by his sloppy appearance. Allen, the man who had always prided himself on his dapper looks, was dressed in loose-fitting worn jeans, a fleece pullover, and dirty sneakers. His face was covered in a scruffy beard and his hair, which he usually wore slicked back with product, was longer and disheveled. Was this his disguise, or was something else going on? She guessed by the anger and rage she saw in his eyes, that it was the latter. He was losing his mind.

And now he had found her. This time, she knew, he would be merciless.

"Don't," she managed to say, "hit me again."

He laughed and she glanced at the door behind him. He'd slammed it closed upon entry, but she usually left it open when she was in there working. Maybe June would notice. Maybe Vaughn would too if she grew worried about her. But the thought scared her more than comforted her. She didn't want them exposed to Allen. He looked maniacal and he had a gun.

He followed her line of sight. "You opened the door for me, Natalie. Was that an invitation? I took it as one."

He staggered as he followed her. She'd taken refuge behind the table, trying to get something between them. But the table, she knew, wouldn't save her from a bullet. He swayed as he blinked watery eyes at her, the gun wavering as if it were too heavy for him.

He appeared to be drunk.

He yanked out a chair and collapsed into it. Then, with the gun in hand, he pointed at the chair in front of her. "Sit," he demanded.

She thought briefly about making a beeline for the door, but he'd shoot her as she ran. She needed another plan. Slowly, she sat.

"Allen," she tried.

"Shut up."

"You don't want to do this."

"Don't I though? Natalie, baby, this is *all* I want to do."

"That can't be true. You have—"

"I have nothing!" Spittle flew from his mouth. "And it's all because of you."

A ball of fire settled behind her sternum. He was drunk, nearly falling down drunk, and he was angry. Not a good combination. Add the gun and she was in serious trouble. She searched for the right words. She had to stall him. Had to keep him talking.

He blinked slowly and set the gun on the table.

"I'm sorry," she tried, thinking quickly. "I didn't mean to cause you any trouble."

He chuckled. Slapped his leg and roared with laughter. "Trouble? That's all you've given me, Natalie. And after I gave you *everything*." He smacked the table. "*Everything!*"

He seemed to have exhausted himself because he quieted and spun the gun around on the tabletop with his finger.

"I know," she said. "And I ruined it. I wasn't…appreciative."

"No. You weren't. You—you're nothing, Natalie. Nothing. I was all you had."

She fought back her rising anger. She'd heard the words before. Too many times and not just from him. Well, she no longer believed them.

"You're wrong," she said, unable to hold her tongue. "All of you are wrong."

He stopped spinning the gun and looked at her closely. "What did you say?"

"I said, you're wrong, Allen. I am something. I am worthy. And I am *so* much better without you."

He lifted the gun again but seemed to have trouble holding it up. He blinked as if trying to maintain focus.

"Go ahead," she said, thinking of all the times she'd been told she was nothing, thinking of all the neglect and emotional abuse she'd suffered at the hands of her derelict foster parents. Then she thought of all the times she felt totally alone. She'd had no one. Not a soul. But she'd survived. And she'd survive now. On her own. With good, kind people who cared about in her life for moral support. She didn't need Allen or anyone. She wanted Vaughn. There was a difference. But if Vaughn didn't want her, that was okay too. She'd move on. She'd find peace. Rebuild her life all over again.

"Do it," she said, feeling fearless for the first time in her life. "Shoot me. Because I'd rather be dead than be with you."

He grinned, but it fell away quickly. His glossy eyes hardened. "Don't tempt me, Natalie."

"Don't tell me what to do."

"What, did you finally grow some balls?"

"No, Allen. I finally grew some ovaries. And I'm ready to go to hell and back to fight you now."

"So, it's true. You've been shacking up with that woman and she's toughened you up, turned you all dyke on me."

"Not that it's any of your business, but I haven't been shacking up with anyone. This is me. All me."

"Bullshit," he slurred. "You left me for her. You're a fucking dyke. No wonder why you were always so difficult. So fucking frigid."

"No, Allen, *that* was all you."

He lunged, like he was going to go for her. She startled but remained seated, heart hammering. She kept talking, driving the daggers home.

"I left you because of you. You were sadistic and abusive and the worst human being I've ever known. And I left this time because you were harassing me, threatening me, and having me followed. None of it has to do with anyone else. It's all you. So, for once in your life take some responsibility."

With that, she stood, slowly and carefully, and walked to the door. Her heart careened in her chest and she felt like she might pass out, but she kept putting one foot in front of the other. Allen screamed at her and she heard his chair scrape across the tile as he stood to come after her. His cries for her to stop grew closer but she didn't. She reached the door and grabbed the handle and turned to pull it open.

There, on the front stoop, was Vaughn, looking as pale as ever and thoroughly concerned as her gaze moved beyond Natalie to Allen behind her. Then, as her eyes widened, a shot rang out and Natalie felt a jolt. She looked down at her hands, to her abdomen and saw blood. She looked back up at Vaughn's horrified face and fell to the floor.

## Chapter Forty-four

"No!" Vaughn shouted, trying to catch Natalie as she fell. She knelt to help her, to try to get her back up. But she was limp in her arms and Vaughn was too weak to pull her away, her back screaming at her in agony.

She looked to the man, who she assumed was Allen. He was staring at Natalie, eyes glossed over, spent gun trembling in his hand. He appeared to be in shock. Vaughn took advantage and charged him, as fast as she could, pain be damned, letting out a low roar as she slammed into him, barreling him backward. He got another shot off before he crashed into the table and she landed atop him, on the floor. She pushed herself up, a burning stab of pain in her shoulder, and began to choke him. But her strength had dwindled from the charge and the tackle, and her shoulder, something was wrong with her shoulder. She squeezed as hard as she could, but he fought her off easily, hitting her in the temple with the butt of the gun. She fell off him and lay crumpled on the ground, fading in and out of consciousness, her blurry vision trying to focus on Natalie's still form, lying in a heap by the door.

"Natalie," she said, blinking back tears. "Run." But Natalie didn't move, didn't acknowledge her. Vaughn heard movement to her right. She shifted her gaze and saw Allen getting to his feet. He staggered, got his bearings, and stood above her, gun aimed at her head.

"Fucking dyke," he said. Drool oozed down his chin as he wavered again. "I'm gonna kill you. Just like I killed Natalie."

"Natalie," she said again. She couldn't be dead. No. She wanted to grab his leg and pull him down. Climb atop him again and strangle the life out of him. Squeeze him until his eyes bulged. But she couldn't move, could hardly manage to blink as darkness threatened. "Fuck you," she whispered.

A raucous laugh came from him and the last thing she saw before unconsciousness took her was June stepping into the doorway, shotgun aimed.

And then, a loud blast.

## CHAPTER FORTY-FIVE

The blast sent June back on her heels and she stumbled over the threshold and fell on her rear. To her horror, the bearded man came for her. Her shot had missed him and blown a hole in the wall above him instead. She clamored backward, catching sight of Natalie on the floor before her, and Vaughn just beyond that. They weren't moving, weren't awake.

Were they—? She didn't have time to think. The man, he was coming. She struggled to grip her gun. She had one shot left. One shot. She lifted it and tried to aim, but he was nearly on her. She closed her eyes, ready to pull the trigger.

Her ears rang as a shot resounded, nearly deafening her. She tensed, expecting the recoil of the gun, but nothing happened. She opened her eyes. The man was down, sprawled on his back, his gun flung at his side.

She blinked, confused. A figure stepped into view from beside her. It was another man. This one was much bigger than the one on the floor. He looked down at her and offered a meaty hand, a spent gun in the other. Tentatively, she took it and he helped her up. He walked over to the bearded man, kicked his gun away, and then kicked him to see if he was dead.

When he looked back to June, he spoke. "I never did like that son of a bitch."

## CHAPTER FORTY-SIX

*Two Months Later*

"Whoa, girl," Natalie said as she tugged on Miracle's reins. Miracle slowed to a trot and Natalie smiled as they neared Vaughn, slowed some more, and stopped. Miracle bobbed her head and stomped her feet.

Natalie slid off her and stepped up to Vaughn, who was smiling as well. "What?" Natalie asked, curious as to her radiant happiness.

"You. Riding in like that. It's exactly how it was in my dream."

"You dreamt about me?"

Vaughn drew her closer. "More than once."

"Really? And these dreams….they were good?"

"Oh, yes." Vaughn tilted her head. "Actually, they never got past you riding in on Miracle."

"Is that so?" Natalie kissed her tenderly and drew away. "We'll just have to make up our own ending then, won't we?"

"If you insist."

Natalie took her by the hand and led her toward the guesthouse, glancing back at her to grin every now and again. They walked slowly, basking in the winter sun, walking amongst the wildflowers that had come back into bloom in the balmy temperatures.

Behind them Natalie saw Em come out and lead Miracle away, back into the corral. She waved and Natalie returned it, glad to have her around. Vaughn had been right about her, she was an exceptionally hard worker and her fondness for Vaughn was just that. Fondness. Okay, maybe a little hero worship. But that was all. And Natalie couldn't blame her. Vaughn was amazing after all. She was doing wonderfully already, just six weeks after surgery, up and walking and going strong, so happy to be relieved of the pain.

Natalie had needed time to heal too, after being shot by Allen. She'd lost her spleen in emergency surgery, but she'd pulled through okay. She'd hated being down the same time as Vaughn and not being able to care for her, but June and Vivian took great care of the two of them.

At one point they'd even shared Vaughn's bed, with Vaughn insisting Natalie join her instead of sleeping on the couch. There they'd watched movies, and talked deep into the night and fallen asleep holding hands.

Now Natalie was back in the guesthouse much to Vaughn's chagrin. But Natalie needed the space, the couch just wasn't cutting it, and she had to have room for her things, Vaughn's room was just too small. So she'd moved back in and Vaughn came to spend every evening with her, with Natalie cooking them supper. They were like two teenagers, dating and spending as much time as they could together, with long make out sessions on the couch, sometimes leading to heavy petting. But they'd always stopped there, wanting to wait until they were better healed, wanting the first time to be special, and without June unintentionally interrupting asking if they wanted pie for dessert.

It was late afternoon now and June would no doubt be getting ready to cook supper, while Vivian helped the ranch hands with the chores. It was the perfect time to sneak away. With Ricky and Pedro in jail and out of commission, thanks to the new private investigator Vaughn hired, the one who'd killed Allen, things were once again peaceful at the ranch, and it seemed they no longer had a care in the world. It was a wonderful feeling, this peace.

Natalie opened the door and led them inside. Vaughn closed the door behind them and locked it, as if reading Natalie's mind. She tried to kiss her once again, but Natalie backed away, tugging on her hand, heading for the bedroom. They entered in silence, the smiles now gone, replaced with serious looks of desire.

"Come here," Vaughn said, drawing her near. She cupped her face and dipped in for a smoldering kiss, one that left Natalie breathless and dizzy. She clung to her when they parted, afraid she would lose her bearings. But Vaughn held her tight, securing her, and urged her to the bed. Natalie felt the mattress on the backs of her knees and she sat, leaning back on her elbows as Vaughn removed her cowboy hat and climbed atop her. They kissed again, this time more fervent, deeply heated, with Vaughn beckoning with her tongue, wanting to explore. Natalie let her, meeting Vaughn's tongue with her own. She moaned into her, gripping her ass as she felt the firmness of Vaughn's thigh press against her aching center. Vaughn sensed her enjoyment and rocked into her, dragging her lips away to kiss and suck on her neck.

Natalie sighed and arched, offering herself up to her heated mouth. "Vaughn," she whispered, running her hands up her sides, careful to avoid her back. She'd never made love like this before, with a passionate but gentle lover, one who wanted to please her, to enrapture her, send her to places she'd only ever imagined. "I love you," she sighed, clinging to her shoulders.

Vaughn stilled and looked down into her eyes. "You…"

Natalie hesitated as fears from her past surfaced, and for the briefest moment, she was unsure if she should repeat herself. But when she saw the raw passion and deep love and affection in Vaughn's gaze, all of those fears vanished into a mist like haze and drifted slowly away. "I do," she said. "I love you."

Vaughn's lips parted. Her eyes searched Natalie's. "I love you, Natalie Brewer."

Natalie reached up and skimmed her fingers along her jaw. "Then show me, as I show you."

Their lips connected again, soft and supple, tasting and teasing, before Vaughn moved lower, taking the time to nibble her neck as she trailed her way downward, inching Natalie's shirt up as she went. When she came to her bra, she unfastened the front clasp and freed her breasts and seemed to delight in the pucker of her nipples. She brushed her lips over them lightly and circled them with her tongue, causing Natalie to clutch her head and arch up in sheer pleasure.

"Oh," Natalie cried, palming her own face, overcome with excitement. A rush of warmth pooled between her legs and she bucked upward, needing more. Vaughn responded, lowered herself farther and unbuttoned her jeans. After she eased them off her hips, she stared down at her and traced her fingers along the outer edge of her panties.

"I'm going to ravish you now, Natalie," she rasped. "Like you've never been ravished before."

Natalie swallowed. She saw the fire in her eyes, the flush in her cheeks. She nodded, wanting nothing more than for her to do just that. She was unable to form words as Vaughn dipped down, dragging her pants off of her completely and rising up to do the same with her panties with her teeth.

Natalie knotted her fingers in her hair, jerking uncontrollably as she felt the soft heat of her breath as she moved down her thighs to her shins and then ankles, where Vaughn stopped long enough to remove her panties and toss them aside. She kissed her way back up, running her tongue up her inner thighs and pausing just before she reached her throbbing flesh.

"Welcome me, love," she said.

Natalie opened her legs with a deep sigh, and closed her eyes and cried out to God above when she felt first Vaughn's breath and her scorching soft tongue on her inner folds, leading up to her oh so sensitive cleft.

"Vaughn!" she called out, lifting her hips up from the bed, wanting, needing, desperate for more. "Oh, Vaughn!" She gripped her head, held her fiercely tight, so tight that Vaughn laughed softly, as she assuaged her clit with first her tongue, then her teasing lips, and then both together at once, sending Natalie into a tailspin of madness and ecstasy, until she was crying out so hard and so deep, that her throat tightened and no further words could escape. She pulsed after that, forcing Vaughn into her flesh, holding her firmly to her, never wanting her to relent.

And suddenly it was all too much and Natalie thrashed her head back and forth and tried with all her might to push Vaughn away. But Vaughn held fast, fastened securely to her, giving until she began to jolt and shake, her body trembling from the intensity of the pleasure. Only then did Vaughn stop, releasing her flesh gently and kissing her delicately as she moved up her body to look down at her.

Natalie stared up into her, her entire body thrumming, a low humming in her ears. She touched Vaughn's face and Vaughn turned into her palm, kissing it. She lowered herself and kissed Natalie, allowing her to taste herself on her warm lips.

"I don't know what's better," Vaughn said as she drew away. "The taste of your lips or the taste of your sweet flesh."

Natalie covered her face and laughed, strangely embarrassed. But Vaughn gently peeled her hands down. "Are you being bashful? Now?"

"I'm sorry, I—This—I've never done this before. Not like this."

"Which part?"

"All of it?"

Vaughn reared back. "You mean you never...no one has ever..."

Natalie shook her head. "That was a first."

Vaughn eased down next to her and traced her fingers along the outer ridge of her nipples. Natalie sighed again, as a new, more needful pressure began to course through her. "Then we must do it again," Vaughn said, dipping down to kiss her erect nipples. "And again. And again."

"Vaughn," Natalie said, dreamy with this new, quickly growing desire. "I want to love you like this."

"Mm, you'll get your chance."

Natalie jerked as Vaughn kissed her way back down to her center. "When?"

"Later."

"Pr-promise?"

"Oh, yes," she said as she flicked her clit. "I promise." She pressed Natalie's legs apart and ravished her...again and again and again.

THE END

# About the Author

Ronica Black lives in the desert Southwest with her menagerie of animals and her menagerie of art. When she's not writing, she's still creating, whether drawing, painting, or woodworking. She loves long walks into the sunset, rescuing animals, anything pertaining to art, and spending time with those she loves. When she can, she enjoys returning to her roots in North Carolina where she can sit back on the porch with family and friends, catch up on all the gossip, and relish an ice cold Cheerwine.

Ronica is a two-time Golden Crown Literary Society Goldie Award winner and a three-time finalist for the Lambda Literary Awards.

# Books Available from Bold Strokes Books

**Back to Belfast** by Emma L. McGeown. Two colleagues are asked to trade jobs. Claire moves to Vancouver and Stacie moves to Belfast, and though they've never met in person, they can't seem to escape a growing attraction from afar. (978-1-63679-731-1)

**Exposure** by Nicole Disney and Kimberly Cooper Griffin. For photographer Jax Bailey and delivery driver Trace Logan, keeping it casual is a matter of perspective. (978-1-63679-697-0)

**Hunt of Her Own** by Elena Abbott. Finding forever won't be easy, but together Danaan's and Ashly's paths lead back to the supernatural sanctuary of Terabend. (978-1-63679-685-7)

**Perfect** by Kris Bryant. They say opposites attract, but Alix and Marianna have totally different dreams. No Hollywood love story is perfect, right? (978-1-63679-601-7)

**Royal Expectations** by Jenny Frame. When childhood sweethearts Princess Teddy Buckingham and Summer Fisher reunite, their feelings resurface and so does the public scrutiny that tore them apart. (978-1-63679-591-1)

**Shadow Rider** by Gina L. Dartt. In the Shadows, one can easily find death, but can Shay and Keagan find love as they fight to save the Five Nations? (978-1-63679-691-8)

**The Breakdown** by Ronica Black. Vaughn and Natalie have chemistry, but the outside world keeps knocking at the door, threatening more trouble, making the love and the life they want together impossible. (978-1-63679-675-8)

**Tribute** by L.M. Rose. To save her people, Fiona will be the tribute in a treaty marriage to the Tipruii princess, Simaala, and spend the rest of her days on the other side of the wall between their races. (978-1-63679-693-2)

**Wild Wales** by Patricia Evans. When Finn and Aisling fall in love, they must decide whether to return to the safety of the lives they had, or take a chance on wild love in windswept Wales. (978-1-63679-771-7)

**Can't Buy Me Love** by Georgia Beers. London and Kayla are perfect for one another, but if London reveals she's in a fake relationship with Kayla's ex, she risks not only the opportunity of her career, but Kayla's trust as well. (978-1-63679-665-9)

**Chance Encounter** by Renee Roman. Little did Sky Roberts know when she bought the raffle ticket for charity that she would also be taking a chance on love with the egotistical Drew Mitchell. (978-1-63679-619-2)

**Comes in Waves** by Ana Hartnett. For Tanya Brees, love in small-town Coral Bay comes in waves, but can she make it stay for good this time? (978-1-63679-597-3)

**Dancing With Dahlia** by Julia Underwood. How is Piper Fernley supposed to survive six weeks with the most controlling, uptight boss on earth? Because sometimes when you stop looking, your heart finds exactly what it needs. (978-1-63679-663-5)

**Skyscraper** by Gun Brooke. Attempting to save the life of an injured boy brings Rayne and Kaelyn together. As they strive for justice against corrupt Celestial authorities, they're unable to foresee how intertwined their fates will become. (978-1-63679-657-4)

**The Curse** by Alexandra Riley. Can Diana Dillon and her daughter, Ryder, survive the cursed farm with the help of Deputy

Mel Defoe? Or will the land choose them to be the next victims? (978-1-63679-611-6)

**The Heart Wants** by Krystina Rivers. Fifteen years after they first meet, Army Major Reagan Jennings realizes she has one last chance to win the heart of the woman she's always loved. If only she can make Sydney see she's worth risking everything for. (978-1-63679-595-9)

**Untethered** by Shelley Thrasher. Helen Rogers, in her eighties, meets much-younger Grace on a lengthy cruise to Bali, and their intense relationship yields surprising insights and unexpected growth. (978-1-63679-636-9)

**You Can't Go Home Again** by Jeanette Bears. After their military career ends abruptly, Raegan Holcolm is forced back to their hometown to confront their past and discover where the road to recovery will lead them, or if it already led them home. (978-1-636790644-4)

**A Wolf in Stone** by Jane Fletcher. Though Cassilania is an experienced player in the dirty, dangerous game of imperial Kavillian politics, even she is caught out when a murderer raises the stakes. (978-1-63679-640-6)

**New Horizons** by Shia Woods. When Quinn Collins meets Alex Anders, Horizon Theater's enigmatic managing director, a passionate connection ignites, but amidst the complex backdrop of theater politics, their budding romance faces a formidable challenge. (978-1-63679-683-3)

**One Last Summer** by Kristin Keppler. Emerson Fields didn't think anything could keep her from her dream of interning at Bardot Design Studio in Paris, until an unexpected choice at a North Carolina beach has her questioning what it is she really wants. (978-1-63679-638-3)

**StreamLine** by Lauren Melissa Ellzey. When Lune crosses paths with the legendary girl gamer Nocht, she may have found the key that will boost her to the upper echelon of streamers and unravel all Lune thought she knew about gaming, friendship, and love. (978-1-63679-655-0)

**The Devil You Know** by Ali Vali. As threats come at the Casey family from both the feds and enemies set to destroy them, Cain Casey does whatever is necessary with Emma at her side to bury every single one. (978-1-63679-471-6)

**The Meaning of Liberty** by Sage Donnell. When TJ and Bailey get caught in the political crossfire of the ultraconservative Crusade of the Redeemer Church, escape is the only plan. On the run and fighting for their lives is not the time to be falling for each other. (978-1-63679-624-6)

**Undercurrent** by Patricia Evans. Can Tala and Wilder catch a serial killer in Salem before another body washes up on the shore? (978-1-636790669-7)

**And Then There Was One** by Michele Castleman. Plagued by strange memories and drowning in the guilt she tried to leave behind, Lyla Smith escapes her small Ohio town to work as a nanny and becomes trapped with an unknown killer. (978-1-63679-688-8)

**Digging for Destiny** by Jenna Jarvis. The war between nations forces Litz to make a choice. Her country, career, and family, or the chance of making a better world with the woman she can't forget. (978-1-63679-575-1)

**Hot Hires** by Nan Campbell, Alaina Erdell, Jesse J. Thoma. In these three romance novellas, when business turns to pleasure, romance ignites. (978-1-63679-651-2)

**McCall** by Patricia Evans. Sam and Sara found love on the water, but can they build a future amid the ghosts of the past that surround them on dry land? (978-1-63679-769-4)

**One and Done** by Fredrick Smith. One day can lead to a night of passion…and possibly a chance at love. (978-1-63679-564-5)

**Promises to Protect** by Jo Hemmingwood. Park ranger Maxine Ward's commitment to protect Tree City is put to the test when social worker Skylar Austen takes a special interest in the commune and in Max. (978-1-63679-626-0)

**Sacred Ground** by Missouri Vaun. Jordan Price, a conflicted demon hunter, falls for Grace Jameson who has no idea she's been bitten by a vampire. (978-1-63679-485-3)

**The Land of Death and Devil's Club** by Bailey Bridgewater. Special Liaison to the FBI Louisa Linebach may have defied all odds by identifying the bodies of three missing men in the Kenai Peninsula, but she won't be satisfied until the man she's sure is responsible for their murders is behind bars. (978-1-63679-659-8)

**When You Smile** by Melissa Brayden. Taryn Ross never thought the babysitter she once crushed on would show up as a grad student at the same university she attends. (978-1-63679-671-0)

Milton Keynes UK
Ingram Content Group UK Ltd.
UKHW030740100924
448141UK00001B/49